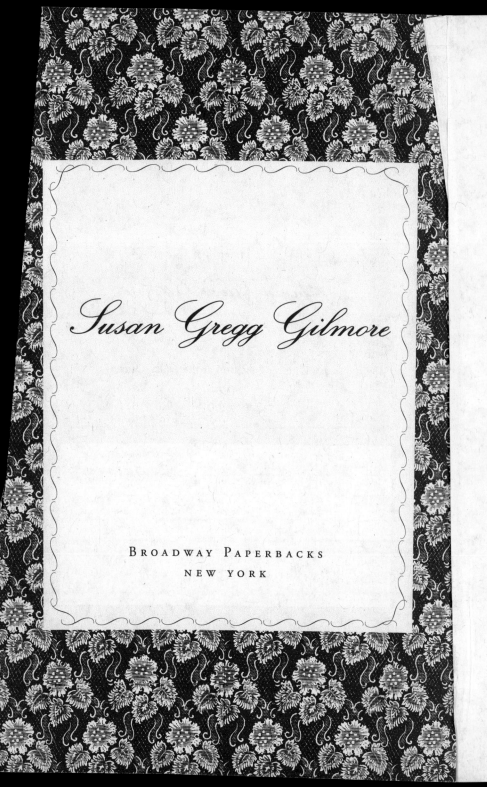

Susan Gregg Gilmore

BROADWAY PAPERBACKS
NEW YORK

The Improper Life of
Bezellia Grove

Also by

Susan Gregg Gilmore

Looking for Salvation at the Dairy Queen

THE

Improper Life

OF

Bezellia Grove

A NOVEL

BROADWAY

Copyright © 2010 by Susan Gregg Gilmore
Reader's Guide copyright © 2011 by Susan Gregg Gilmore

All rights reserved.
Published in the United States by Broadway Paperbacks, an imprint of the
Crown Publishing Group, a division of Random House, Inc., New York.
www.crownpublishing.com

Broadway Paperbacks and its logo, a letter B bisected on the diagonal, are
trademarks of Random House, Inc.

Originally published in hardcover in slightly different form in the United States
by Shaye Areheart Books, an imprint of the Crown Publishing Group,
a division of Random House, Inc., New York, in 2010.

Library of Congress Cataloging-in-Publication Data
Gilmore, Susan Gregg.
The improper life of Bezellia Grove: a novel / Susan Gregg Gilmore.—1st ed.
        p. cm.
1. Interracial dating—Fiction.   2. Family secrets—Fiction.   3. Nashville
(Tenn.)—Fiction.   4. Domestic fiction.   I. Title.
PS3607.I4527I57 2010
813'.6—dc22   2009048110

ISBN 978-0-307-39504-7
eISBN 978-0-307-59233-0

Printed in the United States of America

Book design by Lynne Amft
Cover design by Jessie Bright

10 9 8 7 6 5 4 3 2 1

First Paperback Edition

For Dan
and our girls,
Claudia, Josephine, and Alice

O, be some other name!

WILLIAM SHAKESPEARE,
Romeo and Juliet

GROVE BABY GIRL MAKES DEBUT
FIFTH-GENERATION NASHVILLIAN

Friends and Family Celebrate at Grove Hill

Dr. and Mrs. Charles Goodman Grove V, of Nashville, welcomed their first child, born on March 26. The proud parents officially announced the birth of their daughter, Bezellia Louise, yesterday at a festive luncheon held at the family's Grove Hill estate.

More than one hundred friends and family enjoyed a lavish meal featuring lobster-style eggs Benedict, quiche Lorraine, and cheese strata. The tables were covered with pink damask and decorated with arrangements of pink and white sweetheart roses.

Mrs. Grove wore a one-piece, pale pink linen dress with a coordinating short-sleeved jacket detailed with a pink grosgrain ribbon. Her baby daughter was the center of attention wearing a smocked, white cotton gown accented with soft pink rosettes and trimmed with a pink satin ribbon. Dr. Grove gave his newborn daughter a strand of heirloom pearls, a necklace that was once worn by his great-grandmother.

Guests said the Groves were radiant as they introduced their infant daughter to Nashville society. Mr. and Mrs. George Madison Longfellow Hunt V, Dr. and Mrs. Richard S. Miller, Dr. and Mrs. Joseph Lawrence Hayes, of Birmingham, Ala., and Mr. and Mrs. Albert Lyle Patterson II, of Atlanta, Ga., were among those in attendance.

The Nashville Register
early edition
MAY 1, 1951

chapter one

Apparently among those who consider their social standing some measure of importance, I am to be admired, for I am one of the few Nashvillians who can claim with infallible certainty that a blood relation has lived in this town since its inception. My mother, although a Grove only by marriage, never tired of sharing this piece of family trivia at cocktail parties or morning coffees, convinced that it elevated her own social position far beyond what her birth parents could have guaranteed.

And whether or not she exaggerated the details of our family's history in the hope of impressing her friends, the truth remains that a poor Carolina farmer packed his bags some two hundred and fifty years ago and set out to cross the Appalachian Mountains, heading west with his young bride, determined to claim a few acres of his own and a better life for his family. He probably didn't have a penny to his name by the time he stumbled into Fort Nashborough begging for a hot meal and a place to sleep, but that doesn't seem to matter to the Grove family anymore.

Legend has it that when the Chickamauga Indians attacked the Nashville settlement, they killed my ancestral father as he fearlessly fought to protect his young wife. She grabbed the musket from her dying husband's hands and continued the fight, killing three Indian warriors herself. Then she fell on top of her husband's cold, bloody body and held him in her arms throughout the night.

Her name was Bezellia Louise, and for generations since, the first girl born to the eldest Grove male has been named in her memory. Although most official historians dispute any claims of her heroics, my father donated thousands of dollars to the Nashville Historical Society with the belief that eventually some fresh, young academic would see the past more according to my family's advantage. But whether fact or fiction, I have believed in her courage and passion and was always proud to share her name.

Sadly, the Bezellias birthed before me never cared for this designation, preferring a monosyllabic moniker—like Bee, Zee, or Zell—to their formal Christian name. My own mother disliked it so much that for years she refused to let it cross her lips, calling me only Sister, a generic substitution that summed up her distaste for my name and her inadequate affection for me. I, on the other hand, always wanted to hear it in its entirety, never caring what others thought of it.

But long before I had memorized the details of my family's story, I understood that I was a girl unlike most others. I had a pony to ride and a closet brimming with neatly pressed dresses. My bedroom was decorated with teddy bears that were handmade in Germany and dolls with porcelain heads that I was only to admire and never to touch. And, most important, I was always cooked for and attended to by people other than my mother, by people with dark skin and families of their own.

Maizelle Cooper was a short, round woman with bits of white hair highlighting her forehead like a jeweled crown. She wore the same short-sleeved, light blue work dress every day, summer and winter. And she always kept a stiff white apron tied around her waist. When she hugged me and pressed my face into her full, round tummy, I could smell a faint perfume of flour and cinnamon and grease. Maizelle spent most of her time in the kitchen, keeping a careful watch over a collection of pots endlessly simmering on a hot black stove. She cooked buttery biscuits and sweet, creamy oatmeal to warm my stomach in the mornings and greeted me after school with a cold glass of milk and a piece of homemade pound cake.

She washed and ironed all of my clothes, even my undershirts, and prepared my baths in the evenings, and somewhere in between sang me songs about freedom and grace, swaying from one hip to the other as if the rhythm of her voice kept her body in perfect balance.

I asked her once why she sang those songs considering it had been almost a century since President Lincoln had signed the Emancipation Proclamation. Maizelle just shook her head and said that in all her years on this earth she had seen enough to know that there were many ways one man could make a slave out of another. Then she slowly wiped her brow and pointed to the crooked scar above her right eye. She never told me how it got there, and somehow I knew better than to ask. She imagined it was hard for me to under-stand all that she was saying from where I was standing, but the good Lord, she said, would make things right one day. She just hoped she'd be here to see it.

Maizelle slept in the basement. Her bedroom was small and poorly lit. The gray stone walls always left it feeling cold and damp down there, no matter how hot the temperature was outside. It was furnished very simply, with a single bed, a chest of drawers, a small wooden chair, and a creaky old nightstand with a reading lamp on top. A toilet, sink, and shower spigot were set a few feet from her bedroom door with nothing but a heavy plastic curtain hanging from an old metal rod for privacy. Mother said that was all Maizelle needed, that she was here to work, not to lounge about. And if she didn't keep a close eye on her, then that's exactly what that woman would do. At least that's what Mother said.

I never asked Maizelle how she felt about living in the basement either. I guess I already knew the answer to that too. And even though

I believed that she truly loved me, when she rode the bus home at the end of the week, I knew she loved her own family more.

Nathaniel Stephenson took care of the house, the grounds, and Mother's midnight blue Cadillac. He was a tall, lean man whose skin was so wonderfully rich and dark it looked like night, and when he smiled, his teeth shone like the stars in the Milky Way. His eyes were a deep brown but sprinkled with bits of emerald green. His mama said that the day he was born he had been kissed by an angel. Maybe. He was certainly one of the nicest men I ever knew, and definitely the strongest, and not just because I could see the muscles rippling beneath his cotton work shirt.

Nathaniel was no more than eight years old when he was hired to clean the stables and feed the horses at Grove Hill during the summer months. As soon as the weather turned warm, his father would drop him off at the end of the drive just before daybreak. He'd gently push his small son out of the front seat of an old red pickup truck, so rusted in spots it looked as much brown as red, and then he'd toss him one last wave and go to work for another white family on down the road. When he came to pick his son up at the end of the day, smelling like manure and hay, he'd find him sound asleep on a cot left on the back porch. Nathaniel always said that hard work was good for a man, but a child ought to be left to play.

My own father used to call Nathaniel Bubba, for brother, and in a way I guess that's what he was. He taught my father to saddle a horse and to ease a fish off a hook without even flinching. Nathaniel said Mr. Grove used to follow right behind him from dawn to dusk, more reliable than a shadow on a bright, sunny day. But that was a long time ago now.

According to Nathaniel, Grove Hill was once the prettiest place in Nashville, maybe in all of Tennessee. The earth was green and sweeping, and centuries-old oak trees peppered the landscape, providing plenty of shade from the hot summer sun. And nestled among a thick grove of trees stood my home—a big, gracious house built of deep red brick with a large porch that wrapped across the front. Legend has it that my great-grandfather drank too much whiskey one night and painted the brick a creamy white. He had been to Washington, D.C., only the week before and said if President Grant was going to live in a white house, then damn it, so was he. But now the finish was chipped and worn, and you could see the red brick peeking through its tired old coat of paint.

Six large limestone columns lined across the front of the house seemed to act as strong, stoic guards, not only reminding our guests that Grove Hill was an important place but to this day quietly protecting the family that lived there. You can even see where Union gunfire blasted those columns, nicks and cuts in the stone proof of their effort to stop one bullet after another as it sped toward the house.

Nathaniel told me that Grove Hill was actually considered one of the most beautiful antebellum homes still standing, and it was his job to keep her that way. Her formal parlors filled with expensive antiques, an impressive grand staircase with detailed carvings, and a mahogany-paneled library were often featured in ladies' magazines from Virginia to Alabama. Mother spent enormous amounts of time and money decorating and redecorating the house, always selecting the newest French fabrics and silk-screened wallpapers even before the old ones had a chance to age. To me, though, Grove Hill looked kind of tired and lonely no matter how much attention she was given.

But it was here that my father's father, and his father, and at least his father before him developed one of the best Thoroughbred nurseries in the South. That's right, better than any in Virginia, Tennessee, or Kentucky. Robert E. Lee was even known to visit here every spring just to sip a little sherry and inspect the new foals. Grove Hill was a plantation of sorts really, just without the cotton or tobacco or slav-ery. In fact, my family prided themselves in saying that a Grove never owned another human being. Yet somehow they managed to run a prosperous horse farm with the help of countless black men and women who barely made enough money to buy the shirts on their backs. I guess Maizelle was right. It was just a matter of definition.

Of course by the time I was born, there weren't many Thoroughbreds left, or any other kinds of animals for that matter, most having been sold to settle some unpaid debts my grandfather generously left for his firstborn son. Thousands of green, tree-studded acres that had once belonged to my family had been neatly packaged into neighborhoods of small, three-bedroom homes—Grove Hills, Grove Park, Grove Woods. They all looked the same.

And even though Nathaniel now cared for the house, in reality his most pressing assignment became pleasing my mother—waxing the hardwood floors, sweeping the front porch, washing the windows, polishing the silver tea service, or whatever else she demanded. My father and Nathaniel never talked about fishing anymore. They never talked about much of anything anymore. Truthfully, my father could barely look his old friend in the eye. But Nathaniel always managed a sweet smile on his face, even when my mother talked to him as if he was a child.

"Bless it, Nathaniel, were you dropped on your head when you were a baby?" she'd snap when she found a dirty windowpane or the porch needed sweeping. Mother, it seemed, was convinced that any black man or woman who did something she didn't like had been dropped on the head at birth, assuming that the same men and women she trusted to care for her children were unusually careless and clumsy with their own.

"I'm not paying you to sit around and wait for the stars to come out. Now get that window cleaned so I can see out of it. That strong arm of yours is the only reason you've still got a job here."

Mother never really knew how smart Nathaniel was. He could quote Scripture as easily as he could Shakespeare. She just never took the time to notice. He said his own mama had taught him to read when he was no more than three. She told him that in a book, her son could be anybody he wanted to be.

Maybe so. But by the time I was no more than four or five, I had already figured out that there wasn't a white man in Nashville who would let my mother talk to him the way she talked to Nathaniel. Of course, he always said that when you're right with the Lord nobody's words can hurt you. But I didn't know about that. Neither the Lord nor Nathaniel had to live with my mother day and night.

Poor Maizelle, on the other hand, had to work extra hard to hold her tongue when Mother acted hateful and sharp, like the day she fed one of Maizelle's prettiest pound cakes to a bunch of old, hungry crows poking about the yard. Mother stood on the back porch and crumbled it up into little pieces, said it was too dry for human consumption, said she wasn't even sure the birds would be able to choke it down. Maizelle bit her tongue till it bled, and when Mother wasn't looking, she spit blood right in her coffee. I'd only seen her spit like that once, maybe twice. But I hoped she did it all the time. Truthfully, I was feeling so hurt for Maizelle that day that I added a little of my own expectoration to my mother's face cream. The next morning, I spied her sitting in front of her bathroom mirror, admiring her milky, smooth skin.

Even though my mother was unpredictable at best, Maizelle and Nathaniel always managed to maneuver through the days with such a wonderful sense of sameness that my life felt unaccountably safe and secure. Every morning, at half past seven, Nathaniel would back my mother's Cadillac DeVille out of the garage and drive it to the front of the house. He would pull a white rag out of his back pocket and wipe the car's hood, collecting any dust that might have settled during the night. He said he was caring for more than three hundred horses now, each one of them galloping under the hood of that car, and he had to keep their stable shiny and clean.

A few minutes later, Maizelle would push me out the front door with a lunch box in one hand and my sister's little fingers, sticky from eating a grape-jelly biscuit, clutched in the other. Even when Adelaide was too young to go to school, Nathaniel let her ride along with us for fear she'd stand on the front steps and cry herself into a breathless tantrum, disturbing my mother's morning ritual of sleeping past nine and then sipping her coffee in bed.

Adelaide looked like a little fairy with her soft, curly brown hair and bright blue eyes. She was small for her age, and her features were tiny and delicate. Even her voice was small and gentle. She had been born too early, Maizelle said, but she'd catch up in time. Sometimes Adelaide acted just as sweet and tenderhearted as I imagined a fairy would be. But most days she was cranky and ill-tempered, and it was best to leave her in her own secret world playing with her baby dolls, especially the one with the wiry blond hair she called Baby Stella. Maizelle said Adelaide was just being four. But I was not so sure. Besides, she was almost five.

With my sister and Baby Stella neatly tucked in the backseat, Nathaniel took his position behind the steering wheel and carefully guided the car onto the main road. And while my mother drank her morning coffee and made phone calls from her bed, I'd press my nose against the car window and try to melt into the world on the other side of the glass.

My mother, Elizabeth Mabel Morgan, was the only child born to Mabel and Macon Morgan, simple people whose family tree was rooted as deeply in the Tennessee dirt as the Groves'. But since none of the Morgans had shared a bottle of whiskey with Andrew Jackson or hunted bears with Davy Crockett, no one cared about their family tree, which had been thriving on the same small spot of earth about thirty miles outside of town. Some years ago now, the Army Corps of

Engineers had dammed the Cumberland River, turning their family homestead into valuable lakefront property. And almost as quickly as the water filled that valley, leaving my grandparents' house sitting on the southern edge of Old Hickory Lake, my mother's disdain for her childhood home grew into a much more treasured respect.

Mother never said much of anything nice about her parents until the first of every August, when she announced that my sister and I would be spending the month with Nana and Pop. We ought to be by the water during the hottest days of the summer, she'd say, trying to sound as though she was genuinely concerned about her daughters' welfare. It was good for our lungs and our complexions, she'd say and then hold my chin in her hand, searching for any imperfections. Mother must have truly believed in the healing powers of the water, because the minute Nathaniel loaded our suitcases into the trunk of the car, she packed her own bags and headed to Sea Island, alone.

Actually, I could not imagine my mother, who taught us to recite the rules of etiquette more fluidly than the Lord's Prayer, ever running barefoot in the grass and catching lightning bugs with her bare hands, all the things Nana claimed her daughter did when she was a little girl. Before, my grandmother would say, she turned angry and bitter. All I knew was that my mother ran away from home when she was barely sixteen years old. Nana said she left nothing but a shoe box filled with old letters from her boyfriend and a tearstained note taped to her bedroom door. She said she was going to Paris or Hollywood, but she got only as far as Nashville.

Apparently she was working as a salesclerk at the Vanderbilt University bookstore when a fourth-year undergraduate with a handsome smile and an expensive watch on his wrist came looking for a chemistry book. My mother quickly added it all up and told him that she had taken the semester off to pursue an independent study in Renaissance art and that the chemistry books were on the top shelf in the back of the store. My father bought the book, but I'm not sure he ever looked past my mother's hazel eyes and generous bustline. They were married only seven months later in an elaborate ceremony attended by hundreds of Nashvillians eager to meet the beautiful girl with a supposed interest in art and an obscure past who had mesmerized the future Dr. Grove.

And while my father went to medical school, my mother joined the Junior League and the garden club and anything else she deemed worthy of her new position as Mrs. Charles Goodman Grove V. Nathaniel told me that when Mother first came to Grove Hill, she didn't even know how to set the table properly, hadn't even seen a real cloth napkin. He showed her where to put the fork and the knife and how to sit at the table like a real lady. And in no time at all, she learned to host the perfect luncheon, write the perfect note, raise the perfect children, and all the while, maintain the perfect smile. In the end, she probably worked harder than my father.

At some point along the way, Mother exchanged her afternoon coffee for a gin and tonic, served with a fresh slice of lime and freshly crushed ice that Nathaniel hammered into small pieces on the back porch. He guessed that my mother's volunteer work was real demanding and that she needed a little glass of relaxation in the afternoon. But we both knew that Mother with a coffee cup in her hand was not a particularly kind or attentive person and that Mother with a gin and tonic in her hand was simply mean and withdrawn. I didn't really care for either but learned to tolerate both.

Late at night, when the gin had fully consumed my mother's heart, she would scold me for merely walking past her on the way to my bedroom. She said my feet were too heavy on the floor, and I needed to walk like a lady and not one of those *damn* horses loafing about in the field. I'd tiptoe to my room and throw myself across the bed, pretending to be a beautiful princess waiting for some handsome prince to rescue me from the wicked witch who slept down the hall. But the prince never came, nor did my father, who stayed at the hospital long after dark, preferring to save people he knew very little about.

Actually, I was never really sure if my parents loved or hated each other. One New Year's Eve, I saw them kiss fully on the lips, but most days they merely lived side by side, sharing the same space and nothing more. Father seemed almost awkward around my mother, never quite certain of what to say or do. So he usually said and did nothing. And when he died, I couldn't help but wonder if my mother's tears were from knowing that she would never feel his touch again or from missing the daily habit of disliking him.

Had it not been for my cousin Cornelia, who was three years older to the day, I would never have learned anything about true and lasting love. By the time she was twelve, Cornelia was wearing lipstick and mascara to school and had already kissed several boys behind the coatrack. She didn't have a mother—well, not one that really cared about her. In that way, we were very much alike. She said that she learned all she needed to know about being a woman from reading *Seventeen* and that I would surely benefit from her wisdom and experience. My cousin never threw away an issue of that magazine. It was like some sort of Bible that was specially delivered by the United States Postal Service, one chapter at a time, every word sacred and holy.

Fortunately, Cornelia and her father lived just five miles from my house on ten acres of land that my grandfather left his younger son when he died. It may not have seemed as grand a gift as Grove Hill, but the land came with no liens or judgments attached, leaving some to wonder if Uncle Thad had truly been his favorite. Our fathers were brothers but only thanks to a similar genetic code. Uncle Thad was strong and broad-shouldered with rough, callused hands just like Nathaniel's. He wore his hair long, almost to his shoulders, and laughed and cried freely, never once worrying what somebody else might think.

He went to college in the North Carolina mountains, spending most of his days writing poetry and walking in the woods, searching for the earth's inspiration—at least that's what Cornelia told me. Mother said all he was doing was living in some filthy commune and wasting his father's money. Either way, he met a girl and fell in love, and nine months later Cornelia was born. But Cornelia's mother was an artist and had already planned to study painting in New York with Rothko and Motherwell. She wasn't sure she could care for a newborn as long as her artistic spirit was yearning to be nurtured. So after Cornelia was born, her mother and father parted ways, and Uncle Thad brought his baby girl back to Tennessee, genuinely believing that someday the great spirit of the universe would see fit to reunite the three, who were always bound by a never-ending love—at least that's what Cornelia said.

Uncle Thad always seemed to have plenty of time for his daughter, reading to her at night, taking her on long walks through the woods, catching frogs in the creek. Nothing ever seemed more important to him than being with her. But a man's got to make a living, he said. And before long, he started raising some kind of fancy chickens with a funny name. Buff Orpingtons, I think. Cornelia and I called them Buffy Orphans because they acted more like wayward children, wandering all over the place, even in the house. When they started laying these big brown eggs, Uncle Thad called them his golden geese. At first he gave more eggs away than he could sell or scramble, but before long he was shipping cartons of them all over the country, mostly to California.

A few years later, he started keeping bees and harvesting honey. He called that liquid gold and mixed it into fancy soaps and pretty-smelling lotions. He said he learned that if he could put the word *organic* on the label, he could find some overindulged fool to pay top dollar for it. People called my uncle strange. I knew they did. But I thought he was wonderful. And when Cornelia wanted to wear makeup, Uncle Thad said it wasn't his place to limit his daughter's creative expression, although he always added that she was beautiful just the way God made her.

So needless to say, when I kissed a boy for the very first time behind the coatrack in Mrs. Dempsey's sixth-grade classroom, it was Cornelia I trusted with my secret. Oh, it was not a passionate kiss or an enduring kiss. It was not much more than a quick peck on the right cheek, stolen between recess and reading. But it was the first indication that I would lead my life guided by my heart and a fierce determination to know something other than what circumstance surely would have allowed me.

"Bezellia Grove, I am so proud of you," she said as she leapt onto her bed. "You're becoming a woman right before my very eyes. You'll be starting your period before you know it. You will. Just wait and see. Now that you're kissing and all, it's bound to happen soon." I honestly did feel more like a woman, even if I hadn't started buying pads and tampons.

"When you get a little older, guess what?" my cousin asked as she always did, never waiting for an answer. "You're going to kiss Tommy Blanton with your mouth wide open, tongues touching and everything. It's called French kissing and for a very good reason. You know why? It's very passionate, like everything French. But for now, keep that trap of yours locked tight. You don't want to get a bad reputation before you even get started. Trust me."

I couldn't imagine kissing a boy with my mouth wide open, nor did I understand why opening my mouth would lead to a bad reputation or a love of anything French. What I did know was that Tommy's cheek had felt so soft under my lips that I wanted to kiss him again and again just so I could memorize the touch of his skin. I remembered pulling my head back from his face and standing perfectly still in his presence, afraid to open my eyes, afraid I had scared the boy who had seemed, until now, more interested in playing tetherball than in kissing a girl. But just as that moment of uncertainty lingered into awkwardness, I had felt something warm on my cheek. It was Tommy Blanton's lips, his rough, dry, cracked lips.

"Tommy and Bezellia sittin' in a tree, K-I-S-S-I-N-G. First comes love, then comes marriage, then comes . . . ," sang a chorus of classmates who had suddenly swarmed behind the coatrack, not giving either one of us time to acknowledge the other.

Tossing my hair behind my shoulder, I turned and walked away, ignoring both the song and Tommy's embarrassed plea to them to stop. I took my seat at my desk and opened my arithmetic workbook. *Underline with a red pencil every equation on the page that contains a remainder.* Red. The color of passion and love.

At the end of the day, Nathaniel was patiently waiting for me at the front of the hookup line, reading the afternoon newspaper with one eye and watching for me with the other. Today I desperately wanted him to be the last car in the driveway so I could jump rope with the other girls and whisper in their ears about love and Tommy Blanton, the remnant of his kiss still warm on my cheek.

"Miss Bezellia," Nathaniel cried, his voice dragging me from deep within a cluster of girls gathered on the sidewalk. "Sweet Jesus, child," he hollered as I walked toward the car, "you not see me sitting right here? What'd you learn in that classroom today anyway?"

"Same old stuff," I snapped as I climbed into the back of the Cadillac, slamming the door behind me.

"Uh-uh. Not believing that. You learned something new today. I see it in your face," he said as he leaned into the front seat, all the while studying me real hard like he was trying to break some secret code.

"Nathaniel! Stop looking at me like that!"

"Oh, Lord, I got it now. You're a girl in love."

"I am not."

"You know I've got three girls of my own, Miss Bezellia. I know the look. C'mon, what's his name?"

"I don't know what you're talking about. Just drive the car, Nathaniel," I ordered, my tone suddenly sounding shrill and cutting, just like my mother's.

"Miss Bezellia, there's no harm in liking a boy or him liking you back for that matter," Nathaniel said, gently reminding me that he deserved more respect than I had offered. Then he turned his attention forward and steered the car toward the road. He let out a slow and steady breath and settled into a familiar position—one hand firmly on the steering wheel, the other relaxed by his side.

I had spent a lot of time studying the back of Nathaniel's head. He had thick black hair cut real short. But right on top he had a small bald spot, not much bigger than a quarter. He said it had always been that way, even when he was a little boy. His mother told him that was the very spot where the angel had kissed her son before delivering him to earth. So from where I was sitting in the back of the Cadillac, I wanted to believe with all my heart that this was a head that could be trusted.

I grabbed the edge of the seat with both hands and pulled myself forward and let my secret slide right out of my mouth. "It's Tommy. Tommy Blanton." There. There it was. Now my secret was floating out in the heavens for anyone to know it. I rested against the hot leather seat, feeling proud and breathless all at the same time, waiting for Nathaniel to recognize my truest confession.

He looked surprised at first, as though the name rang a bell. He put both hands on the wheel and drove all the way to Hillsboro Pike, squinting his eyes and occasionally tapping his left hand against the wheel. He must have studied that name backward and forward for three or four miles before nodding his head in revelation.

"That's the boy whose mama and daddy got a divorce last year after she found him with . . . I mean after—" Nathaniel caught himself before he disclosed more than he figured a sixth-grade girl needed to know. "I mean they're the ones who got a divorce. Went and had some judge tear their marriage apart as if it never happened. I heard your mama talking about them on the telephone just the other day. Yep, they're the ones."

The wind suddenly lifted my day's work sheets from my lap. They swirled about the back of the car like confetti thrown at a parade. I started laughing and grabbing for my papers, quickly stacking them neatly in order on the top of my notebook. And there in front of me was a heart, a heart I had drawn when I was supposed to be searching for remainders, a heart that symbolized my love for Tommy Blanton. Tommy and I would never get a divorce. We would love each other forever.

Mother wasn't home when we arrived at Grove Hill. She was probably at the country club lingering over a bridge table with friends, so I begged Nathaniel to drive me to Cornelia's. I needed to tell her about my kiss. I needed to tell her about my newly discovered womanhood. I told Nathaniel we needed more eggs.

Even now I still remember lying on Cornelia's pink-flowered bedspread unraveling the events of my day like a kitten playfully pulling a piece of yarn from a skein. My cousin, with her legs folded beneath her, sat on the bed across from me. She was beaming with pride, as if this kiss had been a reflection of her own efforts. She asked if I had felt a little dizzy, and when I told her that I thought I had, she confirmed that this was indeed a true and lasting love.

She jumped off her bed and hopped over to her vanity, which was looking more and more like the cosmetics counter at Castner Knott. She picked up a tube of lipstick and then turned and stood right in front of me, staring into my eyes so intently I thought she was peering straight into my soul.

"Honey Bee Pink. Brand-new color. Just came out. It's kind of faint but very powerful." Cornelia hummed and then smeared the lipstick across her mouth. She handed me the white plastic tube and indicated that I was to do the same. Then she picked up a mirror with a long pink handle and admired her lips. She kissed the glass and handed the mirror to me, again indicating that I was to do just as she had done. "Remember, be careful, it's very potent stuff. I bet there's real honey in it."

"Thanks," I said in a hushed, appreciative tone, holding the lipstick tube carefully between my fingers. I slowly rubbed some across my own lips and then kissed the mirror just as Cornelia had, leaving a waxy impression of my kiss on the glass. Now this mirror knew my secret too.

At the dinner table later that evening, I sat straight in my chair and tried to cut my chicken without scraping the blade of my knife across the plate. Mother said food was not to be butchered, merely cut. Sometimes I left the table hungry because the thought of cutting anything in my mother's presence made my stomach hurt. And tonight, with the lipstick still hidden in my skirt pocket, I didn't want her scrutinizing my table manners. I just wanted to hide in my room and practice writing my name.

Mrs. Tommy Blanton, Mrs. T. Blanton, Mrs. Tommy and Bezellia Blanton, Mrs. Bezellia Blanton

"Sister, your uncle called," Mother said abruptly, bringing my attention back to the meat held tightly under my fork and knife. "You left a workbook at his house today. He thought you might need it for school tomorrow."

"A workbook?" I answered, adding an appropriate dose of both confusion and innocence to my voice.

"Yes, a workbook." And then my mother stiffened her back and her tone became as inflexible as her body. "You come straight home tomorrow. We don't need any more of his damn brown eggs."

"Yes, ma'am," I whispered, and my knife slid from one edge of the plate to the other, screaming as it made its way across the porcelain. My mother glared at me. She looked so stern and disapproving I was afraid she could see my heart was aching for a boy who kept a piece of gum tucked inside his cheek. I could only hope that, by this time of the evening, Mother's vision was too clouded with gin for her to know my most honest thoughts and that by morning she would have forgotten about a lost workbook.

Thankfully, she was still sleeping when I left for school the next day with Cornelia's lipstick neatly hidden in my pocket. I raced to Mrs. Dempsey's classroom and found Tommy sitting at his desk. I abruptly stopped in the doorway to regain my composure and quickly ran my hands down my pleated blue skirt. Tommy glanced at the door and then lowered his head, choosing instead to focus on the comic book lying open on top of his desk. My eyes started filling with tears, and I was afraid everyone would see my broken heart dripping down my cheeks. But as soon as I took my seat next to his, his green eyes warmed and his blank expression turned into a reassuring smile.

Mrs. Dempsey talked all morning about Columbus and Indians and fractions and prepositional phrases, one subject blending into the next, none of them making any sense to me. Finally, she directed us to close our books. And that day, like the day before, I found myself behind the coatrack primping for Tommy Blanton. I tightened my ponytail and again pressed my hands down my skirt. Then I ceremoniously pulled the tube of lipstick from my pocket and carefully shellacked my lips with a heavy coat of Honey Bee Pink, just like Cornelia had told me to do.

"Gee, Bezellia, you smell good—kind of like honey." Tommy was standing behind me. I hadn't noticed him until he was suddenly there, talking in that deep, raspy voice that should have belonged to a much older boy.

"It's my new lipstick, I guess."

"Huh. Is that why your lips are shining like that?"

"They're supposed to shine."

"Huh."

I closed my eyes. Then I closed my mouth and held my breath, eagerly but patiently waiting for Tommy's lips to find mine. I smelled his skin, a faded hint of Ivory Snow, as he leaned toward my face. His lips felt soft and tender today, gentler than I had remembered. I smiled, a thank-you of sorts, and then straightened my skirt once more and walked back to my desk, my lips tasting like the sweetest clover honey.

For three more days, Tommy and I loved each other as well as any two eleven-year-olds could. We stood next to each other in the lunch line but never said more than hello. And we faithfully met behind the coatrack but never spoke a word about what we did there.

Every afternoon I begged Nathaniel to take me by Cornelia's, if only for a moment. And every afternoon Nathaniel would say the same thing: "If your mama finds out, dear, sweet Jesus, she'll wallop us both." But we both knew my mother was more interested in her bridge parties than in my comings and goings, and so he'd smile and turn the car right onto Davidson Road.

But by the end of the week, the late September air had grown thick and heavy. Nathaniel leaned his head out the open car window. And even though there wasn't a cloud in sight, he said a thunderstorm was surely heading our way. Nathaniel read the sky like my mother read the society page, and he could say with great accuracy when we were heading into violent weather. But today I felt it too.

"That's right, Miss Bezellia. A storm is surely heading our way. Be here by nightfall. Mark my words," he declared, and he gingerly pulled the car into the driveway and continued toward the front of the house. My mother was perched near the top of the porch, her arms folded across her chest. She had never welcomed me home from school, and it did not appear that was her intention today. She stood unusually tall in her high heels, almost like a giant. Her eyes remained fixed on the car.

Nathaniel lifted his foot off the accelerator, being particularly careful not to stir up any dust as he approached the house. He came to a stop and placed the car in park. He eased out of the Cadillac and tipped his hat. Mother just ignored him. He walked to the other side of the car and opened the rear door. Without a word, Nathaniel reached for my arm and tenderly pulled me out of the backseat. He squeezed my hand before letting go, as if trying to secretly inject some hidden strength or courage into my small body.

Mother remained motionless as I climbed the few steps toward her. Standing in her shadow, I shielded my eyes with my forearm. The sun was shining so brightly behind her I couldn't see that she had already raised her right hand. Without saying a word, she slapped me across the cheek. For a moment, I desperately tried to balance myself on the edge of the hard marble step. She could have reached for me. She could have grabbed me. Instead she looked beyond me, as if I wasn't even there, her hands resting behind her back as I fell helplessly against the steps.

"Listen to me, Sister. You are not going around this town acting like some whorish tramp," Mother said with an ugly and bitter tongue. "You hear me? No makeup on your face and no more Tommy Blanton. He is as worthless as his worthless, two-bit parents. Do you understand me?"

She didn't care what I thought, and I knew it was best to say nothing. In my silence, my mother once again folded her arms across her chest and then turned to walk back inside the house. Truthfully, my head was full of so much hurt, I hadn't heard much of anything Mother said except that Tommy Blanton was worthless. And as soon as she stepped through the front door, Nathaniel rushed to my side. I buried my face in his strong, steady arms and began to sob. He picked me up and carried me to the back of the house and through the kitchen door.

"Now, now, Miss Bezellia, you're gonna be all right. You're gonna be all right," he kept chanting quietly in my ear.

Maizelle looked up from her chair and dropped the basket of green beans she was stringing for the night's dinner.

"Sweet Jesus, Nathaniel, what's done gone and happened to Miss Bezellia? Bring her here to me."

Nathaniel placed me on Maizelle's lap, and then he gently held my chin in the palm of his rough, thick hand so both he and Maizelle could better examine my face. He saw the blood trickling from the corner of my lips, where my mother's diamond ring must have ripped my skin. My mouth tasted as if I had been sucking on a piece of metal pipe. Nathaniel handed me a glass of ice water and told me to drink it all.

"What happened?" Maizelle persisted, looking at Nathaniel with bold, determined eyes, afraid that she already knew the answer to her question.

"Miss Bezellia fell down the front steps, lost her footing."

Maizelle understood what Nathaniel was not saying, and she pulled me tighter against her chest. "Get me a cold rag and the baby aspirin there in that drawer." She held the cool, wet rag to my cheek while Nathaniel fumbled with the bottle of aspirin. The only other sound was the kitchen clock that hung over the back door, gently humming as one second poured into the next.

We'd all heard my mother say some pretty ugly things to me, and she had certainly swatted my hand more times than I could count. But she had never hit me. Not like that. Not on the face. For the first time in my life I really, truly believed I hated her. But I didn't hate her because she had hit me or because she'd just stood there and watched me fall. I hated her because she had said such mean things about Tommy.

"He's not worthless," I finally muttered and burst into tears.

"Oh, Lord, child, that boy, that's what this is about?" Maizelle looked at Nathaniel for confirmation.

"You listen to me, honey. It's natural for that heart of yours to feel things. You ain't done nothing wrong. Ya' hear me, Miss Bezellia? Not nothing wrong."

Nothing wrong? I couldn't kiss Tommy anymore. I couldn't stand next to him behind the coatrack anymore. Everything about this felt wrong, very wrong.

Mother didn't come to the dinner table that night. She told Maizelle she wasn't hungry. I sat there and wondered if she might starve to death, even pictured her in my head crawling to the kitchen, begging for food. But Nathaniel carried a small plate of scrambled eggs and a gin and tonic to her bedroom before leaving for the evening. Mrs. Grove had what she needed, he said, and then winked good night at me and Adelaide and walked out the back door. I wanted to go with him so bad I almost cried, even if his house did have dirt floors like Mother said it did. I would rather have been anywhere than here.

But Adelaide and I just sat frozen at the table, staring at each other, eating our dinner alone. Father had phoned, as he usually did, a few minutes before Maizelle was ready to serve our plates to let us know that he needed to care for another dying patient. Fine with me. In fact, I was almost grateful that some poor sick soul had captured my father's attention once again. I was in no mood to endure another meal under my mother's watchful eye or my father's mournful stare. Adelaide sat still and quiet, a chicken leg in one hand and Baby Stella dangling in the other.

By the time I went to bed, the corner of my mouth was swollen and a rich shade of blue. I would tell my friends that Adelaide and I had been playing freeze tag in the house and I ran into the edge of a door. And I would tell Tommy Blanton that I could not meet him behind the coatrack, that I could never again feel his lips against mine. I would try to explain that ours was a forbidden love, like Romeo and Juliet's, at least that's what Cornelia called it. Tears rolled down my face, stinging my mouth where my skin was raw, washing his kisses away forever.

As I slipped into that space between sleep and wakefulness, I heard someone walk into my room. Without even opening my eyes, I knew it was my father. I had felt him by my side so many nights before, leaning over my bed, studying me as if he was memorizing some beautiful painting. He stroked my head and then turned and walked out of the room. I wondered if my father knew what had happened on the steps of his childhood home. I wondered if he hated my mother as much as I did.

After school the next day, I asked Nathaniel to drive me to my cousin's house. He looked at me through the rearview mirror. His eyes were open so wide with surprise and concern they looked like two small saucers placed side by side. I quickly shook my head and told him not to worry. I just needed to return something. I'd only be a minute.

Uncle Thad greeted me at the front door and said that Cornelia wasn't home but that I was welcome to wait in her room and listen to records till she got back. Then he lightly stroked his forefinger against my cheek.

"What happened, Bezellia?"

I mumbled something that not even I fully understood and then ran up the stairs. I should have known my uncle would never have been satisfied with such a cryptic answer, and by the time I got to the top step, he was already walking to the car, motioning to Nathaniel.

Cornelia's bedroom door was wide open, and I could see the pink plastic mirror resting on the top of her vanity. I slowly walked across the room and picked it up, carefully turning it over as if it was a piece of my mother's fine crystal. The impression of my lips was still on the glass, smudged but still there. I dropped the lipstick on Cornelia's bed and then ran back to the car, knowing that Tommy's kisses would soon be nothing more than a precious, well-kept memory.

chapter two

The day the Women's Volunteer League appointed my mother cochair of the symphony's first formal gala was the same day she told her parents to be expecting their granddaughters for the entire summer. She said the Iris Ball, named at my mother's suggestion for the Tennessee state flower, was destined to be the city's premier social event. And since she was creating a legacy for herself and the Grove family, she could not be bothered by anyone or anything until the end of September—unless of course it was her cochair, Mrs. George Madison Longfellow Hunt V, known to my mother simply as Evelyn.

Mother reminded me almost every day that working with Mrs. Hunt was a great privilege and that she was certainly the envy of every woman in town. The Hunts had, after all, lived in Nashville as long as the Groves, but they had invested their money in steel throughout the South, not horses, and now their name was on everything and ours was not—the Hunt Museum of Fine Arts, the Hunt Historical Collection, and the Hunt Botanical Gardens, not to mention Hunt Boulevard, Hunt Valley Road, and Hunt Ridge Lane.

Adelaide always burst into tears when Mother told her she would be spending any time at the lake. She would fall on the floor and cry till she turned a light shade of blue. I, on the other hand, relished the thought of being far from my mother and all the rules involved with being a Grove. There weren't really any rules to speak of at my grandparents' house. Nana didn't care if our shorts and shirts matched or if we brushed our hair in the mornings. She barely brushed her own thin gray hair, let alone noticed if we had taken care of ours.

I spent most of my days fishing for crappie, chasing lightning bugs, and watching a little television while I painted my chigger bites with clear nail polish and drank Coca-Colas right out of the bottle. Adelaide usually calmed down after a day or two. Maybe it was the water that soothed her as Mother said it would, or the special vitamins Nana insisted she take, or the fresh country air that calmed her. I really don't know for sure, but I think it had more to do with Adelaide taking Baby Stella in the lake for a daily swim and making mud pies from dawn to dusk, no one caring whether the mud got caked in her hair or in her ears.

Right before dinner, my grandmother would undress my little sister in the front yard and then soap her down for anyone to see. She'd even wash Baby Stella, scrub her head like she was cleaning a real live human baby. Every now and then, Nana reminded me of Mother, saying something mean and unexpected. But fortunately it wasn't often. And fortunately it was never meant for me.

Mother genuinely tried to convince my sister that she would have a wonderful summer out by the lake, but Adelaide couldn't hear anything comforting amid all of her whining and fussing. Mother finally smacked her hands together and warned her little girl that she did not have the patience or the energy for this ill-timed, overly zealous display of emotion and that Adelaide's dramatics were causing her head to hurt. My sister just lay on the floor kicking and screaming, and Mother went and fixed herself another gin and tonic.

I was never sure if it was chairing the gala or talking to Mrs. Hunt on the telephone every day that delighted my mother most. Mrs. Hunt was a beautiful woman, as all Mother's friends were. Her hair was light blond and stylishly short, curled and teased into a very attractive bob. She never went anywhere without wearing high-heeled shoes and two-piece suits, and always pinned to her jacket's lapel was a large, diamond-encrusted H. My mother admired that pin very much. And before long, she was consulting Mrs. Hunt about everything—invitations, caterers, menus, even her children.

Adelaide and I quickly found ourselves wearing matching taffeta dresses and waltzing every Tuesday afternoon with a bunch of other kids who looked as perfect and as miserable as we did. My sister, however, learned almost on the spot that if she'd stomp and snort loud enough, Mother would leave her at home. Oh, Mother would threaten Adelaide with a spanking that she would never forget, and my sister would retaliate by screaming even louder and clutching Baby Stella tightly against her chest. Then Mother would, inevitably, leave them both behind, but only as she reminded me that I was very privileged to be dancing with Mrs. Hunt's children.

One afternoon I simply refused to go. I told my mother that there was nothing particularly privileged about holding some boy's sweaty hand while he stood on my left foot. She immediately lowered her body so her face was directly in front of mine. And with her finger pointed sharply in front of my nose, she said that when she was a little girl she would have *given* her left foot to dance with a Hunt. And I obviously did not appreciate what had been handed to me on one very old, albeit slightly tarnished, silver spoon. Then she grabbed me by the arm and dragged me to the car.

Besides, she said, I was now old enough to understand that worthwhile relationships were not rooted in the foolish affairs of the heart. She had learned the hard way that there were only three things of value to look for in a man. One, he wears cashmere. Two, he drives a convertible. And three, he glides across the dance floor. Anything more than that, Mother said, should not be of any importance to me, now or ever. I asked her if that was all she had looked for in my father. She simply tilted her head back and laughed. But from where I was sitting, it seemed that being a good wife had much more to do with impressing other wives than it did dancing with your own husband.

Mrs. Hunt flew to New York to buy a triple strand of pearls with a diamond clasp. She came to Grove Hill straight from the airport so she could flaunt her bejeweled neck in front of her dear, envious friend. My mother took one look at that necklace and then demanded that my father send her to Tiffany too. It wasn't right, she shouted later that night behind their closed bedroom door, that her neck was always bare. It was simply embarrassing that the only pearls she owned were fake—cheap, cultured impostors. And it was very, very rotten, she screamed, that the one strand of pearls my father had ever seen fit to give to anyone had been presented to his baby daughter. Mother must not have liked what he had to say, because I heard a loud *thud* and the sound of shattering glass. A week later, a turquoise blue box arrived at Grove Hill.

Mother was determined that her daughters possess the skills she believed necessary for our own social survival—writing that seemingly sincere thank-you note, needlepointing one's monogram in the same turquoise blue thread that Mother confirmed was in fact Tiffany's signature color, and of course, maintaining that perfect smile whenever you're dining at the club or having cocktails with friends. It was as simple as that.

So it was really no surprise to me when I came home from school one day and found a strange man with dark black hair and a silver mustache standing on the front porch. He greeted me as if we were old friends, enthusiastic and warm, even if I didn't understand a single word he said.

"*Bonjour. Je m'appelle Monsieur Gadoue. Je suis votre le nouveau professeur. Votre mère veut que vous parlez français. Elle est au club de loisirs en discutant le menu pour la boule avec Madame Hunt.*"

I understood nothing but "Madame Hunt," which was all the explanation I needed. Mrs. Hunt believed that any modern, educated child should speak French fluently. I had heard her say it myself. After all, it was the language of international diplomacy and of sophisticated, glamorous women like Jackie Kennedy. And Monsieur Gadoue was now here to make certain that someday I could politely converse with the former First Lady in both English and French.

I'm sure my mother's motives were more mundane than the thought of sending her daughter to the White House or abroad with a needlepointed peace treaty to engage in foreign affairs. But I rather liked Monsieur Gadoue, and the thought of engaging in any type of diplomacy, even buying a café au lait on the banks of the Seine someday, sounded exciting and wildly exotic to me. Besides, Mother never seemed as happy as she did now. And dancing and sewing and speaking French all seemed like a very small price to pay for her happiness, fleeting or not.

By the first of June, however, I was growing very tired of doing whatever Mrs. Hunt judged important, and I found myself counting the days until I would leave Grove Hill. Even my father seemed to think I had needlepointed enough pincushions to last me a lifetime and maybe my fingers needed a rest. I had hoped that poor little Adelaide would be ready to go too, but when Nathaniel carried her trunk into her bedroom, she started crying and kicking her feet. She cried when Maizelle packed all of her neatly folded matching short sets. She cried when Maizelle told her to collect her books and babies. And she cried when Maizelle closed the lid of her trunk and fastened the lock. Finally, even Maizelle put her hands on her hips and told my sister to hush. Not until Adelaide was much older did I realize that it wasn't that she loved Grove Hill so much. She was just afraid to be anyplace else.

My father came into my room late that night to tell me goodbye. He stood awkwardly by my bed and said he was going to miss me. He said he didn't know what he was going to do all summer in this big, empty house without his darling daughters there to liven things up a bit. He said he would be at the hospital when we woke and then kissed me on the forehead. He lingered for a minute, seeming unsure of what to do or where to go next. I stroked the top of his hand and told him not to worry, that I'd be home soon. Then I went to sleep as I had so many times before, wondering if my father was happy, wondering if he had ever been happy.

Just as the sun began to light my room, I heard the telephone ring. The house was so quiet and still that the abrupt sound of the phone rolled through my body like thunder, and I could hear my mother speaking as plainly as if she was standing next to me.

"What? When?" There was a long pause. "The doctor said what? Damn it. Well, what am I supposed to say, Mama?" And suddenly I knew my plans for the summer had changed. There was another pause, and I could hear my mother tapping her foot on her bedroom floor as though she was sending out some angry message in Morse code.

"Of course I care about Daddy. It's just that this gala is very important. Well, I'll try. I cannot promise a thing. I said I'd try. Don't bring that up again, Mama; that was a long time ago and doesn't have one damn thing to do with Daddy's heart."

Mother slammed the phone down on her nightstand and then began slamming doors. She was mad, and every door in the house was her victim. I pretended to be asleep, tightly closing my eyes and sliding farther under my covers. And even though I was desperate to know what had happened to my grandfather on the other end of the telephone, it was ten o'clock before I braved leaving my room and wandered downstairs.

I found Mother sitting at the breakfast table with a cup of coffee in one hand and the telephone receiver in the other. A lit cigarette was resting on the edge of a round, silver ashtray, a gift from Mrs.

Hunt. She'd bought it at Tiffany. Mother had never held a cigarette before she met Mrs. Hunt, but now she could balance one perfectly between her long, thin fingers no matter what she was doing, even while she was combing her hair. When the surgeon general announced that smoking caused cancer, Mother only laughed, saying that a government-paid doctor is hardly one to be trusted with your life.

"Evelyn, it's absolutely unbelievable," she moaned, sniffling a bit for added effect. Mother always sounded like another person when she was talking to her friends, particularly to Mrs. Hunt. She sounded like somebody I wished I knew.

"I'm still in shock. She just called this morning before I'd had a chance to have even one cup of coffee. I mean the girls' trunks are packed and everything. They're ready to go."

Mother tapped her cigarette on the edge of the ashtray.

"The poor man, yes, I'm sure he was working too hard. I've tried to get him to sell that farm, but he won't hear of it."

Mother put the cigarette to her mouth and drew the smoke into her lungs. "Camp? In North Carolina? No, I really hadn't thought of that. Oh, but you're right. It probably is too late to send the girls this summer." She sighed, blowing smoke in my face as if I wasn't even standing there. "But yes, do remember us for next year. The mountain air would be so good for Sister's complexion. Yes, yes, I know. Thanks, Evelyn, so very much. You're such a dear friend."

I stood cautiously by my mother's side, afraid that even the slightest movement might annoy her. She finally waved her left hand, motioning for me to sit down while keeping the receiver tightly clutched in her right. I wondered for a moment if my grandfather was dead, maybe lying motionless in a field surrounded by stalks of young corn he was nurturing into adulthood. But Mother sharply slapped her hand on the table in front of me, and my thoughts and attention quickly fell back to her.

"Well, you know Charles has Nathaniel tied up all summer

building that damn barn, and for what, a couple of old horses that should be in a bottle of glue.

"Maizelle? Lord, no. I can't trust that woman to get anything right but a hot buttered biscuit. I swear I think her mama dropped her on her head when she was a baby. Did you know, Evelyn, that I found her in Adelaide's bathtub the other day taking a hot soak?"

I hated it when Mother talked about Nathaniel and Maizelle that way. Nathaniel was only building that *damn* barn because Mother wanted every inch of Grove Hill looking its best come September since she would be hosting several luncheons at the house in the weeks before the ball. She even wanted the horses looking their best and had told Nathaniel to start giving them better feed and to brush their coats every day. And poor Maizelle, she had only taken that bath because her back was hurting from kneeling on the kitchen floor, scrubbing the baseboards with something not much bigger than a toothbrush. I was the one who suggested the hot soak. I even gave her some of my bubble bath.

"Oh, yes, I was going to fire her, excuse my French, colored ass right then and there, but Charles wouldn't let me. She's been with us since the day Sister was born, and Charles said it wouldn't be right to fire her after all these years." Mother sat there nodding her head, agreeing with whatever was being said on the other end of the line. "I know it. She and Nathaniel both have to be reminded of their place from time to time. I think they've been listening to that damn Martin Luther King again. Anyway, dear, remember we have a meeting at the club at eleven. The chef hopes to have the menu prepared for a final tasting. I'll see you then. Bye bye."

Mother gracefully placed the receiver back on the telephone base and pulled her ashtray toward her. The smoke from her cigarette was drawn to my face. I closed my eyes and saw my grandfather waving his arms, begging for help. I turned away and hid in the smoke, shielding my cheeks behind the palms of my hands and wondering why my complexion was suddenly my mother's concern. I had seen only one pimple on my chin, and Mother had grabbed me and squeezed it dry, telling me to hush as she pinched my skin between her nails.

"Mother," I said very cautiously, not wanting to upset her any more than she already was, "what happened to Pop?"

"What? Oh. Yes. Well, it seems, at least according to your grandmother, that your grandfather has had a heart attack—or something like that," she said flatly, not sounding as though she was truly convinced that her father was ill at all.

"I know, I'm worried sick about him too," she added, more out of a sense of obligation, I imagined, than any real concern. Then she pulled another breath through her cigarette. "Your grandmother said he is going to need lots of quiet and rest. Doctor's orders or something like that. So it seems you girls will not be going to the lake this summer, and Lord knows I have a thousand meetings between now and September twenty-sixth." Mother stared at the kitchen wall, again blowing smoke in my face, as if she had yet to notice I was sitting there next to her.

"Honestly, I do think your grandmother is being a bit ridiculous about the whole thing," she said, as much to herself as to me. "You girls spend most of your days outside anyway. Besides, I just don't know where all this love and concern is suddenly coming from. I've always said she'd be the one to put that poor man in his grave, picking on him the way she does."

My mother and I rarely had a conversation about anything. And now it felt as though she was looking to me for some kind of comfort or advice. I patiently listened to every mean and mocking word she had to say about her mother, and then I scooted my chair slightly closer to hers and made her an offer. "I can watch her for you, Mother. Adelaide, that is. I can take care of her. I'm fourteen now. Cornelia started babysitting the Jamesons' little boys when she was only thirteen.

Besides, you know Adelaide, all she wants to do is play with her babies anyway."

My mother's eyes darted from left to right as she considered my proposition. The Iris Ball was, in Mother's very own words, the single most important event in her life. I truly didn't understand why she was hesitating to accept, unless, of course, she thought it best to call Mrs. Hunt first.

"Okay, Sister," she finally said, pulling the cigarette back to her lips. "If you think you are up for the job, you can have it. You'll be on your own for the most part. And you have to stay out of sight and out of trouble. Nathaniel is going to be very busy, so you can't get in his way or ask him to drive you all over town. That barn has to look good, and I don't think that man can do two things at once and get either one of them right." She paused for a moment, as though she was rethinking her decision. Then she sat back in her chair and released a slow, steady breath, the smoke forming loose rings as it filtered through the air. "Be sure and keep an eye on Maizelle too."

I nodded my head as if I understood her concern.

"Well, go on and get dressed. It'll be noon before you know it. And just because it's summer doesn't mean you can walk around here looking like an orphan child. This is not your grandparents' house. Put on those Bermuda shorts I bought you in Atlanta." She waved her hand in my face again, this time motioning for me to leave.

I ran up the stairs, skipping every other one, eager to tell Adelaide of our new summer plans. My little sister jumped up and down when I told her she would be staying at Grove Hill, and then she ran to wake Baby Stella and share the news with her. I told them both that if she didn't mind me, Mother was going to ship Adelaide off to some camp in North Carolina where baby dolls were not allowed. My sister threw her arms around my waist and promised to be a very good girl. She said Baby Stella would be good too.

I couldn't stop smiling, knowing that it was me, Bezellia Louise Grove, who had been the one to rescue my mother. Not even Mrs. Hunt could help her *dear friend* this time. And giving up one carefree summer at the lake would all be worth it, because maybe, come September, my mother would love me a little bit more.

$\mathcal{M}$other left shortly after breakfast almost every morning, not even taking the time to linger in bed and drink her coffee. She was gone until dinner, sometimes not coming home then, choosing instead to stay at the club and eat with her friends. Some afternoons Mother and Mrs. Hunt arrived at Grove Hill, and the two of them sat on the porch, nibbling chicken salad sandwiches and sipping gin and tonics, all the while talking about the ball, devoting much of their conversation to the design of their gowns and the final invitation list.

Mrs. Holder would be invited. Her husband was a prominent attorney in town. He took her to Paris for their tenth wedding anniversary. Mrs. Warren would not. She was fake and inconsiderate. She bought her clothes at Castner Knott but told everyone they came from Neiman Marcus, shipped all the way from Dallas.

Father stayed home a little longer in the mornings. Most days we'd sit on the front steps together, waiting for Nathaniel's truck to pull in the drive. I'd lean against my father's stiffly starched shirts and fill my head with the musky aftershave he had sprinkled all over his face. He said he needed to check Nathaniel's work, but I think he was just enjoying the opportunity to visit with his old friend. The two of them would stand by the barn and point toward its roofline every now and again, but mostly they just talked about horses and fishing and long afternoons spent down by the creek when they were young.

As for me, I spent most of my time tending to my little sister, just as I'd promised my mother I'd do. I helped her bathe and dress her babies and set up tea parties on an old, worn quilt under the oak tree in the front yard. Maizelle wouldn't let Adelaide put tea or lemonade or even water in her little plastic teapot unless we went outside to play. She said she was not cleaning up any more of Adelaide's messes in the house. That was my job now. But when Adelaide was napping in the afternoons, I would sprawl across the chaise lounge on the porch and read the collection of Nancy Drew mysteries that Uncle Thad had given me for my fourteenth birthday. He had written a short message inside the first book.

> *Dear Bezellia, hoping you solve life's mysteries. Happy Birthday, Uncle Thad*

I must have looked kind of puzzled when I read his inscription, because he patted me on the back and told me not to worry. He said I'd figure it out someday because I was a smart, plucky girl just like Nancy Drew. I loved that he thought I was *plucky*, although I wasn't really sure what that meant. I just hoped it had nothing to do with his chickens.

At the very end of June, Mother announced at dinner that she and Mrs. Hunt would be traveling to New York to buy some imported table linens for the Iris Ball. She would be gone for four or five days, and Adelaide and I were to behave. Then she turned and looked at my father, and with the stern and serious tone a parent would use to caution a child before crossing the street, she warned him that she would be spending an afternoon at Tiffany. Mrs. Hunt had already scheduled a private appointment with the store's manager.

When Mother left, she hugged me good-bye. Even now, when I close my eyes, I can still feel her arms wrapped tightly around my shoulders. She looked so beautiful, dressed in a coral silk suit and her hair tucked neatly under a matching pillbox-shaped hat. A large diamond brooch in the shape of a *G* was attached to her lapel. Father had given it to her that morning at breakfast, pinned to her napkin. They had even exchanged a brief kiss.

As the Cadillac headed down the driveway, Mother looked back at her daughters and waved a final good-bye. I ran behind the car as it made its way to the road. Mother watched me from the rear window. She smiled so sweetly. Surely she was going to miss me. Then the car turned to the right, and my mother was suddenly out of sight.

Adelaide kicked up some dirt with her new white tennis shoes and then turned and walked back to the house. Before she got into the car, Mother had warned Adelaide not to get this pair of shoes dirty. Of course, when Maizelle saw them, she snorted something about a mother buying a child anything white to wear must be a mother who never has done a load of laundry. Then she shook her head and walked down the stairs to the basement carrying a basket full of our dirty clothes.

Adelaide wasted no time in telling me that her babies needed a good bath and a long nap. I warned her not to get water on the bathroom floor again, because I, like Maizelle, was not cleaning up another mess today, and then I stretched out on the chaise lounge and opened my book. My eyes were already heavy, and I found myself staring at the same words over and over again.

Nancy Drew began peeling off her garden gloves as she ran up the porch steps and into the hall to answer the ringing . . .

Nancy Drew began peeling off her garden gloves as she ran up the porch steps and into the hall to answer the ringing . . .

Somewhere I could hear the sound of a car pulling up the drive, the tires crunching over the gravel as they rolled forward, the noise forcing its way through my sleep. Drowsy and confused, I dropped my book on the floor and started looking for my mother. But it was only Nathaniel this time, perched behind the wheel of his old blue pickup truck, with his worn brown hat pulled low on his forehead. I squinted my eyes a little tighter and sat up a little straighter, trying to wake myself. It was Nathaniel all right, but somebody else was sitting next to him, somebody I had never seen before.

He looked about my age, maybe a year or two older. He had chocolate brown skin and deep, dark eyes. He was wearing a pair of worn-out blue jeans that rested low on his waist and made his legs look slender and long. He was almost as tall as Nathaniel, but he didn't really look like him, at least until he smiled. And it was a smile I had known since I was a baby.

"Miss Bezellia. Hey, I saw you up there behind that book. Hope that sister of yours hasn't gone and drowned a baby doll or two by now. I can hear the water running in the upstairs tub from here." Nathaniel laughed, pointing to the open window on the second floor. "Come on down here and meet my son before we need to start building Adelaide an ark of her own."

Nathaniel had three girls and a boy. He'd told me so. He talked about them every now and then, always with a brightness in his eyes. But for some reason, I'd never really believed they were real. Or maybe I just didn't want to.

"Samuel's going to help me this summer. I promised your daddy I was going to get that barn looking like new before the end of the month, and I need Samuel's strong back if I'm to keep my word." Nathaniel was grinning from ear to ear, clearly so proud of his strapping, good-looking son.

Samuel smiled too, obviously enjoying his daddy's praise.

"It's nice to meet you, Samuel," I said.

"What you reading there?" he asked as he buckled an aged leather tool belt around his waist.

"Reading? Oh, Nancy Drew."

"Never heard of her."

"She's more for girls, I guess. You probably read the Hardy Boys."

"Nope. Never heard of them either. Nice meeting you, though," he said, and smiled again, leaving my body feeling anxious and relaxed all at the same time. He hoisted some boards over his right shoulder and followed his father into the barn. I stayed on the porch, hidden behind my book.

Nancy thoroughly enjoyed herself and was sorry when the affair ended. With the promise of another date as soon as she returned from Twin Elms, Nancy said goodnight and waved from her doorway to the departing boy.

I lingered on the chaise lounge for a while longer, letting the sound of their hammers slapping against the wood lull me in and out of a light sleep. Maizelle was calling my name from somewhere deep within the kitchen, but I kept drifting away from her voice and finding myself floating across the field behind the house. The grass was dotted with Queen Anne's lace and black-eyed Susans. The sound of the water rolling through the creek was pulling me downstream, and the sun was warming my face. Samuel was ahead of me, waiting on the other side of the cherrybark oaks, extending his hand toward mine. The water isn't deep, he said, motioning for me to follow him. Then Maizelle tapped her foot on the porch floor, and I fell right back onto the chaise lounge.

"You better go check on your sister. You promised your mama you'd look after her, and the minute your mama leaves town, I find you out here sound asleep. I haven't heard a word from Adelaide in the last twenty minutes. She's either done fallen asleep like you or is cutting that poor doll's hair again. That baby's not looking quite right, if you ask me. Something in her eyes is just plain evil."

"She's only a doll, Maizelle," I told her, and I laughed and cocked my head to the right like I always did when I wanted her to know that her imagination was getting the best of her. Maizelle could be brave and fiery one minute and then skittish and scared the next, sometimes falling from one extreme to the other like a yo-yo dancing on a string. I sat up and rubbed my eyes and realized Maizelle was carrying a tray piled with sandwiches and fresh fruit and a large bowl of potato chips. I rubbed my stomach and waited for her to offer me something to eat.

"This ain't for you, girl. This is a meal meant for those who have been working hard. Now get up from there and find your sister. You promised your mama you wouldn't take your eyes off her. I'll feed you two in a little bit."

Maizelle stepped off the porch and slowly walked toward the barn. She never rushed anywhere, said there was nothing on this earth worth running to anyway. But as soon as Samuel saw her coming, he ran to greet her and quickly shifted the tray into his own two hands. "This is the best-looking sandwich I've ever seen, Miss Maizelle," he declared, and grinned real big, revealing a band of perfect white teeth. Even from where I was sitting, I could see Maizelle's cheeks turn pink as a rose and her hips jiggle from side to side.

"Oh, your mama better not hear you say that, Samuel Stephenson, or she's gonna have you bringing a sack lunch tomorrow," she answered, and then she laughed real hard and playfully swatted him on his arm.

"Oh, Miss Maizelle, my mama is a wonderful cook, but she don't make sandwiches like this. Is this bread homemade?" he asked her, and then winked, as if to reassure her he wasn't telling lies about her cooking.

"Lord, son, you got your daddy's smile, something dangerous for sure. I bet you got yourself at least a girlfriend or two, hmm, don't ya?"

Samuel only smiled. He seemed to know that was all he needed to do. Then he glanced up toward the house, and I suddenly felt like his teasing was as much for my entertainment as it was for Maizelle's. I dropped my head against the back of the chaise lounge. I didn't think it was really right for a colored boy to be flirting with me, even if I did kind of like it.

Maizelle swatted Samuel on the arm again and then pointed to the barn. "You better get your daddy's lunch delivered before that man passes out from hunger," she told him. She laughed to herself as she walked back to the house, every now and then stopping to pull a weed thriving among my mother's flowers. I snuggled farther down on the chaise lounge and closed my eyes again and listened to the hammer, and the saw, and Samuel's laugh, and Nathaniel's singing, all woven together and drifting through the air like a redbird coming to offer me some lonesome morning trill. If Mother'd been here, she'd have told Nathaniel to quit singing that Negro music.

"You're not a slave, old man," she'd snap. "You're not working on some cotton-picking plantation." And Nathaniel would look at my mother and tip his cap and say the same thing he always said. "No, Mrs. Grove, you're right. This *ain't* no cotton-picking plantation."

For the next two days, I woke to that same soothing sound. And by the time I'd made my way downstairs and taken my place at the kitchen table, Maizelle would already be carrying a tray loaded with sandwiches and fresh chips to the barn. She said when you've been working since daybreak, lunch comes early, and it might do me some good to remember that. "The early bird is the one that ends up getting the worm every time."

Maybe. But I didn't care too much about that worm. All I knew was that when I wasn't tending to Adelaide or Baby Stella, I found myself right back on that porch, drawn to it like a moth to the light. Samuel and I would exchange glances every now and then, never more than that. But it was all the encouragement I needed to keep coming back.

"Bezellia, whatchya doin', child?" Maizelle asked late one afternoon as she stood in front of me, swaying from one foot to the other. Mother's body was stiff and rigid, but Maizelle's body was never still. Even when she was standing in place, her body was always moving. And even when she was trying to be stern, she could never completely hide the smile in her voice.

"Nothing," I answered, keeping my eyes closed and my nose buried behind my book.

"Uh-huh, I can see that," Maizelle said. "When I was your age I had been taking in ironing for more than a year. Never had the time to do nothing. Now take this lemonade out to Nathaniel and Samuel. And then take your little sister down to the creek for me." I had left Adelaide sitting on the grass feeding her babies some crackers and ice water. Now the garden hose was pulled to her side and water was trickling onto a patch of dry, dusty earth. Stacked between her legs sat a pile of newly made mud pies.

"While your nose done been buried in that book, your little sister's been out playing in the mud again." Hearing herself spoken of, Adelaide looked up and grinned. Her arms and legs were covered in a fresh, wet coat of mud. "I don't want her inside getting anywhere near your mama's furniture. She'll take a switch to all three of us if one tiny speck of mud finds its way into this house," Maizelle told me sternly.

She nodded her head as if to punctuate her point and then handed me an old wooden tray. A large plastic pitcher full of lemonade and two Mason jars left it feeling heavy and awkward in my hands. I had never been served lemonade or tea or anything for that matter in a Mason jar. Maizelle said it wouldn't be proper.

My little sister jumped up as I walked down the front steps. She wiped the hair out of her face with her dirty hand, leaving her cheek streaked with mud, Baby Stella dangling as usual by her side. It was as if the two of them had been hand-dipped in a vat of melted chocolate. Adelaide was whining, wanting me to come and admire her mud pies. But my arms were already aching, and I was afraid the tray might spill from my hands before I got to the barn. I told her to run up ahead and let Samuel know I was bringing him and his father some lemonade. But Samuel didn't run to help me like he had Maizelle, and by the time I got to the barn, my arms were shaking.

"Well, lookie here! Look who's come and paid us a visit, Samuel. And she's bringing refreshments. I always knew you were my favorite, Miss Bezellia." Nathaniel laughed, winking at Adelaide. She winked back as if they had already agreed that she was his true favorite. I spied a worktable a few feet in front of me, but my legs grew suddenly stiff, no longer willing to listen to my head. And the pitcher of lemonade began to slide toward the edge of the tray.

"Son, grab that before she drops it!"

Samuel threw down his hammer and ran toward me. He steadied the tray in his own hands and then nodded his head, reassuring me that I could let go.

"Shoo. That was a close one, Miss Bezellia. Sure would hate to lose Maizelle's lemonade before even getting a sip. Don't think she'd make me any more if it wound up on the ground." Nathaniel laughed, now seeing that the tray was safely in his son's hands. "Bezellia," he continued, scratching his head as he talked, "you ever met my son before this week? I just can't remember you two ever meeting. Samuel and I were talking about it on the way home last night. I've talked about each of you to the other for so long, I just assumed that you had."

"No, I don't think so," I said, my arms falling heavy and tired at my sides. "But it was nice finally getting to meet you," I told Samuel, and then crossed my arms in front of my waist to keep them steady.

"I've always kind of wondered what a Bezellia looks like," Samuel said, barely even bothering to really look at me.

"Samuel," Nathaniel snapped in a surprised but serious tone. "You know he's going to be playing football at Pearl this year. Straight A's too. I guess he's gotten a little big for his britches and done forgotten his manners, Miss Bezellia."

"I didn't mean no harm. It's just that, like Daddy said, I've been hearing about you all my life, and to be honest, I've never heard of anybody with a name quite like yours."

"It's definitely different, no denying that," I said. It even sounded a little funny to me as I listened to it roll off the tongue of a stranger. It was almost as if I was hearing it for the first time. But I liked the way it sounded. I liked the way he said it. "Well, you'll never forget me. My name, that is."

"I guess we'll see about that, won't we." Samuel laughed so warm and easy, as if he already knew something he wasn't quite ready to share.

Nathaniel tossed his hammer down next to Samuel's and then reached for the pitcher and poured two glasses of lemonade. "Bezellia, I think if your sister don't get down to that creek soon, she's going to dry hard as a nut, and we might have to crack her open like a pecan growing on one of those trees back behind the house."

Adelaide immediately started crying and jumping up and down. And even though she did need to be soaked and scrubbed, I couldn't help but wonder if Nathaniel had done that on purpose. I wondered if he could tell that I liked it when his son said my name. I wondered if he could tell that I liked it when his son looked at me. I wondered if he could tell that I was looking back.

By the time we got to the water's edge, the mud was starting to dry hard on Adelaide's skin. She stood on the bank, waving her arms in the air and screaming, "Get it off. Get it off. I don't want to be a peanut!"

"A pecan," I corrected her and then reached for a branch hanging low over the bank's edge and sidled my way down the grassy slope and into the creek. The water felt cool around my ankles, and I quickly found my footing in the pebbles that covered the creek's floor. I stretched out both arms, and Adelaide leapt toward me, still clutching Baby Stella in her right hand.

Before she had both feet firmly planted beneath her, she plopped her bottom down in the water and started rubbing her arms and legs with her muddy hands. I crouched behind my little sister and untied her braids, carefully working my fingers through her curly brown hair. I cupped my hands, lowered them into the creek, and poured the water over her head.

"How 'bout that, you're starting to look like a little white girl again," I said, gently cleaning her shoulders and back. "I was beginning to wonder if you were one of Nathaniel's daughters and not a Grove after all."

Adelaide giggled and continued to wash the mud off her legs, rubbing her knees so hard I was afraid she might make them bleed. Then she locked Baby Stella between her thighs and started pouring handfuls of water over the doll's plastic head.

"I think that'd be nice," she said.

"What would be nice?"

"Being Nathaniel's daughter."

I laughed out loud. But when I saw Adelaide's serious expression, I hid my smile behind my hands.

"Why's that so funny?" she asked.

"I don't know. I guess if you were Nathaniel's daughter, you'd be as dark as that mud, and that just seemed kind of funny to me."

"Yeah, so? That mud's a pretty color. Besides, I like Samuel."

"Samuel?" I was surprised to hear his name, and for a moment I wondered if even Adelaide had caught me admiring him.

"Yeah. Samuel. I'd like Samuel to be my big brother. And if I was Nathaniel's little girl, then Samuel would be my brother, right? I think that'd be real nice."

I retied my sister's hair in one short braid and then softly stroked her neck, rinsing the last traces of mud from her tiny body. "Well, there's no big brother that's going to wash the mud out of your hair like I just did." And then I playfully poured one more handful of water over her head.

Adelaide stretched her feet out in front of her and started kicking. She giggled and waved her arms, tossing water in every direction. I closed my eyes and asked her to stop, but she only kicked harder and giggled louder. I leaned back on my forearms and started kicking my own two feet. Adelaide's laugh grew strong and full. It was a sweet, unbridled sound that came straight from the bottom of her belly. I had never heard such a rich, beautiful melody. I think that day Adelaide washed the mud and a whole lot of sadness right down that creek. All these years later, I can still hear her laughter ringing in my ears.

But Maizelle would be looking for us before long. She'd want to give Adelaide a hot, soapy bath before she started cooking the evening meal. She'd want to scrub her down one more time for good measure. I reluctantly guided my sister out of the water. And while I stretched out in the sun to dry my clothes, Adelaide crawled under the willow tree and started making a bed for Baby Stella. She needed another nap, Adelaide said, and we couldn't leave until she'd had one.

The sun warmed my body, and I raised my arms above my head, offering myself completely to its touch. A bee buzzed back and forth across the field, and I could hear Adelaide humming a lullaby to her baby. I wondered if that doll, all snug in my sister's little arms, felt as relaxed as I did. And for once, I really didn't care how long Baby Stella needed to sleep.

A cloud moved in front of the sun, and the sudden dose of shade left my body feeling chilled and exposed. I opened my eyes and found Samuel sitting in the grass by my side. He was holding his hat over my head, staring down at me.

"What are you looking at?" I asked, now feeling very out of place by the creek I had known since I was a little girl.

"Your face. It's all red."

I touched my cheeks with my fingertips. My skin was hot and tender.

"That's funny. How your skin can go from white to red in no time at all?" Samuel said. "You really ought to wear a hat," he went on, and he pointed to his own tattered blue ball cap.

"Guess so," I quipped. But Samuel just sat there, shading my face.

"Daddy said there was some water here along the tree line where I could clean up a bit. Said he used to fish down here when he was a boy. We're heading straight to the bus station to pick up my grand-mother. She's coming up from Birmingham."

"Nathaniel's mother?" I asked, feeling more and more surprised by the discovery of Nathaniel's very own family tree.

"Yep. Nana comes up every summer for two weeks."

"Nana? Huh, that's funny. That's what I call my grandmother."

"Why's that funny?"

"I don't know, just seems funny. Besides, I didn't even know his mother was still living." The way Samuel looked at me I figured he thought I was saying more than I was, and I didn't care for that ei-ther. "Didn't you come here to clean up? Well, go ahead. Help your-self. It's not my creek."

But he just sat there, staring at me, holding his hat over my head. I looked down and saw that my shirt was still damp, and my bra was showing as if I wasn't wearing any shirt at all. I crossed my arms over my chest and sat straight up. Samuel politely smiled, understanding that he had taken in a little more of me than he should have. I really didn't think it was right for *any* boy to be noticing my breast size. Mother would definitely not approve, and yet I found myself puffing my chest out as far as I could to convince Samuel that there was more to see than he had first thought.

He smiled again, and his forearm grazed my hand. He leaned forward and tugged off his tennis shoes and socks. Then he rolled up his blue jeans to his knees, revealing strong, muscular calves. He grabbed the back of his shirt and yanked it over his head, exposing his bare back. And now I felt like I was taking in more of Samuel than I should have.

He tossed his cap on the ground next to me and walked to the edge of the creek. He stepped into the water and sat down on his bottom, just like Adelaide had. I could hear him exhale, the heat and sweat of a long day pouring out of his tired, hot body. He leaned back on his elbows, the cool water rushing past him, and stared up at the sky.

"Hi, Samuel," Adelaide cried from behind a curtain of branches. "Look! Look at my baby. I made her a crown, just like a real princess. See?"

"That's real pretty, Adelaide," Samuel answered, as he turned his body around so he could admire my sister's handiwork. "Hey, why don't you make your sister a crown while you're at it? She's kind of a princess, too, you know." He looked back at me and smiled, but I didn't feel like this boy was paying me much of a compliment.

"Adelaide!" I yelled. "C'mon now. We better be heading back to the house." I jumped to my feet and straightened my blouse.

Adelaide started fussing and telling me that Baby Stella was not good and awake yet. I told her she'd be sitting in a tent somewhere in North Carolina if she didn't pick that baby up right now and come with me. I was feeling anxious and clumsy, queasy and light-headed, and I was certain that the only other time I remembered feeling this way was when I was standing behind Mrs. Dempsey's coatrack and waiting for Tommy Blanton's lips to find mine. But a white girl doesn't kiss a black boy, just wouldn't be right. Everybody knew that. Then he smiled again. And for a minute I almost forgot who we were.

I walked toward the creek and up to Adelaide's secret spot underneath the willow tree. Samuel was still leaning back in the water, staring straight up at the sky, as if he was lost in a dream.

"You know, someday I'm going to own a big piece of land with a big, wide creek running right through the middle of it, just like this one here, only bigger," he said, as much to himself as to me.

"Uh-huh," I mumbled, as I tried to retrieve my sister from deep within the willow tree.

"You can uh-huh me all you want, but it's true. I'm going to have me some land. Yep, sure am. And a big house too. Maybe even bigger than yours."

"Better be careful what you wish for, Samuel," I warned, and again focused my attention on my little sister. "I mean it, Adelaide. We've got to go. I'm taking Baby Stella myself if you don't move it. And I'm going to pack your trunk and call that camp in North Carolina as soon as I get back to the house."

"No!" she yelled through the branches.

"Then come on." And I blindly reached through the willow branches and grabbed Adelaide by the arm. She let out a sudden cry and tugged hard to try to free herself. But I held on tight to my sister's tiny wrist and pulled her up. Samuel jumped out of the creek as if I had ordered him back to the house too. He had nearly buttoned his shirt by the time we started walking back across the field, and he indicated he was going to escort us home whether I wanted him to or not.

Adelaide was tripping along next to me, my hand clutched tightly around hers. Samuel quickly fell into place on my other side. We walked toward the house without saying much of anything, except for Adelaide interrupting the awkward silence with whiny comments about the gnats flying around her head or about the grass sticking to her legs. We stopped in a patch of clover so she could make another crown for Baby Stella, since the first one had fallen off somewhere along the way. Samuel made one, too, and then placed it on my head.

"There," he said. "You are a princess after all."

Adelaide looked at me and giggled. "You do look like a beautiful princess, Bezellia."

"Why do you keep calling me that, Samuel? Why do you call me a princess?" I demanded, snatching the clover ring from the top of my head.

"Okay, you live in a castle for one thing. You have people waiting on you for another. And you sit on that porch and read while everybody else is working to make you happy. Sounds like a princess to me, at least what I know of one."

"Well, if everybody's working to make me so happy, I'd say they're not doing a very good job."

"Then maybe you're more like that spoiled princess that had to sleep on all those mattresses because of that one tiny pea keeping her up all night," he said, with that now-annoying smile stretched across his face.

"I love that story, Samuel. That's my favorite," Adelaide shouted. I quickly glanced at them both and with a blunt cutting stare told them to hush.

No one had ever accused me of being spoiled, or a princess, and he was making me feel like I had done something I should be apologizing for. He did not understand how much sadness could fill a big old house. He had no idea what it meant to be Bezellia Grove. But I guess at the end of the day, I had no idea what it meant to be Samuel Stephenson either. And so we walked the rest of the way in silence, each not really caring to understand what the other one knew to be true. Then every few steps his arm would brush against mine, and a shiver would run straight down to my stomach.

Adelaide wrenched her hand free and started running ahead of me. "Mother! Mother!" she cried.

My heart stopped when I spied my mother talking to Nathaniel. He was pointing to the barn, showing her the shingled roof he and Samuel had nailed in place in the few days since she had left. She smiled and nodded, but when her eyes caught mine, the smile swiftly drained from her face. Nathaniel seemed as surprised as my mother to see Samuel by my side. But I stepped steadily toward them both, trying not to interrupt my stride with any expression of fear or concern, desperately attempting to pretend that Samuel was someplace else.

"Hello, Mother. You're home," I said, sounding more like I was asking a question than making an observation. "Maizelle said you wouldn't be back until tomorrow evening."

"Maizelle was wrong, Sister," she said curtly and then stared at Samuel. "I assume this fine-looking young man is your son." Mother was obviously speaking to Nathaniel, but her eyes were fixed on Samuel.

"Yes, ma'am, I am. I'm Samuel Stephenson. Nice to meet you, ma'am," he said, not waiting for his father's introduction. He held out his hand to shake my mother's. But she kept her hand, protected in its white cotton glove, at her side.

"Sister, you better be getting in the house. Looks as though Adelaide needs a bath. Remember, you have a job to do."

"But . . ."

"No, no. No buts."

I walked up the front steps, passing both Samuel and Nathaniel, none of us willing to speak. Mother refused to exchange a warm hello or a welcoming hug like I had dreamed we might do. And from the top of the porch, I could see Samuel standing stiff by his father's side.

He was staring through my mother as if he was boring a hole right through to her soul. He wasn't the least bit afraid of this white woman shielded in her cotton gloves and fancy silk suit. But I was. A part of me was afraid, afraid I'd never see Samuel Stephenson again. And a part of me was afraid that I would.

IRIS BALL IN FULL BLOOM AT HUNT ESTATE
MOST LAVISH SOCIAL EVENT IN CITY'S HISTORY

Symphony to Benefit from Gala's Success

More than five hundred guests attended the Iris Ball Saturday night at the Hunt family estate in support of the Nashville Symphony Orchestra. Mrs. George Madison Longfellow Hunt V and Mrs. Charles Goodman Grove V hosted the debut fund-raiser. The Women's Volunteer League of Nashville sponsored the evening's festivities.

Guests were serenaded by orchestral music as they made their way down a candlelit path and into an opulently decorated white tent, the interior of which had been transformed into a lavish Paris garden scene.

Streamers of purple irises and red roses were strewn from the center of the tent. Under a canopy of flowers and twinkling lights, guests dined on an elaborate five-course dinner featuring potage crème de cresson, canard en croûte, escalopes de veau, chocolate soufflé, and French champagne.

Beautifully appointed tables were draped in a soft lilac-colored French silk and were centered with impressive arrangements of deep purple irises, red roses, and white tulips. Silver and crystal candlesticks were wrapped in ivy and held long cream tapers.

Mrs. Hunt, who greeted all of her guests in French, wore a red sequined gown with an empire waist and cap sleeves. Her dress was designed and fabricated in Paris. Mrs. Grove chose a purple silk worsted sheath with an elegant back drape and heavy beading around the neck and sleeves. Both women received a standing ovation for their fund-raising efforts.

Patrons had been treated to a cocktail supper at the Groves'
historic home earlier in the week.

Guests at the ball included Dr. and Mrs. Thomas Walter
Purdy; Dr. and Mrs. Anson Franklin Johnson, Jr., of Memphis;
Mr. and Mrs. Richard Ottowell Haase II; Mr. and Mrs. Francis
Parsons Watkins, of Chattanooga; and Mr. and Mrs. James
Dickson Holder III.

The Nashville Register
early edition
SEPTEMBER 27, 1965

chapter four

$\mathcal{M}$other did not wake up until noon the day after the ball. Father took her a cup of coffee and the morning paper as she intended to spend the afternoon in bed reading the society page and calling friends. He stayed by her side for hours, and I could hear them talking and laughing as they swapped stories, retelling the events of the previous night. I had never known my parents to enjoy each other's company as much as they seemed to that day. Father was very proud of my mother, and I think she was finally very proud of herself.

Everyone, including me, agreed that Mother looked absolutely beautiful, much prettier than Mrs. Hunt in her French couture gown. And with photographs of Mother splashed across the society page, we all assured her that she was now certain to be the envy of every woman in Nashville. "Purple is, Sister dear, an unforgettable color," Mother gushed.

By Thanksgiving, the Women's Volunteer League had hosted a lovely luncheon at the country club in honor of my mother and Mrs. Hunt and then very promptly named two new women to chair the next year's Iris Ball. And just as quickly as the glasses had been raised to toast my mother, the attention she had so desperately craved slipped into the gloved hands of another.

The president of the hospital's auxiliary committee asked Mrs.

Hunt to chair the gala fund-raiser for the new pediatric ward, another elaborate evening of dinner and dancing. I'm sure Mother expected her dear friend to invite her to cochair the event. After all, they were the talk of the town, and her very own husband was sure to be the hospital's next chief of staff. But the phone never rang, and Mother finally read of Mrs. Hunt's decision in the afternoon paper. Mrs. Holder would be her cochair. Her husband had just been named managing partner of the city's oldest and most prestigious law firm, a position that apparently impressed my mother's dear friend even more.

So by Christmas, Mother found herself feeling very forgotten. She spent most of her days at the club, playing bridge or lunching with a few so-called friends, trying desperately to remind them that she was a very important person. But this was a job that now seemed to overwhelm her, and she began drinking more and more, not only at dinner but sometimes even at breakfast, pouring gin into her orange juice when she thought no one was looking. Most afternoons, the manager at the club would call Nathaniel and politely tell him to come and retrieve Mrs. Grove, as she seemed to have fallen ill, yet again. By Easter, few of Mother's friends bothered to call, and she rarely left the house, spending most of her days hiding in her bedroom.

I had grown somewhat accustomed to my mother's cruel behavior when she drank, but now she didn't even seem to notice us—and that scared me even more. And although Adelaide and I saw no more of our mother than we had when she was working endless hours with Mrs. Hunt, designing table decorations and engraved invitations, our house now seemed shrouded in a sickening chill that nothing, not even an unexpected thunderstorm, could wash away.

Then one brilliantly clear spring evening, Nathaniel announced that rain was surely heading our way. He could smell it in the air. He tipped his head back and took another deep breath. "Yes, sir, the rain is coming," he said and then walked out the back door, probably wanting to check on the horses or put the Cadillac in the garage before leaving for the night. Maizelle was in the kitchen cooking some caramel icing for a yellow layer cake she had made earlier in the afternoon. Adelaide was stirring the pot of thick, sugary syrup as it slowly boiled on the stove. I headed up the stairs to study for an English test.

I could see Mother sitting in the den, staring blankly at the television set as she often did, the sound of David Brinkley's steady, commanding voice leading her into a deep, sound sleep. Maybe she got up to change the channel or make herself another drink. I don't really know for sure. But I do know that when she lifted herself out of the chair, drunk and half-asleep, she tripped and fell to her knees, dropping her Waterford tumbler and grazing her forehead on the corner of the glass-topped coffee table. I heard the muffled thud and quickly ran down the stairs to see what had happened. But when I spotted my mother kneeling on the floor, clutching Baby Stella in her hands, I carefully dropped behind the banister. Adelaide came running out of the kitchen. Maizelle was just a few steps behind her.

Mother immediately began yelling and cursing, spitting out words I had never heard, words I later had to ask Cornelia to define. And as she steadied herself on her feet, with Adelaide's doll still dangling from her right hand, Mother spied my little sister. Adelaide slid behind Maizelle, but she couldn't hide. Without much warning at all, Mother stormed toward her, yelling something about it being time she grew up and quit living in her childish, make-believe world. It was time she quit playing with baby dolls and making those damned mud pies. Adelaide pressed her face into Maizelle's bottom, desperately trying to disappear.

"The real world is not very nice, little missy, not fucking nice at all. And you might as well learn that right now," Mother screamed, looking so red-faced and twisted I thought the devil himself had swallowed her whole. Mother pushed Maizelle aside and yanked my little sister by the arm, her fingernails piercing Adelaide's pale, tender skin.

Adelaide started crying and shaking uncontrollably, which only seemed to further fuel Mother's rage, like a match thrown into a bucket of kerosene.

"Shut up! Do you hear me! Shut up! I don't want to hear any more of your damn screaming."

But Adelaide couldn't stop. Her heart was broken into too many tiny pieces. And Mother didn't care. She slapped her across the face and then grabbed her small frail-looking arms and shook her back and forth, back and forth, my sister's curly-haired head looking like it might snap right off. Maizelle tried to squeeze her body between Mother and Adelaide. But Mother slapped her too, fortunately only sweeping the top of Maizelle's shoulder. I saw Maizelle's right hand go up as if she was intending to hit my mother back. Then, just as quickly as she had raised it, her hand fell behind her back.

"Get your nigger ass out of my house!" Mother screamed. But Maizelle didn't move. I thought for a minute she really might strike my mother, just punch her square and hard in the mouth. And I hoped for a minute that she would. Then the back door slammed shut. Maizelle relaxed her stance a little bit and took a full step back, carefully pulling Adelaide along with her. Nathaniel walked into the front hall. I guess he was coming for his hat or to tell Maizelle good night. But there he stood, tall and strong, trying to make sense of the confusion that was unfolding right before his eyes.

He stepped toward my mother, who snatched Adelaide in her arms and charged up the stairs, not even noticing me crouching in the corner of the landing. She threw my sister on her bed and slapped her thigh over and over again. I shook every time I heard the sharp sound of her hand striking Adelaide's smooth, fair skin. Then she started slamming drawers and doors, one right after the other. It sounded like a tornado was ripping through my sister's room, and in the midst of it all, Mother just kept shouting at Adelaide, demanding she take one good, last look at her baby dolls as she stuffed yet another one into her arms. Adelaide would never see them again, Mother promised. Never. Then she stomped out of the room, with her arms full of plastic arms and heads and legs, not even bothering to look back at the little girl left crumpled on the bed.

As soon as Mother slammed the door to her own room, directly across the hall, Nathaniel ordered Maizelle to run and check on Adelaide. She turned and grabbed onto the handrail, pulling herself up the stairs with such strength that I thought she might knock me down. I could feel her feet almost on top of mine and her breath, heavy and labored, against my neck. She was desperate to comfort her baby girl.

My little sister was lying on her side with her knees tucked against her chest. She wasn't crying anymore. She was just staring at the wall.

Maizelle said she had been shocked into silence, said she'd seen it before. She quickly dampened a cloth and washed Adelaide's face. She gave her a couple of baby aspirin and then opened her top dresser drawer and pulled out Adelaide's favorite pink pajamas. I sat down next to my little sister and put my arm around her shoulders. She was so thin and small I could feel her bones poking through her skin. I patted her back and told her not to worry about Baby Stella and the others. Nathaniel would find them. And Maizelle promised she would wash their faces and give them some baby aspirin too.

Adelaide suddenly started crying with such force and conviction that I wasn't sure she would ever be able to stop. "Baby Stella. Baby Stella," she moaned, repeating this tearful, tiny plea as she rocked herself back and forth. She finally closed her eyes, and Maizelle and I held our breath, hoping she had fallen asleep. But then her body jerked forward, and she started sobbing again, repeating the same tearful refrain.

Nathaniel opened the door just enough to push his head into the room. He winked at us and smiled, trying to reassure us that everything was going to be okay. Then he told Maizelle to stay with the children until she heard Dr. Grove come up the stairs. He said he'd be sitting on the front porch. My eyes must have widened with surprise, because he looked right at me and told me not to worry.

"It'll be all right, Miss Bezellia. I just need to have a few words with your daddy." Then he closed the bedroom door, motioning for Maizelle to lock it behind him. Maizelle stood up and whispered something to Nathaniel and then locked the door. I knew right then she hated my mother as much as I did.

From Adelaide's bedroom window, I could see Nathaniel sitting perfectly still in the green wicker glider, gazing up at the stars, patiently waiting for my father to pull in the driveway. He sat there for what seemed like hours, with his hands resting on his thighs and his head slightly tilted toward the sky. I wondered what all he saw when he looked at those stars. Then Adelaide's room suddenly filled with light as my father's car eased its way to the house, the headlights boldly announcing his arrival. I ran to the window and hid behind the heavy floral draperies, carefully spying my father as he stepped out of his car.

Nathaniel stood up and walked to the edge of the porch. "Good evening, Dr. Grove," he said with a firm, direct voice, not even waiting for my father to make his way to the front steps.

"Good evening, Nathaniel." My father answered slowly and carefully, suddenly looking like a buck who had been grazing in the field at dusk. It was as if he could sense some sort of danger, hidden but surely there. He probably wanted to run for cover, but instead of scanning the horizon for a thicket of trees or some heavy brush, he just froze in place. "What are you doing here so late? Everything okay?"

"No, sir, it's not. Nothing here is okay. But you already know that," Nathaniel said and then paused for what seemed like a very long time. I guess he was searching for the right words to say to the man he had once taken fishing down by the creek, steadying his fishing cane so he'd be certain to get a bite. But now, Nathaniel sounded more like a parent chastising a naughty child than an old friend or a colored man careful of his position. And even though my father would have had every right to make him stop, he did not.

"I have known you for a long time, and maybe 'cause of that I feel I can say what's in my heart. Or maybe I'm just plain afraid if I don't, one of your girls is going to end up in that hospital you're at all the time.

"You know as well as I do that Mrs. Grove's taken to drinking every day, pretty much from the time she wakes up in the morning till she falls asleep at night. She sneaks that gin into her orange juice like nobody knows what she's doing. But you do. You know. And you ought to know by now that she can't care for herself, let alone those two sweet baby girls of yours. That's bad enough for sure. But today she hurt Adelaide, could have killed her, I think, judging by the look in her eyes. And I'm afraid, Dr. Grove, if you don't start paying attention to what's going on inside that house of yours, well, you may come home one day and find something really tragic has happened right here under your very own roof."

Nathaniel didn't wait for my father to respond. "There. I've said my piece. I best be getting home now. My family's probably worrying where I am," he concluded, and he tipped his hat and walked down the front steps to his old blue pickup truck.

"Nathaniel, wait a minute," my father stammered. He wrung his hands and lowered his head. Whatever he wanted to say seemed stuck somewhere deep inside his throat. He coughed a couple of times, as if he was trying to force the words out. "I didn't really know things had gotten this bad. I mean I knew Elizabeth hated me, but I guess I thought the girls were . . ."

Nathaniel slipped in behind his steering wheel. "Charles, this really isn't about you anymore," he said, and he shut the door of his truck and drove away, leaving my father standing motionless at the bottom of the steps.

The next day all of Adelaide's babies reappeared, each one shiny and clean and wearing a neatly pressed dress. Baby Stella even had a pink satin ribbon tied around her plastic head, making her look prettier than she had in months. Maizelle never said a word about where they had been, and Mother acted as though she didn't remember what she had done. But Adelaide never forgot. And a few days later, Mother left for a vacation of sorts. Father said she needed to go to a special place to get better, someplace in Minnesota. I think it was near a lake.

Father still worked long days at the hospital, but with Mother gone, he was always home for dinner. And there, at that perfectly polished mahogany table, my father tried at last to get to know his daughters. He seemed uneasy at first, unsure of what to say to the two little girls who were so thirsty for any tiny bit of his attention. He talked about family mostly, about the first Bezellia fighting the Indians at Fort Nashborough and about a young Teddy Roosevelt kissing his grandmother when her fiancé was too busy looking at his horses. He said a small heart was engraved on the bottom of the silver teapot the future president gave his grandparents on the eve of their wedding, a heart that represented his own hidden love for my great-grandmother. I wanted to run and see if it was there just as he said it would be, but I guess it really didn't matter if what he was telling me was true or not.

Father said our mother would not be back until September. He said he was sure we were missing her but we needed to be patient. Sometimes it took a long time to get well. I tried to miss her. I wanted to miss her. But to tell the truth, I didn't think about my mother much, except when Maizelle made me get down on my knees and say my prayers before going to bed. And even then, sometimes, I forgot to mention her name.

Mrs. Hunt started coming by not long after Mother left, just to

check on us girls and let "our daddy" know she would love to do anything to help us in this truly difficult time. She loved our mother, she
said. She couldn't have chaired the Iris Ball without her, she said.
Now she only wished her dear friend the very best and a speedy recov-
ery from this most difficult condition—all the while the most perfect
little smile remained painted across her face, a smile I had seen on my
own mother's face, a smile that surely hid at least a thousand perfect
little lies.

Our father really appreciated Mrs. Hunt's special attention, and
one night he invited her to stay and have a drink. They talked for
hours while sitting on the front porch sipping whiskey sours and listening to Frank Sinatra albums left playing on the record player in
the living room. I couldn't hear the specifics of what they were saying,
but I did understand the laughter and ease in their voices. And before
long, Mrs. Hunt started visiting at least twice a week to check on the
poor little Grove girls and deliver another chicken noodle casserole
that her Emma had baked just for us. Maizelle didn't like Mrs. Hunt
coming by any more than I did, and she certainly didn't like her
thinking she couldn't care for her own family. She'd tell Mrs. Hunt
how much she appreciated her thoughtfulness, and then she'd walk
right through the kitchen door and dump that casserole in the trash
can out back. Father always hugged Maizelle and reassured her she
was the best cook in town. Then he made a couple of whiskey sours
and joined Mrs. Hunt on the porch.

Of course when the two of them had tired of polite conversation,
Father started coming home well after dinner, just as if Mother were
here. Naturally he was very sorry about *needing* to be away so much.
He said the hospital was short-staffed, and everyone was working
much longer hours this summer than they'd like. Adelaide and I obediently nodded our heads and said we understood, but we both knew
it wasn't the hospital that demanded our father's attention. He never
mentioned sending us to the lake, as Mother surely would have. I
guess he was trying to keep his wife's condition a secret even from her

own parents, although I'm sure everyone in Nashville knew the truth, or at least some mangled version of it. And even though Maizelle was always nearby, Adelaide and I found ourselves, once again, feeling very alone at Grove Hill.

I was going to run away from home that summer. I schemed and plotted but never managed to pack my bags. Maybe I didn't want to leave Adelaide, or maybe at the end of the day even I was too scared to consider a life beyond Grove Hill. I hated myself for thinking that. But then one afternoon my plans, imaginary or not, abruptly changed. Cornelia called the house blabbering something about her father and the Buffy Orphans.

"Cornelia, slow down," I told her. But she didn't. "Cornelia! Stop! I can't understand a word you're saying!" Nothing she said was making any sense, not one word, until she said *Samuel*.

"Bezellia, you have to come over. Now!"

"Why?"

"Listen, just do what I said. Tell Nathaniel to bring you. Tell him I need you to help me, um, um, bake some brownies or something. I don't know. Tell him anything you want. No! Ride your bike. Yeah, yeah, that's better."

"My bike? Are you kidding me? It's kind of far, Cornelia, and only about a hundred degrees out there."

"What else have you got to do? Hell's bells. Get here however you like, but just come on. Daddy has gone and hired Samuel to help him rebuild that god-awful-looking chicken coop. Apparently he was really impressed with that dumb barn of yours. Come on. I'll be waiting for you in my room."

Click.

chapter five

*A*lmost a year had passed since I had seen Samuel Stephenson. Now my heart was racing and my palms were sweating, and I wasn't really sure why. But I did exactly as Cornelia told me and ran downstairs and started looking for Nathaniel. He was in the backyard carefully watering the impatiens that bordered the walk leading to the kitchen door. Mother had Nathaniel plant flowers there every spring. She said even those of us coming to the back door deserved a proper welcome. Two fuchsia, three pink, three white, and repeat. This year she hadn't been here to tell him what to do. But he did it anyway. Out of respect, he said.

"Nathaniel," I hollered, my voice sounding much too high-pitched to hide my excitement. "Will you drive me over to Cornelia's?"

At first he ignored me and continued tending to the flowers. I took a few more steps toward him and cleared my throat. But he was already suspicious. I could see him looking at me out of the corner of his eye. He put the watering can down next to his feet and stared directly at me. "Why all the sudden do you need to be going to your cousin's house, anyway?"

"She called. Didn't you hear the phone ring?" I spoke very quickly for fear that even the slightest hesitation would reveal my true intention. "Well, it did. The phone rang, and Cornelia wants me to come help her make some brownies for some church youth group thing she's going to tonight."

Nathaniel was a regular churchgoing man. He had earned a gold pin for perfect attendance every year since he was twelve years old. He brought them all to the house once to show me, hoping, I think, it would encourage me to find my way to church at least once a week. He probably should have shown them to Mother. But I knew that any man with all those shiny pins in his pocket would never want to keep me from helping my cousin do the Lord's work.

"That girl can't make those brownies on her own?"

"Nathaniel, will you take me or not? I'll ride my bike if you won't," I said and then turned around and started walking toward the garage.

"All right, hold on. I'll go get the keys. But what do you want me to tell your daddy when he gets home for dinner and you're not here?"

I just stared at Nathaniel. He and I both knew that my whereabouts were no longer my father's first concern, and so, out of either duty or heartfelt pity, he emptied the watering can and slowly walked inside the house. I had grown quite accustomed to lying to my mother—and my father, for that matter. I could do it with the most sincere and honest expression, but I was having a hard time even looking at Nathaniel. So I climbed into the backseat of the Cadillac and focused my attention on a long thread hanging down from the hem of my denim shorts.

A couple of minutes later, Nathaniel tossed his hat onto the front seat and stepped into the car, releasing a slow, almost desperate moan as he settled behind the steering wheel. He carefully placed the key in the ignition and then found me in the rearview mirror. "You know, Samuel is working at your uncle's this summer, helping him with his chicken coop."

My awkward silence surely confirmed what he already suspected.

"Yes, he is. He's working real hard. Wants to go to college, Miss Bezellia, just like you. Except he's going to be the first Stephenson to do that. His mama and I are mighty proud of that boy. He's talking about Fisk or maybe Grambling State, if he can get a scholarship, that is. He's making the grades all right." And then he paused for a minute as he eased the car out of the dark garage and into the bright sunlight. "You know his mama and I sure are looking forward to that day."

I wanted to tell him not to worry. I wanted to tell him I understood what he was saying, but I really didn't. And I really didn't know why I was going to my cousin's house, but I didn't see how it had anything to do with Samuel going to college. So nothing came out of my mouth, not one word. I just slumped down in the backseat and rode in silence, never brave enough to say anything at all.

Cornelia was downright giddy when I walked into her bedroom. She was already dressed in a blue, two-piece bathing suit and had another one, a deep raspberry pink one with little white ruffles across the seat, in her other hand, waving it like a flag. Mother would never let me buy a suit that revealed my stomach. She said those were for tramps. Cornelia didn't look like a tramp, but she sure did look like a girl who knew what she was doing.

"Here, put this on," she ordered and tossed me the suit.

"I brought one."

"Yeah, I know. Wear mine," she repeated, giving me that I-know-best look that Cornelia had perfected. "Bezellia, I can see why you like him. He is so cute, so powerful-looking, like some kind of African prince."

"Lord, Cornelia. What in the world are you talking about?"

"Oh, come on, Bee, you with Samuel. It's so cool. It's like your own little march on Selma."

"Damn it, Cornelia. This is not some kind of sit-in. I haven't even seen him since last summer. And we didn't particularly hit it off then, if you remember."

"Uh-huh. Yeah. But if we hang out by the swimming pool, we'll have a great view of the chicken coop and anybody who happens to be working on it, if you get my drift."

"I'm not sure I want to get your drift."

"What do you mean you don't want to? You're here, aren't you? Shit, put the suit on, Bezellia. Lord, it's not like you two are getting married. Although I would give anything to see the expression on Aunt Elizabeth's face if you brought Samuel home to announce your engagement. I wonder if the *Register* would run your picture on the society page or the front page."

"Cornelia, just shut up!" I exclaimed, and then threw a towel over her head and walked into the bathroom. She was still laughing as I undressed and slipped into the bathing suit. I looked in the mirror and rubbed my stomach, and then turned to the side so I could admire the little white ruffles stretched across my bottom and the two full breasts now neatly covered in two small pieces of raspberry fabric. Mother would not like the way I looked in this suit. But the girl looking back at me in that bathroom mirror suddenly felt a little bit older and a little more certain of what she wanted.

We each wrapped a towel around our waist and grabbed some of the magazines piled on the floor beside Cornelia's bed. We raced down the stairs like we did when we were little. She pushed her body ahead of mine and took the lead. As we passed through the kitchen, Cornelia tossed me a bottle of Coppertone and handed me a cold bottle of Tab out of the refrigerator. She practically lunged through the screen door, laughing and singing, making plenty of noise so that Samuel was sure to hear us.

And as soon as I stepped onto the patio, I saw him. He had a large roll of chicken wire resting on his right shoulder and was headed back inside the coop. He was much taller and thicker than he had been only a year ago, looking much more like a grown man than the boy I had known down by the creek. Cornelia, who was just ahead of me, poked me with her elbow and instructed me to stick my chest out a little farther.

"Hey there, Princess," Samuel hollered from the other side of the yard. Funny, I thought, how the sound of that word felt good to me now. "Don't let that face of yours get burned again. Sun is mighty strong today." Then he tipped his same tattered blue ball cap, just like Nathaniel would do, and walked inside the coop, the roll of chicken wire still resting on his shoulder.

"I'll see you later," I yelled back, but Samuel had already disappeared.

"Cool, Bee, very cool," Cornelia chanted. "Remember, you have to act a little disinterested. Boys always want what they can't have, especially the black ones."

"Cornelia Grove! Where in the world are you getting this crap?"

But my cousin just rolled her eyes, wanting me to think I was the one with no sense. I stretched out on a lounge chair and opened a magazine. And by the time the sun had made its way across the swimming pool, I felt as though I had read every copy of *Seventeen* Cornelia owned, some dating back to 1961. I had painted my toenails pink, drunk three bottles of Tab, and polished off almost an entire tin of Charles Chips. I was lying on my stomach and slipping into a satisfied, contented sleep when I heard a loud splash and felt cold drops of water stinging my back. I looked up and found Samuel standing in the swimming pool with his arms crossed, resting on the concrete edge.

"I told you not to stay out in the sun too long. Looks like your back has done gotten red as a ripe tomato."

As I shifted my weight onto my left shoulder, I could feel my skin, hot and tender. But just like that day down by the creek, I acted as though I didn't care. "What are you doing in the pool? I thought you were here to work."

"Sounding a bit like your mama, Miss Bezellia. But just so you know, we're done for the day. And your uncle always lets me swim here. You know this ain't a whites-only pool," he added, with a touch of sarcasm in his voice.

"Sorry. I didn't mean it to come out that way." I slowly flipped onto my back and lifted my left leg, carefully bending it at the knee, hoping to look more like Brigitte Bardot than a self-conscious, prejudiced teenage girl.

"Why don't you get in? I bet that back of yours could use some cooling off."

Cornelia looked up from her lounge chair, and even though there was a full bottle of Tab under her chair, she said she needed to run inside and get something cold to drink. She told Samuel she'd bring him a Coca-Cola. And then with her eyes, she told me to get up and walk toward the concrete steps at the shallow end of the swimming pool.

I dipped my toe into the cold blue water and quickly yanked my foot back onto the hot concrete. Samuel walked toward the steps and held out his hand. He wrapped his cool, wet fingers around mine, and like a preacher guiding a sinner into the waters of salvation, he led me into my cousin's swimming pool.

"That sure is a pretty bathing suit you got on there."

"It's Cornelia's."

"Well, it sure looks pretty on you." But I was too cold or too nervous to respond to his compliment. I pulled myself up on my tiptoes, trying to lift my body out of the water, and stretched my arms across my bare stomach. "Girl, you got to move around a little." Samuel dropped my hand and started swimming, gracefully extending one arm above his head and then the other, turning to the side to take in a full breath of air.

Mother had always told me that black people couldn't swim. She said their bodies were too thick and they just sank to the bottom like a lead weight. But Samuel swam right to me, and when he put his feet on the bottom of the pool, we were standing face-to-face.

"Come on, Bezellia."

"I'll swim when I'm good and ready, thank you very much."

"We'll see about that," Samuel taunted, and then he dove under the water. He swam directly beneath me and put his head between my legs, lifting me out of the pool.

"Damn it, Samuel!" I screamed.

"Yeah," he answered, ignoring my protests. "Now stand up on my shoulders and dive into the water."

"No!"

"Go on, Bezellia, you can do it. I've got you. Besides, there's no other way down from here." He started hopping from one foot to the other, jostling my body from left to right. "Come on. Like I said, there's only one way down from here."

"Okay, okay." I took a deep breath and carefully lifted my right foot onto his right shoulder, pausing for a moment to regain my balance. "I hate you right now, Samuel Stephenson," I snapped and held his hands tightly in mine. I slowly lifted my left leg up and onto his left shoulder, crouching on top of his back, again trying to balance myself before pulling my entire body up and out of the water.

"Good going, Princess, I knew you could do it."

I stood up straight and tall just long enough to yell at Cornelia, begging her to stick her head out the back door and take a good look at her cousin. And then I dove, arms straight above my head, into the water. When I came up, Samuel was cheering for me, and I swam right back to him like a piece of iron drawn to a magnet. He grabbed my hands and pulled me into the shallow end, dragging me across some line that we both knew had been drawn deep in the dirt beneath that swimming pool long before the two of us were ever born.

I started spending as much time as I could at Cornelia's house. And with Mother gone and Father preoccupied with Mrs. Hunt, it wasn't hard to find my way there. Samuel worked on the chicken coop until late in the afternoon. But before he went home, we met by the edge of the swimming pool. Cornelia and Uncle Thad were always nearby, but somehow neither one of us ever seemed to notice them being there. And with our feet dangling in the water, we talked about school and family and movies and growing up. I had always figured our dreams would be as different as the color of our skin, but they weren't really.

Samuel dreamed of marching with Dr. King, although he wasn't convinced that sitting at a lunch counter was going to get his people where they needed to be. He dreamed of getting married and raising a family. But he said, more than anything else, he dreamed of having children who could do and be what they wanted without people spitting on them or calling them names.

I simply dreamed of living in a house where it didn't matter whether your linens and towels were monogrammed and your friends were members of the Junior League. I dreamed of living in a house where your mother called you by your name, saying it with genuine love and affection. I dreamed of being a woman who didn't need a husband who owned cashmere and convertibles. So I guess, in the end, Samuel and I wanted pretty much the same thing, just to be ourselves.

He asked me one afternoon, as the sun fell behind the house, if I remembered that day down by the creek when he first called me a princess. I told him I did. He asked if I remembered the promise he made to buy some land of his own and a big house just like mine. He wondered if I believed him now—believed that he was going to be more than the son of a house servant. I told him I did.

"Good," he said, and then he reached into his pants pocket and pulled out a thin gold bracelet. He clasped it around my wrist and made me promise not to take it off until that land and that house was his.

Cornelia cooed when she saw it. She said our love was Shakespearean, a love to last for all time, a love greater than Samuel and I could ever comprehend. I reminded her that she had told me the very same thing about Tommy Blanton. Cornelia ignored me and rolled her eyes again and continued with her talk of Romeo and Juliet. But when Nathaniel came to get me at the end of the day and saw a tiny flash of light bouncing off my wrist, I understood that my cousin was right—just like the love between a Montague and a Capulet, ours was dangerous and forbidden.

Nathaniel asked me to collect my things and meet him at the car. Even though his voice was calm and steady, his eyes were suddenly dark and fearless. And for once, I felt nervous standing next to him. He left me by the pool and marched toward the chicken coop. I wanted to warn Samuel, but I just stood there, not knowing what to do. Cornelia rushed to my side and tried to convince me that Nathaniel knew nothing about us. Something else must be bothering him, she said. "You know how emotional *they* can be."

"Cornelia! I cannot believe you said that—you of all people."

"I didn't mean anything by it. Come on. Don't get mad at me. I'm not the enemy here."

"I'm not so sure about that, Cornelia. Damn it, if you hadn't called me in the first place, none of this would be happening right now. Some things are just better left alone." I grabbed my towel and swimsuit, nudging my cousin out of the way, and headed out the back gate. I was almost to the car when the sound of my uncle's voice, urgent and plaintive, drew my attention back to the side of the house.

"Nathaniel, I promise you, nothing inappropriate has gone on here. I've been here every minute of every day."

"I'm not calling you a liar, Mr. Grove. You're a very good man. Samuel's just got other obligations to tend to. If you need help with that coop, I'll come by after leaving your brother's and finish what my son started."

"Nathaniel, please hear me out."

"That's not necessary, Mr. Grove. You're a real good man, a fair man, but I sure would appreciate it if you would have my son's wages for the week ready by the time I come back to get him." Nathaniel tipped his hat toward my uncle and then threw Samuel a stare that left even me feeling scared and uncomfortable. I ran to the Cadillac just ahead of Nathaniel. We both stepped into the car without looking at each other and rode back to Grove Hill in silence.

The air grew instantly thick and stale, and even I knew that a thunderstorm was heading our way. I hid in my room for two whole days, just trying to catch my breath. Nobody attempted to coax me out, not Maizelle, not even Adelaide. When I finally left my room and wandered downstairs, I found Maizelle sitting on the front porch stringing another bowl of green beans, moving her hands in a predictable and soothing rhythm. She never sat on the front porch unless Mother was out of town. I guess she knew Mother wouldn't like it, and I guess that's why she did it. But I was glad she was there, and I sat down next to her, looking for some kind of unspoken comfort.

"Where you been, child?" Maizelle asked.

"I think you know where I've been," I snipped, sounding more like a wise-mouthed teenager than a girl with a broken heart.

"That's not what I asked. Where you been?" she said again. Her words seemed to float through the air, filling the empty space between us.

I felt safe next to Maizelle, and without even realizing it, I started pleading my innocence. "Maizelle, I didn't do anything wrong. Neither did Samuel. We just talked, that's all. I didn't do anything wrong," I cried, all the emotion of the past two days suddenly spilling out of my mouth.

"I know. You were just talking."

"Mostly. I promise. He understands me better than anybody I've ever known. We talk about everything. He loves me for being me, for being Bezellia, not Bezellia Grove."

"Loves you." Maizelle repeated my words exactly as I had said them, and then she put the bean she was holding in her hands back in the bowl and handed me a pile of my own. She nodded at my lap, instructing me to help with the evening's last chore.

"Bezellia, someday you and me may live in a world where a girl like yourself and a boy like Samuel can be together and *just talk*. But we ain't there, sweetie. You know that."

"But—" I tried to interrupt, but Maizelle just smiled and again nodded at the beans, reminding me to pick one up and pull its green, thready string.

"You know, when I was a little girl, even smaller than you, I used to follow my mama for miles every day as she walked from one house to another doing laundry for the white people in town. I'd sit there and watch her rub their pretty clothes over an old metal washboard till her knuckles bled. That lye soap just made 'em burn something awful. She'd sit there waving her hands in the air crying 'Oh, sweet Jesus. Oh, sweet Jesus.' And after all her work was done, she'd walk home with no more than a dime or two in her pocket." Maizelle snapped another bean and continued with her story:

"One day a woman told my mama that her work wasn't good enough, that there were still stains on her husband's shirts. There weren't any stains on those shirts, Bezellia. I'd seen 'em with my own eyes. That woman threw those clean clothes in the dirt, told my mama she wasn't going to pay her for sloppy work.

"My mama got so mad. I'd never seen her get mad like that. She pushed that woman down in the dirt and rubbed her face in the mud. Oh Lord. That woman's husband came flying out of his house and beat my mama unconscious, right there in front of me.

"Now here comes Samuel, so young and handsome, and he believes he can change the world. And we all need him to try, baby—for me, for my mother . . . even for you."

Tears were collecting in the corners of my eyes. I desperately tried to soak them up with the edge of my cotton blouse before they spilled down my cheeks. Maizelle handed me a fresh white handkerchief that she pulled from somewhere deep inside her sleeve.

"Listen, honey, I thank Jesus every day that we haven't seen the kind of violence here in Nashville like they done down in Birmingham. Still, there's just too much hate floating in the air. Don't you feel it? Don't you feel it even way back here behind all these big, old trees?"

Yes. I felt it. I did. Sometimes my lungs were so full of it I wondered if I would choke on it. My chest would tighten and ache with it. But by Cornelia's swimming pool, with Samuel sitting next to me, the air had felt so pure and so clear.

"Bezellia, people like Samuel believe they can make this world a better place just by peacefully standing their ground. Not me. After seeing my mama lying there in the dirt, bleeding so bad I thought she might die, I knew I could never just stand there and watch, never again," Maizelle said, and then she picked up another bean.

"Throwing rocks became my specialty," she announced, her tone a little lighter and more relaxed. "That's right, a strong right arm can teach a mighty powerful lesson in my opinion. Now don't you ever repeat that, or old Maizelle might just wind up in jail—again." She said it so matter-of-factly that I almost started laughing. But her face was again stern and serious, and I knew she wasn't kidding, leaving me to wonder what all about Maizelle I didn't know. "You don't need to be giving that boy any ideas that could get him into trouble. You understand what I'm telling you?"

"I'm not giving him any ideas, Maizelle," I stammered, trying to convince myself as much as her.

"Sweetie, just being with you is giving him ideas. Worse than that, it might give other people ideas too, people who might think Samuel needs to be taught a lesson for simply sitting by the swimming pool with a girl like you."

"He's just my friend, I swear," I insisted, my voice now flooded with tears. Maizelle shuffled her glider right next to mine. She put her round, thick arm around my shoulder and pulled me a little closer.

"Sweetie, Nathaniel's not mad at you. He's just afraid for his son. Surely you can understand that. And you know, if I had my way, it wouldn't be like this. Of course, if I had my way, I wouldn't be living in some other woman's basement." Maizelle smiled and snapped another bean.

"'Red and yellow, black and white, they're all precious in his sight.' That's my way of thinking," she said, her voice now sounding full and upbeat. "Funny how some churchgoing folks I know see things a little differently. They sing the song, but I'm not sure they're really listening to the words. And I'm not sure we're ever gonna be able to change that. All I do know for sure is that this old arm of mine is getting tired." She laughed right out loud. Then she stroked my hair and held me a little closer, a little tighter.

"Honey, it's a sad thing when a child ain't loved right. But you will be. It won't always be like this. So hard, I mean. You're turning into a beautiful young woman, Miss Bezellia. And I know that heart of yours is aching to be loved. And I also know that you and me ought to be down on our knees thanking the good Lord that your mama wasn't here." We both started laughing, realizing that, for once, my mother's special condition had indeed been a blessing. I relaxed against Maizelle's arm and picked up another bean.

Nathaniel and I never talked about that day by the swimming pool. In fact, there were a lot of things Nathaniel and I never talked about anymore. And sometimes I wondered which was worse—never seeing Samuel again or seeing Nathaniel every day, each of us feeling guarded and awkward around the other. But I knew what Maizelle was saying was right. Samuel needed to find his dream as much as I needed to find mine.

Mother came back a week or so before school started. She seemed timid, almost shy at first. Even I could tell that her improving health sometimes frightened her more than a full bottle of gin. But I think she wanted to be a better wife and mother. She called my father "dear" and brought Adelaide a beautiful new baby doll with soft blond hair and a white satin dress. She even seemed to treat Maizelle and Nathaniel with a bit more kindness and patience, although by five o'clock, when she would have been soaking in a gin and tonic, she tended to grow sharp and bitter.

A couple of her friends came by to welcome her home, although I think they were more curious than concerned. Of course, we never saw Mrs. Hunt again, and not much of our father really. Our mother grew painfully aware of their absences and, after a while, unsure of what to do with her long, quiet days at Grove Hill, started spending more and more time at the club. Sadly, by Easter, she was *sick* again, and by June she was heading back to Minnesota, not well enough or concerned enough to call her parents and schedule an impromptu summer vacation at the lake for her two young daughters. So Adelaide and I spent another summer at home alone, neatly out of our parents' sight.

My little sister locked herself in her room and played with her dolls when she should have been playing hopscotch and phoning her friends. The doll my mother had given her last year sat on the floor by her bed; its hair had been cut short and the eyes painted with markers. I hid Baby Stella in the back of my closet for a few days, hoping Adelaide would leave her behind and start playing with *real* girls her own age, but my little sister pitched such a tearful fit I had to give her the doll back. Maizelle said she was just being Adelaide. She figured that even though my sister was now twelve years old, Adelaide was still a little girl in many ways, too afraid to grow much beyond her make-believe world. And I guess, in a way, Maizelle was right.

I spent more and more time with Cornelia, going to the movies and shopping for clothes. And I spent long afternoons in the kitchen with Maizelle, making pound cakes and canning tomatoes. But mostly I spent my days alone—needlepointing, reading, wading in the creek—trying to convince myself that I'd never really cared for Samuel Stephenson.

Maizelle said Samuel was spending the summer in Atlanta, organizing civil rights demonstrations. I imagined him sitting with his hands folded in his lap at some dime-store lunch counter or standing shoulder to shoulder with Martin Luther King. But Maizelle said those days were over. She was afraid Samuel was taking up another kind of fight, and I could hear her and Nathaniel whispering on the back porch, both sounding nervous and uneasy.

I kept Samuel's bracelet wrapped inside a silk slip and tucked under some sweaters in my bottom dresser drawer. I never wore it during the day, never wanting to upset Nathaniel. But every night, before going to sleep, I prayed that Samuel would find his dream. And then I'd clasp his gold bracelet around my wrist and live mine while I slept.

AU REVOIR!
MISS HARDING'S SCHOOL TO SEND GROUP ABROAD
FOR SUMMER STUDY

Mrs. Hunt to Accompany Girls

Twenty rising seniors from Miss Harding's Preparatory School for Girls will be traveling to Paris to further their fine arts education. The United States Ambassador to France, Mr. William H. Monroe III, extended the invitation to study and paint at Parisian museums, most notably, the Louvre and Musée d'Orsay. Mr. Franklin's wife is an alumna of Miss Harding's Preparatory School and will personally oversee the girls' studies.

The students will leave Nashville on June 2 and spend three days in New York City before traveling on to Paris. Mrs. George Madison Longfellow Hunt V will accompany the group abroad along with Mrs. David Hensley, the school's art history teacher, Miss Laura Nelson, the school's French teacher, and Miss Polly Clements, head of the city's prestigious preparatory school.

Miss Clements believes this unique opportunity to study in France will greatly enhance each girl's academic and cultural education. "These girls will be shining stars in our community, forever changed by this life-altering experience that awaits them," said the head of school.

Misses Mary Margaret Hunt, Abigail Lynne McAniff, Francesca Claire Burton, and Mary Constance Lewis will be among those traveling abroad.

The Nashville Register
late edition
MAY 17, 1968

chapter six

The evening paper arrived just as I was coming home from school, but I had already heard the news. It was all my friends had talked about for the past two weeks, ever since Miss Polly Clements, the school's headmistress, had assembled the junior class for a special meeting in the auditorium to announce a unique and surely life-altering experience.

We had all been invited to Paris. Yes, Paris, France. The ambassador's wife was apparently the school's most prestigious alum, and we were going to paint and study for three weeks under her watchful eye. We would embrace Notre Dame at daybreak and capture the warm, golden sunlight dancing across the Seine at dusk. We would study Monet and Manet, Matisse and Seurat, all the while absorbing everything French, from the Brie to the croissants.

After the meeting, Miss Clements pulled me aside. She told me that my painting had depth and passion, and that my French was authentic and ripe with emotion. (And although Monsieur Gadoue never cared for my mother and her feeble attempts to greet him in French, he was quick to say that my accent was pure and honest. He even admitted, in a perfect Parisian dialect, that Mary Margaret Hunt butchered the language like a side of beef.) Miss Clements said she hoped I would take advantage of this unique opportunity, and then she handed me a stack of papers outlining the details of the trip.

I rushed home to tell my parents. For once, I thought, mother and daughter would be in total agreement about what was best for Bezellia Grove. But when Mother discovered that Mrs. Hunt had been slated as the trip's official chaperone, she threw my father a look, a gnashing, bloodshot stare. And Father, well, he simply glanced at the wall, too afraid or maybe too ashamed to look either of us directly in the eye.

"No," Mother said abruptly, breaking the silence that had quickly permeated the room. "Sister will not be going to Paris," and then she slammed her fist down on top of the papers that now appeared wilted and worn under her hand. She quickly turned her chair toward me and caught the disappointment clouding my eyes. She seemed almost startled that her words had delivered such a devastating punch. And even though she left no room for argument, she added in an uncharacteristically kind and empathetic tone, "Maybe later, maybe you can study abroad when you're in college. It will mean so much more then anyway—when you're older and all."

I knew she expected me to sit there quietly and nod my head in agreement, to accept her decision without question—deferential, respectful submission, nothing more. But that was not possible.

"Are you kidding?" I shrieked, this time not willing to surrender without a fight, no matter how futile the outcome was destined to be. "I *have* to go. I've taken all these stupid French classes for *you* . . . because *you* thought I should speak French just like Mrs. Kennedy! I even spent two whole days teaching you how to greet all those snobby friends of yours at that stupid ball. Damn it! I read Voltaire . . . in French . . . twice.

"And God only knows how many stupid apples and pears and purple irises I've painted, hoping that just one of them would be pretty enough for you. Miss Clements tells me my brushstrokes are gifted. Did you hear me? Gifted! I have to go to Paris! Miss Clements is counting on me. I am going!"

My voice was loud and demanding. It was a voice until this very moment I had never dared use when addressing my mother or my father, let alone both at the same time. And they just sat at the kitchen table looking oddly bewildered, as if they were staring at some crazed hippie high on marijuana or maybe tripping on some LSD.

"I'm sorry, Sister, but this is an impossible situation," my mother finally snapped, regaining her composure and ending my charge as quickly as it had begun. Then she got up from the table, tossed the newspaper in my father's lap, and walked away.

"Quel dommage," my friends sighed when I explained that I preferred to stay home for the summer. *"Quel dommage,"* they repeated in obvious disbelief when I said that June was a stifling time to be in Paris. *"Quel dommage,"* they said and then ran off giggling and chattering about French-kissing a French man under a French bridge.

"Screw it," I whispered under my breath, in English.

I knew good and well why I was not going to Paris, and for the first time in my life I found myself hating my father as much as my mother. So when the newspaper came that afternoon announcing my classmates' "life-altering" trip abroad, I took a big red Magic Marker and wrote a message for my father right across the headline, thanking him for this missed opportunity to finally step foot out of the state of Tennessee.

> *Merci, Papa merveilleux. Je vous remercie pour ceci?*
> *Bezellia~*

That night I dreamed of the first Bezellia, clinging to her husband's dying body, his blood soaking her clothes, the rain washing her hair. I'm not sure why she came to me like that, but she did from time to time, never with any warning or notice. The next morning at the breakfast table I announced that I would not be staying at Grove Hill for the summer. Instead, I would be spending my vacation at

Old Hickory Lake, with my *grand-père* and *grand-mère*. Furthermore, I would be traveling alone. Caring for Adelaide and Baby Stella was not going to be my responsibility this year, whether Mother *vacationed* in Minnesota or not. Then I stood silent before my mother and waited for her to say no, to reject my plan, to put her foot down with such force that she would rattle the house.

But she simply nodded her head in agreement. And without thinking, I flung my arms around her neck and hugged her so tightly she gasped in surprise. Then I ran up to my room, fell across my bed, and threw my arms over my head like an athlete who had just won the race or a teenage girl who had finally gotten her way. Maybe this trip to Paris was going to be a life-altering experience after all.

The sun came up particularly bright and clear on that first day of June. My trunk was already packed and waiting for me by the front door. I pulled on some jeans cut off just above my knees and a short-sleeved cotton blouse, an ensemble I knew my mother, already dressed in a crisp blue linen suit, would not approve for traveling, not even to the lake. That afternoon she inspected me as she always did, slowly, from head to toe, and then sighed and said, "Fine. I'll call Nathaniel."

My father had ducked out of the house earlier than usual, surely feeling guilty that his poorly disguised affection for Mrs. Hunt had cost his daughter a trip abroad. It was just as well, because I was in no mood to act as though I was going to miss him. And even though I still felt rather sorry for myself, for the first time, I felt even sadder for my mother. She had apparently married a cheat and a coward, and I wasn't really sure which was worse.

Mother stood quietly outside the front door with nothing but a cold cup of coffee in her hand. Maizelle and Adelaide were lined up beside her, each one waiting her turn to hug me good-bye. I think, of the three, my mother was going to miss me the most. She seemed almost afraid to be left at Grove Hill, to be left in charge of a household she really didn't know anymore. For a moment, I wondered if I should stay. But almost as if Nathaniel sensed my hesitation, he revved the engine and yelled through the open car window that it was time to be on our way. Mother, Maizelle, and Adelaide walked to the edge of the porch and stood there together waving good-bye until the car pulled out of the drive. I looked at them and smiled and then fell back against the seat and closed my eyes.

The trip to Mount Juliet was less than an hour, but we were traveling much farther than that, back through time somewhere, exiting onto Route 171, fifty years or more before we left Grove Hill. A gas station on the far corner of the intersection looked abandoned except for an old man dressed in blue coveralls stacking cans of Quaker State motor oil in the front window. Seeing how there were no other cars in sight, I figured it might take the man the rest of his life to sell all that oil.

I rolled down the window and smelled the wildflowers and the cows that were grazing in the pastures. Mother was right. The air was cleaner and sweeter here, and when I exhaled, every bit of anger and frustration that had been stored in my body floated into the backseat and was sucked right out the rear window.

"There's nothing like that, is there, Miss Bezellia?" Nathaniel said as he drew in a full breath and held it in his lungs. He scratched the back of his head with his right hand, keeping his left firmly on the steering wheel. Nathaniel's hair was thinning and turning whiter, and the tiny bare spot where the angel had kissed him so long ago had grown a little bigger. For a minute, I was on my way to elementary school again, sitting as I always did right behind Nathaniel and hoping Tommy Blanton was still waiting for me behind the coatrack. I couldn't help but wonder if Nathaniel would still be driving me around in my mother's Cadillac when my hair started turning white like his.

Nathaniel and I hadn't talked about Samuel since that day I left Cornelia's house wearing the gold bracelet his son had given me, the bracelet I still wore when I slept at night. Maizelle had told me that Samuel was doing very well at Tennessee State University but was still hoping for a scholarship to Grambling State. He had been elected freshman class president and had a perfect A average. That scholarship seemed sure to come soon, and he was thinking he might be a lawyer or a doctor or maybe even a preacher. A cow mooed in the distance as if he understood what I was thinking.

"Miss Bezellia . . . Miss Bezellia . . . hey, are you there?" Nathaniel called, instantly placing me right back on the warm leather seat in my mother's Cadillac.

"I'm sorry. Did you say something?"

"Heavens, child, I said all sorts of things. But most recent I was saying that I bet your grandparents are mighty excited about you spending the summer with them."

"Yeah, I guess so." But to be honest, I wasn't really sure. Nana said Pop hadn't been feeling too good since Easter. She told me on the telephone that my visit would either perk his spirits right up or put him in his grave, only time would tell. I wasn't exactly sure what she meant by that, but Mother told me to ignore it. My grandmother had always had a twisted way of saying things, she said. I'd just been too young to understand that till now. Maybe, she added, it was a good thing I was spending the summer with them after all.

Nathaniel honked the horn three or four times in rapid succession as he pulled into the narrow gravel driveway in front of my grandparents' house. A small wooden sign staked low in the ground had two words burned into it—THE MORGANS. Pop had never seen much sense in cutting a drive big enough to hold anything more than his red Ford truck, so Nathaniel steered the car onto the grass.

The day's laundry, including my grandmother's bras and panties, was hanging from a line she had strung along the front porch. My grandparents had an old washing machine in the basement but saw no need in owning a dryer as long as the wind was sure to blow. Nana came barreling out the front door, untying her apron as she hustled toward the car. Her thick gray hair was falling free from a loosely wrapped bun low on the back of her head, and two or three wooden clothespins were still clipped to the sleeve of her dress.

Pop, thinner than a stick and not much taller than I was now, came wobbling behind her, using a cane to steady himself. In the wake of my grandmother's force, he suddenly looked very fragile and small.

"Lord, child, get out of that dang car and give me a hug. Oh, Lord, Macon, look how this child has growed. I bet she's gonna be taller than the two of us combined," Nana said, pushing me back from her arms so she could get a good, full look. "Now don't go and get too tall, hon, or you gonna scare them boys off."

Cornelia had always said my legs were one of my best features, but now I found myself turning my ankles in toward the ground so I could shorten my body by an inch or two. Pop was standing beside me, holding my elbow for added security.

"Hey, how ya doing?" I asked as I drew my grandfather into my arms.

"Hanging in there, sweetie. Hanging in," he repeated, sounding lonesome and tired. "My, my, you are something to look at, just like your mother." He squeezed me again before turning his attention to Nathaniel. "Nathaniel, sir," my grandfather said, "sure is good to see you too. Been too long, old man."

But before Nathaniel could answer, Nana interrupted. "How's that daughter of mine treating you these days? Judging by all that white hair you got, I'd say not so good."

"No, ma'am. Mrs. Grove is doing good, doing real good," Nathaniel said, and he smiled at my grandmother and reached out to shake Pop's hand. Mother *was* doing better. He wasn't lying about that. But in all the years I'd known him, Nathaniel had never said one unkind word about either my mother or my father, and he wasn't going to start now. "I've got Miss Bezellia's bags here in the car. Where would you like me to put them, Mrs. Morgan?"

"Miss Bezellia," my grandmother repeated in an exaggerated, drawn-out tone. "Just put *Miss Bezellia's* bags in the front bedroom, Nathaniel. You know the way." She pointed at the house. "Cain't you stay and have something to eat with us? Already got the pork chops fried, and the corn bread's browning in the oven."

"I'd love to, ma'am, but I best be getting back to Nashville. Took me a bit longer than usual to get here today, and Mrs. Grove's needing me to get the summer cushions out on the porch furniture this evening. She's expecting a couple of ladies from the country club tomorrow, and she's wanting everything to look extra special. It's been a while . . ." He paused. "Well, it's been a while since Mrs. Grove has done any outdoor entertaining what with the cold winter and all. Like she always says, there's no point in putting your best foot forward till the daffodils have done come and gone."

Nana just rolled her eyes and tossed Nathaniel a quick good-bye. Then she grabbed my grandfather's forearm and started dragging him back toward the house. I looked at Nathaniel and smiled. He stepped toward me, and in a very soft voice, to make certain that my grandmother would not hear what he was saying, made me promise to call if I needed anything or just found myself wanting to come home sooner than expected. He said it as though he thought I might need him. I said I would and then hugged him real tight. Nathaniel and I had kept our distance for too long, and it felt good to wrap my arms around his big, strong back. Standing next to Nathaniel was about the safest place on earth.

My grandparents were waiting for me in front of their little white, wood-frame house. Nana had patiently watched our good-bye from the porch, but now she was waving her right arm, signaling for me to move it along. "Food's on the table, and it's getting cold," she hollered and then reached for the handle on the screen door and disappeared inside the house.

The table was set with nothing more than a checked vinyl cloth and some worn, white china. The food was served in a variety of mixing bowls, and a stack of white paper napkins was left piled right in front of my plate. "Oh, Nana, this looks so good," I said, trying to be gracious, picking up a piece of fried okra between my thumb and forefinger, and popping it in my mouth. "Mmm. This is even better than Maizelle's. But I swear if you tell her, I'll have to call you a liar."

"Well, sweetie, that's quite something. Did you hear that, Macon? I can fry okra better than Elizabeth's colored woman."

"Nana!" I said, noticeably surprised.

"What, honeybee?" she asked, sounding both shocked and innocent in return. "We all know the colored can fry anything better than anybody. Ain't that right, Macon?"

"I've always said that your nana is the best cook God ever put on this earth," Pop answered obediently, and then he licked his fingers clean, leaving his paper napkin untouched by his plate and my grandmother's words simmering in the air.

After the dishes were washed and left to dry on the counter, the three of us took our places on the back porch, where we watched the moon's reflection as it poured itself across the lake. We sat in flimsy old folding chairs Nana had bought at the Kmart at least ten or fifteen years ago. Wherever a strap had broken, she had mended it with a piece of gray duct tape that stuck to your legs, especially when the air was heavy and thick, like it was tonight. I wondered if my mother had sat on chairs just like these. Heck, I wondered if she had sat on these very chairs, judging by the amount of tape holding them together. Maybe that was why Mother liked her wicker furniture with the big, thick cushions so much. Maybe she got tired of her legs sticking to this old tape.

Pop lit his cigar and blew smoke rings into the black night sky.

He said he'd been studying the clouds since daybreak, and as best as he could tell, now looking at the stars, nice weather was going to last all week long. He said he planned it that way just for me. Nana said my grandfather knew no more about the weather than that damn fool they paid to look into the future on the Channel Four evening news. Then she glanced at her watch and let out a howl.

"Oh, my Lord, it's after midnight, Macon. We got to get to bed or we're gonna be worth nothing tomorrow." And as if we were singing in a church choir, the three of us stood in unison and said good night.

My grandparents slept in a small bedroom next to the only bathroom in the house, at the end of a short, narrow hallway. I slept in the other bedroom, the one that had belonged to my mother. And even though my eyes were tired and heavy, I forced myself to stay awake long enough to soak in the few remaining details of her childhood still scattered about the room.

A dark wooden plaque with a picture of Jesus glued in the middle was hanging on the wall by the switch plate. A signature down in the right-hand corner confirmed it was hers, although I could never imagine her doing crafts of any kind. Nana said Mother had made it at Vacation Bible School. She said she had even burned the edges of the picture with a match to make it look ancient or something. She said my mother used to love to go to church when she was a little girl, rededicating her life to Jesus every chance she got. Mother rarely went to church anymore, unless she was parading a new Easter hat.

On the old oak dresser was a baby's silver drinking cup, dull and tarnished from years of neglect, surely a gift from some generous distant relative or a dear well-heeled friend, as I'd never known my grandmother to buy anything this nice or expensive. I held it in my hands, trying to imagine my mother's tiny fingers wrapped around the very same cup. It was so pretty, surely my mother had meant to take this with her.

Nana said she had kept everything in this room exactly the way it was the day my mother left home, the day she taped a note to the door explaining that there was nothing left in this town for her except beaten-down dreams and broken hearts. Nana didn't say it quite like that, but that's what I imagined Mother meant to write.

When I was small, I'd thought this room was strange, like some kind of memorial to a fallen soldier. I figured Nana was afraid that if she put anything away she might forget one precious memory after another until they were all gone forever. Now I wasn't so sure, but finally I closed my eyes, knowing that it would all be the same in the morning.

chapter seven

*P*op was already down at the corner market buying some fresh minnows and a gallon of gasoline so we could go fishing later out on the lake. I heard his truck rolling over the gravel just after the sun came up and knew where he was headed without anyone bothering to tell me. Nana was in the kitchen cooking. I could smell the bacon frying on the stove.

She hollered from the kitchen door, asking if I wanted a cup of coffee. Nathaniel always said drinking coffee before you were good and grown would stunt your growth. But Nana said it would make you smart. She said she gave it to my mother as soon as she was big enough to hold a cup. And when I walked into the kitchen, my grandmother was standing by her worn metal percolator with an empty mug in her hand, the words ROCK CITY now barely visible on the dull white porcelain. Nana and Pop had gone to Chattanooga seven or eight years ago, the first trip she said they'd taken since Mother left home. She said it wasn't much of trip, but she always drank her coffee out of that mug.

"I guess this explains Mother's love for her morning coffee," I said, thinking my grandmother would be pleased that she had affected her daughter in such a habitual kind of way. "Nathaniel always takes Mother two cups before she gets out of bed. Mother says she just can't face the day without it."

"Before she gets out of bed? No fooling. Sounds like a spoilt princess to me. Lord, sometimes it's hard for me to believe that child is mine," Nana puffed, the word *princess* leaving a familiar and unsettling ring in my ears. "She didn't always think she was better than everybody else. Big city done gone to her head. Hardly acts like she even knows who we are anymore. Hell, that girl never once appreciated what she did have." Nana was suddenly spewing all sorts of foul, nasty words about her only daughter, sounding like an old, leaky pipe that had finally burst, flooding the room with anger and disappointment. She stomped out of the kitchen muttering something about needing to have her bath before Macon got home.

Sometimes I used to wonder if I was adopted. Cornelia said most kids do that at one time or another. She'd read that in *Seventeen*. For a time, I was certain that my real mother was a sweet, quiet woman with a kind smile who loved to work in her garden and greet me after school with a shower of hugs and kisses and questions about my day. Now seeing my grandmother, dressed in her worn-out chenille housecoat and dirty terry-cloth slippers, with pin curls clipped against her head, I wondered if my own mother had ever shared the same dream.

I sucked a tiny bit of the coffee over the rim of the mug and let it set in my mouth, but even doctored with milk and sugar, it was too strong and bitter. Nana said I'd come to like it if I kept at it. But as soon as I heard the water running in the tub, I poured the coffee down the drain.

From the open kitchen window, I could see Pop's dilapidated green tractor still sitting in the lake. After the engine blew a few years ago, he just rolled it right down into the water. He said that a nice tasty fish would love to make a bed under that John Deere. I used to think it looked wonderful out there in the lake, half of it sticking straight up like some kind of crazy artist's sculpture, the other half mysteriously hidden below the surface. Now it looked like nothing but a piece of junk that desperately needed to be hauled away.

"Bezellia, hey, honey, is that you?" I knew that voice without even looking to see who was calling my name. Mrs. Clara Scott had lived next door to my grandparents, well, since I could remember. I believe she may have been the kindest, sweetest woman I ever knew. And whenever I spent any time with Mrs. Scott, I swear the sun even shone a little brighter.

She had spied me from her own kitchen window and was practically falling out the small opening above the sink, contorting her body to get a better look, her large bosom pinched against the windowsill. The Scotts lived next door in the only brick house on this side of the lake. Mr. Scott worked at a bank down in Nashville and made the hour-long drive to the city and then back home again every single day. Mother never could understand why they chose to live so far from town, but Mrs. Scott simply said this lake was the most beautiful place on earth. Mother couldn't help but wonder where *all* on earth she had been.

The Scotts' only daughter, Megan, was a year older than me and one of the prettiest girls I'd ever seen. She was every bit as pretty as those models in the magazines, and Cornelia always figured she could have gone to New York City and modeled professionally except that Megan couldn't say or hear a single word. During the week she went to the Lebanon School for the Deaf and the Blind, where she learned to talk with her hands. Nana said the real reason the Scotts lived out in the country, and not down in Nashville, was so they could hide their misfortune from the rest of the world.

As I stepped onto the brick walk that led to the Scotts' front door, the loud roar of a riding mower drew my attention back to my grandparents' yard. I turned around so hurriedly that I lost my footing and almost landed in the bed of bright red geraniums that were planted near the front steps. I expected to see Pop on top of his new

John Deere, maybe taking it for a quick spin so I could admire it, ooh and aah over it. But there on top of my grandfather's tractor sat a boy about my age. He was wearing a navy blue T-shirt and khaki shorts. A bright green ball cap covered his head, but his arms and legs were already a golden tan. He tipped his cap in my direction and then went about mowing the grass.

"Oh, my Lord, Bezellia, look at you. Oh my, I cannot believe that's you," Mrs. Scott shouted, forcing her small, almost childlike voice to be heard over the lawn mower. She pulled me into the entry hall and folded her thick, warm arms around me. Then she pushed me back, like my grandmother had, to get another good, long look. "You are so grown. Oh my, you are such a beautiful young woman. Looking more like your mother every day. Oh, my Lord. Get in this house and tell me what is going on with you." No one had ever told me that I looked like my mother, until yesterday. Now I'd heard it twice and was surprised how much I liked it.

"Oh, how I wish Megan was here to see you," Mrs. Scott continued, hardly pausing to take a breath. "She is going to be sick when she finds out that you are here. We didn't know you were coming till just the other day."

"Oh," I said in a slightly wilted tone. "I really wanted to see her. Where'd she go?"

"Lord, that girl has gone to California for the summer."

"Really?" I asked, obviously surprised. Suddenly it seemed very unfair that Megan's parents would let her travel clear across the country and she not being able to speak one single word while my parents wouldn't let me go to Paris, and I spoke the whole damn language— with an honest and authentic accent! I wondered how you said *quel dommage* with your hands.

"Yep, she just left day before yesterday. She's staying with my sister down in some place called Marina del Rey and won't be back till the middle of August. She's learning to surf. Can you imagine that? She is just going to be sick when she hears you're here and she's there. Come on in and sit down and tell me what's going on with you."

Mrs. Scott put her arm around my waist and led me into a pleasant, sunny room with a large picture window. Beneath it was a long yellow sofa that reminded me of a big stick of butter with matching yellow lamps framing either end. The Scotts were definitely, as my grandmother would say, "highfalutin city people," even if their address indicated otherwise. We sat side by side in the middle of the sofa, and Mrs. Scott laughed out loud as she repositioned the pillows behind her, admitting that her newly found passion for needlepoint might be becoming something of a hazard.

I told her that I, too, had done my fair share of needlepointing lately, and then I continued from there, spilling my story in tedious detail. Mrs. Scott sat patiently next to me, staring intently into my eyes, at least acting as though she was listening to every syllable spoken. I wondered if most mothers were this attentive or if she was such a good listener because she had to work extra hard to understand Megan.

I told her about my classmates' *life-altering* trip to Paris and mine to Old Hickory Lake. I told her about Adelaide and Baby Stella and all the other blue-eyed dolls that demanded my sister's attention. I told her about Mother going to Minnesota every summer, and about Mrs. Hunt sitting on our front porch—first with my mother, then with my father. I knew my mother would die if she knew all the secrets I was sharing. But I didn't care. I just kept talking, except about Samuel. I kept Samuel to myself.

Mrs. Scott offered me a bowl of homemade banana pudding, the kind that's full of Nilla wafers and fresh bananas, the kind she said can help soothe an aching, troubled heart. I had two helpings while I flipped through the photo album of the Scotts' family trip to Destin. The three of them looked so happy standing on the beach with their feet buried in the sand like one of those families you'd expect to see on a picture postcard inviting you to come and vacation on Florida's sandy, white beaches. They sure didn't look like they were trying to hide any kind of misfortune.

As I turned the last page, I realized that the lawn mower had stopped.

"Mrs. Scott," I asked, still holding the album in my hands, "who's that boy mowing my grandparents' yard?"

"Oh, Lord, isn't he a doll?"

"I can't really tell from here. Just wondering who my grandfather would trust with his new John Deere."

"Oh, believe me, Bezellia, he is precious. Megan just loves him. I mean like a brother and all. And he is just as good as they come. He is so sweet to her. He's even learned to sign enough words that the two of them can carry on a conversation." Cornelia would say that kind of sensitivity in a man is a rare and wonderful gift and should not be overlooked. I knew that's what she'd say.

"Rutherford. Rutherford Semple," Mrs. Scott continued. "But he hates Rutherford, so we all call him Ruddy. His daddy runs a small farm on the other side of Old Cove Road. Lived up here all his life. Lord, your mama surely must know him. They might have gone to school together. Anyway, Ruddy's mama takes in sewing. She's the one who put all these pillows together for me. They don't have much, but they're good people. Real good church people."

"How long has he been working for Pop?"

"Oh, my goodness. I guess it's been ever since your granddaddy had that big heart attack. When was that? Two, three years ago now? Lord, has it been that long since I've seen you? Anyway, he's been doing it ever since then," Mrs. Scott said and paused for a moment. "Kinda thought I would have seen your mama up here at some point. But I know she's real busy with all her volunteer obligations. Your grandmother tells me that she's a very important woman in town."

I smiled, knowing that mother would be so pleased to know that someone still thought that she was important.

"But you ought to go and meet him," Mrs. Scott suggested. "It would be nice for you to know someone your own age way out here, particularly since Megan is gone for the summer. In fact, you better get going. Go introduce yourself. I've kept you long enough now."

Mrs. Scott scooted me right out the front door, of course not before my promise to come for dinner one night soon when Mr. Scott would be home. He would love to see me too, she said.

"Go on, girl, before your granddaddy pays him and he gets gone." Mrs. Scott gently laughed, kindly urging me in the right direction. She stood in the doorway with a smile on her face, watching my every step, making sure I stopped to introduce myself to the cute boy in the bright green ball cap. I was almost running to my grandparents' house, even though I had this odd feeling in the pit of my stomach that I might be cheating on Samuel by the time I got there, cheating on a boy I hadn't even talked to in almost two years.

The riding mower was already parked under the aluminum carport. It was still ticking and pinging, trying to cool its engine in the late morning heat. I slowed down in case Ruddy happened to be looking, not wanting to appear too eager or obvious. I caught my breath and pushed my hair behind my ears and then stepped onto the front porch. But as I reached for the screen door, it suddenly swung toward me, almost knocking me to the ground. And in that moment, as I teetered on one foot, it seemed that all those thoughts about Samuel I'd been carrying around for so long were knocked to the back of my heart, just far enough to make room for one more boy.

"Oh, man, I didn't see you there. Sorry about that."

"It's a screen door," I said and grinned.

"I'm real sorry. Just wasn't paying attention, I guess. You okay?" Ruddy asked, standing right there in front of me with his ball cap in his hand but trying to look anywhere except at me. He scooted toward the edge of the porch, and I wondered if he was attempting to stage his escape.

"You must be Rutherford Semple," I said, calling him by his full name. Cornelia said it was very alluring when a woman called a man by his full, God-given name. But this Rutherford tightened his eyes, letting me know he didn't care for that much.

"I am. But I'd just as soon you call me Ruddy."

"Sure thing, Ruddy."

"And you must be the granddaughter I keep hearing so much about," he said, now staring down at his work boots. "I knew you was coming. Mr. and Mrs. Morgan been talking 'bout you for weeks."

"I guess I am. And I guess you're the boy I've been hearing about, the one my grandfather trusts with his new John Deere."

"Yeah, guess so. But it ain't exactly new. He bought it used from a man on the other side of the cove."

"Well, anything less than ten years old is new to my grandfather."

Ruddy laughed, nodding his head in agreement. His deep brown eyes relaxed, and when he smiled, a little dimple on his left cheek appeared out of nowhere. I stepped closer to the house, brushing past him in a slow, deliberate way, and then carefully pulled the screen door toward me. "Maybe I'll see you around," I said, and then I stepped inside and let the door slam shut behind me.

Cornelia would be so proud. I'd been flirty and coy but vague and slightly disinterested, and I hadn't required the Parisian sun bouncing off my cheeks to do it either. I needed to write my cousin and tell her about this Rutherford Semple. And I needed to write Mary Margaret Hunt and let her know that the best-looking men were not, it turned out, in France.

"I see you met Ruddy," I heard my grandmother shouting from the kitchen.

"Yeah. He was coming out as I was coming in."

"Don't be getting too friendly with him." Nana stepped outside the kitchen door just far enough so I could see her face. She was holding a knife in one hand and an onion in the other. She wiped her eyes with the hem of the ratty old apron she had loosely tied about her waist.

"He's a nice boy and all, but he spends way too much time with Megan, and something about that just ain't right."

"I think it's nice that he hangs out with Megan. Besides, they're just friends, Nana. Mrs. Scott said so herself."

"Just friends? A girl who can't talk. Lord, child, are you kidding? That boy could only have one thing on his mind, and that's getting into her pants. Just like his daddy."

"Nana!" I said, surprised to hear my grandmother talk about any boy getting into any girl's pants. "Mrs. Scott says Ruddy is very nice. And what do you mean 'just like his daddy'?"

"Forget it. It's not important. But remember this, Bezellia, I didn't just crawl out from under some rock the way your mama would like you to think I did. Mark my words, the only reason he spends time with that girl is because he likes the way she fits into those blue jeans she's always wearing. God almighty, you can see everything the good Lord gave her."

I didn't even bother to argue with her because I was beginning to realize, just as it was with my own mother, that an argument would be nothing but a waste of words. I honestly didn't care what my grandmother thought. It felt good to be interested in a boy again, and I liked Ruddy Semple, whether he wanted in my pants or not. And I wasn't so sure that was a bad place for him to be.

Turned out, Ruddy was everything Mrs. Scott had said he would be. He was kind, a little shy, but patient and very handsome. His chest was broad and strong, and his eyes were the warmest, deepest brown I had ever seen. His dark hair was cut short and parted over to the side. And when that little dimple on his left cheek surfaced, I found myself wanting to curl up in his arms.

Before long, Ruddy and I were spending most every afternoon together paddling around in my grandfather's rowboat, checking his fishing lines that were tied to empty plastic milk jugs and scattered about the lake. We drifted through the summer doing nothing more than talking and holding hands. And when he finally kissed me, he hoped my granddaddy would understand that his feelings for me were true and honest. I really didn't care what anybody thought. I just wanted Ruddy to kiss me again.

To tell the truth, Pop thought Ruddy kept coming around the house because he needed extra spending money. But Nana knew better and just stared him down like a hungry hawk circling her prey. When my grandmother was in the room, poor Ruddy spent most of the time talking to his feet.

He said that when he was singing and playing his guitar he had more courage than a lion and that he was heading to Nashville as soon as he graduated from high school. He was going to be a famous country music star someday but had promised his mama he would finish school first. He'd be only the second Semple to get his diploma, his daddy being the first.

We were almost to the other side of the lake, probably already had fifteen fresh catfish in the metal tank at the end of the boat, when I started telling Ruddy about my uncle and his Buffy Orphans. As soon as I mentioned those silly hens, Ruddy jumped to his feet and clapped his hands, almost dumping me right into the water.

"Lord, girl, I don't believe it. You know something about the chicken business? Man, you have got to see my daddy's prizewinning cock, a blue-ribbon winner, twice over. Prettiest cock in the county. Maybe you could come to supper tomorrow night and take a good look at him?" Ruddy clapped his hands in excitement and then just as quickly turned a deep shade of red. He sat back down and fixed his eyes on the water. "You do know I'm talking about a rooster, don't ya?"

I reassured him that I did, even if I did live in the city, and that I would love to see his daddy's prizewinning bird.

Nana was not too happy about my invitation to Ruddy's house. She said his parents barely had a pot to piss in, and she didn't think my mama would be too happy either about me going anywhere near the Semple farm. Nana was probably right. Ruddy did not own one expensive sweater, and he certainly did not drive a convertible, unless you counted my grandfather's tractor. And since he was born and raised in the Church of God, I could guarantee that he did not know how to dance. But I told my grandmother not to worry. I was only going to see a bird.

Ruddy picked me up in his daddy's truck a little before four. I was wearing a white cotton skirt and a thin cotton blouse with little pink and green flowers all over it. Nana thought the skirt was too short. But Ruddy smiled when he saw me, said I looked real pretty, and then he helped me into his daddy's truck. We drove a couple of miles without saying anything, my hair blowing in my face. I'd catch Ruddy staring at me and then looking away, shy and yet real curious all at the same time. He finally slowed the truck down and pulled off to the side of the road. He inched a little closer, put his arm around my shoulders, and pointed to a field spotted with Queen Anne's lace and black-eyed Susans. It looked a lot like the land back behind my house, except now a rooster was crowing in the distance, urging us along.

"That's Mister Jackson," Ruddy said with a big grin on his face. "He knows you're coming. See, down there, that's my house." On the other side of the field stood a small yellow house topped with a red tin roof. It looked like a speck of paint from where we were, and even up close it didn't get much bigger. Ruddy said his mama had been cooking all day. She was real anxious to meet me, so Mister

Jackson would have to wait till after supper to make my acquaintance.

The smell of pot roast and green beans filled their tiny house. The windows were wide open, but it was still so hot and sticky inside I could feel the sweat dripping down my back. Three or four pots simmered quietly on the stove, and a pan of biscuits sat warming in the oven, the door left open so they wouldn't burn. I wondered how Ruddy's mama stood there cooking all day without fainting from the heat.

The living room and kitchen were one large room, no walls separating one space from the other. The kitchen table was nicely set with a faded blue checked cloth and a handful of that Queen Anne's lace plunked down in an old glass milk pitcher. As soon as I stepped through the door, everyone's eyes turned toward me—Ruddy's mother's, his father's, his little sister's, even their dog's eyes were fixed on the girl who'd come all the way from Nashville. No one said hello until I did. No one sat at the table until I did or placed his napkin in his lap or picked up his fork, until I did. And somewhere swirling about my head, I could hear Samuel, sitting down by the creek under the cherrybark oaks, calling me a princess.

Mrs. Semple apologized that her meal wasn't very fancy, like I was surely used to eating back home. I told her it was wonderful, better than anything I'd had in Nashville or anywhere else for that matter, and then took another bite of pot roast. She smiled at me and then at Ruddy and asked if I'd like another biscuit. Mr. Semple took his place at the head of the table without saying a word. He sat there either staring at me like he was trying to recall an old friend or ignoring me altogether, every now and then stopping to look at his plate while he dragged his biscuit through the last bit of gravy. He waited for his wife to clear the dishes from the table and seemed relieved when Ruddy and I finally got up and left.

After supper, Ruddy took me into the front yard and introduced me to Mister Jackson. He stood near the edge of their beaten old barn, beaming like a daddy who's just been told his baby girl is the prettiest child in town. He clucked like a rooster and then threw Mister Jackson a few kernels of corn. The rooster waddled right up to Ruddy and ate out of his hand. I told him that Mister Jackson was the best-looking bird I'd ever seen, much more handsome than Uncle Thad's pack of orphaned hens.

We walked back to the house and said our good-byes. Ruddy's mom told me to come again real soon, that it had been a pleasure meeting me. I assured her that the pleasure had been all mine. His daddy just sat in a tattered old reclining chair reading the newspaper, never once bothering to look our way. Ruddy kissed his mother on the cheek and said he was going to show me the sights. I started to laugh but then realized he meant what he said. We hopped in his daddy's truck and headed back down the narrow gravel road that led to his house. But he turned left and onto a little dirt path I hadn't noticed before and shifted down into first gear. He drove real slowly, the lush green growth on either side of the road rubbing up against the truck. A branch popped inside my window, and I squealed and moved closer to Ruddy, resting my head on his shoulder.

"I've got a present for you," he said, pulling off the road and gesturing for me to look out the window. And there, glistening in the remnants of the late evening sun, Old Hickory Lake stood perfectly still, its glassy surface reflecting the tall oaks and cedars that trimmed the water's edge.

"Oh, it's absolutely beautiful, Ruddy. You know my mother would say there's nothing quite like being on the water."

"That's not the best part," he said excitedly. "Come on and I'll show you. You know your grandparents' house is just right over there. I'm surprised you've never been over here."

Ruddy jumped out of the truck and practically ran to my door.

He reached for my hand and guided me off the seat, giving me time to pull my skirt down before fully revealing my panties. Then he led me through some tall grass and onto a white, sandy beach. We stood there holding hands while our feet instinctively burrowed down into the cool, smooth sand. Ruddy fidgeted for a while and finally pointed to the ground. "This! This is what I wanted to show you."

"The sand?" I asked, suddenly realizing that it was odd to see a white, sandy beach in the middle of Tennessee.

"Yeah, the beach," he said excitedly. "The Army Corps of Engineers carried in all this sand last summer so everybody out here could pretend like they were in Florida or Hawaii. I guess they figure most of us aren't ever gonna get anywhere near a place like that so they decided to bring it to us. I told the Scotts there was no point in them making that long drive to Destin anymore," he said, and then laughed, pulling me down onto the beach next to him. He said it was the biggest thing that had happened in Mount Juliet in years, next to Mister Jackson winning a blue ribbon at the state fair and Mr. Patterson setting his own house on fire so he could collect the insurance money.

We nestled our bodies next to each other and watched the stars come out, every new spot of light further decorating the night sky. Ruddy said there'd be rain later in the week. I told him that was exactly what my grandfather had said, even though that wasn't true. He laughed just a bit and wrapped both arms around me, pulling me so close that I could hear his heart beat. He said he'd never met a girl like me and sure hated to think of my leaving soon. Then he stroked my lower lip with his finger before pressing his own mouth against mine, his kiss so warm and perfect that I couldn't help but wonder if he read *Seventeen* too. Every time he touched me, I found myself digging my foot deeper and deeper into the sand, as if I was hopelessly trying to bind my body to the earth.

I snuggled deeper into his chest, and without warning or announcement, he reached under my blouse and tried to unfasten my bra. Now Cornelia would say that a man with any experience at all with a girl's undergarments could unfasten a bra in one swift flick of the wrist. But Ruddy struggled with the clasp, and I finally reached behind my back and helped him with the last hook and eye. He apologized for his clumsy fingers. I told him not to worry about it, that sometimes even I had a hard time getting those hooks undone. He pulled off his own shirt with ease, and I watched him as he carefully unbuttoned mine. Ruddy didn't seem so shy right now.

My breasts felt warm against his chest and my back cool against the sand. His tongue touched mine, and he kissed me a long time, as if he was trying to pour every ounce of love he had right down my throat. Tommy Blanton and I had never kissed like this. Samuel and I had never kissed like this, like Cornelia had promised I would do someday. A part of me wanted to tell him to stop, that I had been saving this moment for another boy. And a part of me wanted to tell him to move a little faster.

Ruddy rubbed his hand up and down my leg and then into my panties. Nana was right. He *had* wanted in my pants, but I gently caressed his hand, reassuring him that he was headed in the right direction. Then he led me to a place that I was not familiar with, and he stroked me until I shook in his arms. He kissed my forehead and my nose and my cheeks and my chin. He whispered in my ear that he wanted to love every inch of my body—someday. I told him that he better not wait too long because I would be leaving soon, and then I tugged at his belt. Ruddy took my hand in his and kissed it over and over again.

"Bezellia, you're makin' it real hard, but it just wouldn't be right, here and all."

"I didn't know the location had that much to do with it."

"I guess the beach is better than doing it in the back of the pickup, but I think you oughta have a ring on that finger before you, uh . . ." And he hesitated finding it hard to say the word. "You know, before we do everything God intends for a man and woman to do."

"You don't think God's going to have a problem with what we just did?"

"That just ain't the same thing. Besides, I think God understands that a girl and boy got to have some fun along the way. But the big *it,* well, that needs to wait till after the wedding. Daddy says you can really make a mess of things if you don't wait till it's proper."

Proper. Suddenly I pictured myself standing at the tiny stove in his tiny house fixing fried chicken for Sunday supper, his mama and daddy sitting on lawn chairs out in the front yard watching Mister Jackson and waiting for me to call them to the table, which was still covered in that same tattered old cloth with a can full of dead Queen Anne's lace sitting smack-dab in the middle.

An uncomfortable feeling washed over me, one I felt ashamed to claim as my own. I didn't want to marry Ruddy Semple, and for no better reason than that he was a poor boy from the middle of nowhere. Maybe there was just too much Grove in me after all and not enough courage to marry someone who couldn't live in the only world I'd ever known—even if it was a world I often didn't like. Maybe I was more like my mother than my grandfather or Mrs. Scott or even I had imagined.

"Hey, Bezellia, hey, you in there? Hey, girl, you hear me? I got one more thing to show you." And Ruddy stood up and drew me toward him in one swift, smooth motion. "We're gonna take us a little walk, so you better button up that pretty little blouse of yours or you're gonna be giving those cows something to talk about."

"Walk?" I asked as I straightened my blouse and pulled the hair out of my face, trying to make sense of where we were headed now.

"Daddy always says that if it ain't worth walking to, then it ain't worth seeing. C'mon, it's worth it, I promise."

We walked at least a mile with nothing but the croaking of the tree frogs reminding us that we were not alone. Sometimes we'd stop in the middle of the road and Ruddy would lean forward and kiss me lightly on the lips, and then we'd start walking again. The moon was fairly bright, and I could see up ahead where the road curved to the left. Beyond that, there was a glow, some kind of light rising up out of nothing. I asked Ruddy if that was where we were headed, toward that light. Instead of answering, he stopped and kissed me on the lips one more time, a reward for faithfully following him into the night.

As we came to the bend in the road, I could see a big red barn all lit up against the dark sky. White letters mounted just below the roof-line read Bradley's Barn. There were probably two dozen cars parked in the driveway. But other than the frogs still singing their songs, there wasn't a sound to be heard.

"Is this some kind of bar, Ruddy? Like a honky-tonk? I'm not sure we ought to be going in there. Who's Bradley anyway?"

"Bezellia Grove, damn, girl, do you even know what a honky-tonk is? All that fancy learning of yours and you don't know a thing about Owen Bradley or his big red barn, do you?" I just gave him a look like *why should I?* And Ruddy shot me a smart look right back. "Because he's only one of the greatest record producers ever and that place is full of musicians right now making an album."

"Country music?" I asked.

"What other kind is there? Lord, it seems that any girl born and raised in Nashville ought to know something about country music. Daddy says it's our heritage."

"Not everybody in Nashville picks a guitar, Ruddy," I said, sounding unkind and defensive. "Besides, my mother always called that hillbilly music. She says it's not good for the ear." Truthfully,

Mother didn't listen to much music of any kind, and she certainly never listened to country music. She said she'd had enough of that when she was little. All at once Ruddy's eyes looked a bit wounded and sad. "I *have* heard of Johnny Cash," I said, trying to soften my blow.

"Listen, Bezellia, I don't mean to sound disrespectful, but your mama don't know what she's talking about. And Lord, I sure hope you have heard of Johnny Cash, seeing how he lives just on the other side of this big old lake. One of these days, just so you know, I'm gonna have me a whole bunch of gold albums just like Mr. Cash. And I'm gonna live in a big house on the lake too. Maybe even bigger than his."

I had heard this dream once before, and I imagined I was going to hear it again. I guess no matter who we are or where we're starting from, we all want something other than what we've got. Maybe that's what keeps us moving forward, but I'm not sure I fully understood that back then, standing in the middle of that country road in the dead of night.

"Wow, what a special occasion this is," Ruddy said. "Looks like I'm about to teach the city girl a thing or two she'll never forget." And then he took me by the hand and once again led me somewhere I'd never been.

We walked right up to a small door cut into the back wall of the barn, not framed with any kind of trim, making it hard to find in the dark. Ruddy tugged on a long wooden handle, cracking the door just wide enough to wedge his body through the opening, and then he pulled me in behind him.

"Is this okay, being here and all?" I whispered, already feeling a bit anxious and out of place.

"Oh, yeah. I sweep the floors and take out the garbage for Mr. Bradley every Monday morning. He doesn't mind as long as I'm quiet," Ruddy said and then paused for a moment, "and he doesn't know that I'm here." And he put his finger to his mouth, signaling for me to hush.

We felt our way down one dark hallway and then another. I could barely see my hand outstretched in front of me, holding tightly on to Ruddy's arm. We stopped behind a heavy curtain that was hanging from the ceiling, its other end dragging on the ground. Ruddy pointed to the floor, now signaling for me to sit down. Then he pulled the curtain back just enough to reveal a small group of people, some sitting on stools, some standing, but all of them together forming a circle around a cluster of silver microphones.

One man was crouched behind a set of drums, a couple of others had guitars strapped over their shoulders, and one real skinny man was holding a shiny red guitar plugged into a big black box. There was another man tuning a banjo and a couple of others with violins tucked against their necks. Ruddy said that out here they were playing fiddles, not violins.

"This ain't some fancy orchestra, Bezellia."

And in the middle of all these men was one small, beautiful woman with long black hair cascading down her back. She had a dainty little mouth and a dainty little nose. Even her smile was dainty. But her eyes were a bright, piercing blue. She was standing behind a microphone singing the same line to herself, over and over again, like she was trying to find the right note.

> *"I'm here to tell ya gal to lay offa my man.*
> *I'm hear to tell ya gal to lay offa my man."*

A gray-headed man was in another room behind a large plate-glass window. He was seated in front of a desk covered with all sorts of knobs and lights, and the minute he positioned the microphone in front of his mouth, all the musicians in the other room grew silent. He directed everyone to stand by. Ruddy kissed the back of my neck while the man with the red guitar counted with his fingers. One, two, three. Music immediately filled the room, and the little woman with the brilliant blue eyes stood up straight and tall in front of her microphone and thrust her chest slightly forward.

She started singing about some floozy who had been spending too much time with her husband and then bragging too much about their affair. She called her nothing but trash and promised if she didn't stop "a lovin'" her man, then she would have no choice but to come looking for her. Yes, that tiny little woman was going to punch that tramp right in the face and take her to a place she called "fist city." And to tell the truth, she sang those lyrics with such power and emotion that I actually believed she could do it too.

"Who is that?" I whispered.

"That's Mr. Bradley behind the glass."

"No, I mean who's singing?"

"That's Loretta Lynn. You never heard of her either? She grew up poorer than dirt, lived up in the hills of Kentucky somewhere. Now look at her. Just proves anybody can do anything," Ruddy said with a smile, obviously referring to his own big dreams for the future.

I'd heard Loretta Lynn's name and seen some pictures of her in the newspaper from time to time, always outfitted in some fancy gown that had too many sequins and too many ruffles on it, at least that's what Mother said. But I'd never heard her sing. And now, sitting on the floor of that barn, hearing her rich, twangy voice, I felt like I was listening to some wise old sage or prophet. I just wished my own mother would listen to her sing, would find her on the radio, maybe even find the courage to go looking for Mrs. Hunt and take her on a little trip to "fist city."

After Mrs. Lynn sang the last note, everyone stayed real still and quiet until Mr. Bradley nodded his head. He turned a knob on his desk and then pulled the microphone right up close to his mouth.

"That was great, everybody, but I'd like to hear the second verse one more time. And, Loretta, hold that last note just a beat or two longer."

I wanted to jump up and clap right out loud, but Ruddy grabbed my hands and led me back through the darkened hallways and out the barn door.

"Why'd we have to go? That was incredible! Her voice is so beautiful, absolutely beautiful. I've never heard anything like it."

"Well, I think you better take a look at that sky for one thing, Bezellia. I got to get you home."

The horizon was turning a light shade of black, almost starting to look blue along the edge. It wouldn't be long till Mister Jackson would be sounding his alarm, informing everyone, including my grandparents, that night had come and gone.

"Come on!" Ruddy said as he grabbed my hand and started running. We couldn't help but laugh and sing as we barreled our way headlong into the morning, straight to Ruddy's pickup truck. His voice was so unexpectedly rich and strong. It was as if that sound coming from his mouth scooped us right up and carried us along, leaving us both feeling daring and bold. By the time I got to my grandparents' house and reached for the screen door, I was nothing less than brave and fearless, ready to tell my grandmother that Ruddy Semple was a good man, that she had sold him short, that I probably had too. And I had a funny feeling that Loretta Lynn would be standing right there beside me.

Nana and Pop were already sitting at the kitchen table, each one holding a mug of coffee. Nana rubbed her finger across the rim of her mug, and even I could see that her eyes looked more wet and confused than worried or angry.

"Sit down, Bezellia," my grandfather said, still refusing to look directly at me. I was suddenly afraid to sit anywhere, somehow knowing that, once I did, they were going to tell me something I did not want to hear. So I just stood by the table, stiff and straight, not even willing to bend my knees.

"Honey," my grandfather said as he reached for my hand, "you need to sit down," and then he used what strength he had left to drag me into the chair next to his. "There's been an accident. At your house."

"What do you mean an accident? What happened? Is Adelaide hurt? Is she okay?"

I wanted my grandfather to talk faster, and I wanted him to hush. I wanted to be back on the beach, in Ruddy's arms, drifting off to sleep. I wanted to be at Grove Hill, playing with Adelaide and Baby Stella down by the creek, helping Maizelle roll out biscuits and string green beans. I wanted to be kissing Tommy Blanton behind the coatrack. I wanted to be sitting with Samuel by the swimming pool. I wanted to be painting my toenails on Cornelia's bed. Please, I screamed, let me be any place but right here. But nobody heard me.

"Bezellia, your daddy fell down the stairs, sometime after he come home from the hospital last night. Apparently nobody heard him fall. Maizelle done found him this morning." My grandfather stopped and choked back some tears. "I'm sorry, sweetie. There was nothing that could be done. Broke his neck. Never woke up—"

"Nathaniel's on his way to get you," Nana interrupted. "We'll come on later. We got to take care of a few things here first. Your mother won't talk to no one. Won't come out of her room. Your uncle Thad thought it might be good if you come on right away. Of course, if I know my daughter, she's probably done gone and drowned herself in a bottle of gin. Cain't say that I blame her this time, though."

I sat there not saying one word, just drifting in and out of that still, muggy kitchen. My father was dead. I heard my grandfather say it, and yet all I could think about was my mother. I scooted my chair back from the table and looked my grandmother squarely in the eyes.

"That's just it, Nana. You don't know Mother. You don't know her at all."

DR. GROVE DIES
CHARLES GOODMAN GROVE V PASSES AWAY AT HOME

Nashvillians Mourn Loss

Dr. Charles Goodman Grove V, died in his Grove Hill home today. He was 42.

A member of one of the city's most prominent families, Dr. Grove will best be remembered for his dedicated service to Methodist Memorial Medical Center, where he served as a doctor of internal medicine since 1950 and was recently named the hospital's chief of staff. In his newly appointed position, Dr. Grove was spearheading the development of the new pediatric ward, scheduled to open in the fall of 1970.

Dr. Grove was also a loyal and generous supporter of the Harpeth Hills Botanical Garden and the Nashville Museum of Art, the city's symphony and the Nashville Historical Society. Last month, he personally established the Bezellia Grove Scholarship, to be given to a Vanderbilt University student majoring in American history with a keen interest in researching Nashville's own rich past.

Visitation with the family will be held at the Grove Hill estate tomorrow. Funeral services will be held Saturday at Broadway United Methodist Church. Pallbearers and flower ladies will be selected from friends.

Dr. Grove is survived by his wife, Elizabeth Mabel Morgan, and his two daughters, Bezellia Louise and Adelaide Elizabeth. He is also survived by his brother, Thaddeus Lee Grove, and one niece, Cornelia Dutton Grove.

The Nashville Register
final edition
AUGUST 13, 1968

Strangers had taken their places inside my house by the time Nathaniel and I got to Grove Hill. Ladies dressed in black were carrying casseroles from the kitchen to the dining room table, each one wearing a sweet but ingenuous smile that was intended to provide some unspoken comfort. Men, dressed in black, stood about the living room swapping stories, seemingly not as interested in their newly departed friend as they were in Orlando Cepeda's chances of leading the Cardinals to the World Series.

Maizelle and Adelaide were huddled in the kitchen, trying to occupy themselves by walking from the refrigerator to the stove and back again. Their shoulders were slumped forward, and their eyes were red and swollen. When I stepped into the room, they both rushed toward me, and we stood there in one another's arms, supporting our bodies as they heaved in sorrow.

"I'm sorry, Miss Bezellia. I didn't hear a thing. Down in that basement I can't hear an elephant sneeze. I'm so sorry, child." Maizelle finally broke the silence, needing to confess something she couldn't have done anything about.

"Me too, I'm sorry too," Adelaide sobbed. "It was my fault. It was all my fault. If I'd been a good girl, then Father would still be here—"

"Adelaide, child," Maizelle interrupted. "Hush up. I want you to stop that now. This was not your fault." And then she turned to me. "Your mama had me give your sister one of those Contac pills before going to bed. Knocked her right out."

"Where is Mother?" I asked as I held Adelaide tightly in my arms, reassuring her that this was certainly not her fault.

Nathaniel, who had been standing quietly by my side, suddenly interrupted and announced that Mrs. Grove was still in her room. "She won't come out. She knows what all of those people out there are saying about her. She won't show her face. Says she won't even go to the funeral."

"What? What are they saying about her?"

Adelaide turned to Maizelle and dropped into her arms as if she was burying herself in some deep, faraway hole. Nathaniel and Maizelle finally lifted their heads, both obviously wanting to say something but neither having the courage to say it.

"What? Damn it, Nathaniel, what are *they* saying?"

"Uh, well. I really shouldn't be the one telling you this."

"If you don't, nobody will. Now what is it? Tell me."

"Well, you see. Thing is, Miss Bezellia, your daddy came home late last night."

"So? So what? He always comes home late, for one reason or another. I'm sure some dying patient needed him desperately, or maybe Mrs. Hunt had him all tied up in her arms. Which was it this time?"

"Bezellia!" Maizelle said with a rush of surprise.

"I don't think now's the time to pretend Father was a loyal and devoted husband, Maizelle," I snapped, finding it much easier to be mad at Father for cheating than sad and brokenhearted that he had died. After all, my father wasn't the first married man to screw another woman. And my mother was like so many other upstanding, country-club-going women who had lived with infidelity. She acted as though she knew nothing about it. God, I thought to myself, if she had only listened to Loretta Lynn.

"Yes. That's right," Nathaniel continued. "We all know about Mrs. Hunt. Your mother does, that's for sure. And probably most of Nashville knows it by now. That's the truth. But see, Miss Bezellia, the police found a bottle of gin in your mother's bedroom. Apparently she done finished it off. I told them she hadn't been drinking lately. But they couldn't wake her when they came to pronounce Mr. Grove . . . Well, they couldn't wake her." Nathaniel paused, clearly afraid to finish what he had to say.

Maizelle stood by my side, patting my back in a smooth, simple rhythm. "Miss Bezellia, I think you better sit down."

"Why does everybody think sitting down is going to make any of this any better? Damn it. I am not sitting down, Nathaniel, so just go ahead and tell me what you have to say."

Nathaniel repositioned himself so he was standing directly in front of me. He adjusted his weight from one foot to the other and then back again, as if finding the perfect balance was going to ease what needed to be said. Maizelle gently nudged Adelaide toward the butler's pantry. She said she needed to find more linen napkins, but I knew she really wanted to keep Adelaide from hearing too much. I leaned against the kitchen counter, now wondering if I should have found a place to sit.

"Some people," Nathaniel continued, "knowing of your mother's lingering condition, are wondering if your mama had something more to do with your daddy's dying. Some people think she pushed him down the stairs. The police haven't come out and said that, and I don't think they ever will. At least that's what your uncle Thad said, and he spent several hours down at the police station talking to some old friends of his. But people around town, they're saying something different."

I reached behind me and gripped the counter till my knuckles turned white. I tried not to fall, to keep my knees locked in place. But I sank to the floor in silence. I couldn't scream. I couldn't cry. I couldn't make sense of anything Nathaniel was saying to me. He knelt down in front of me and took my hands in his.

"Everybody standing out there eating cheese thins and casseroles is going to think what they want, child. Some of them may want to believe your mama pushed him. Some of them may think she had a right to. But at the end of the day, nobody knows what really happened here last night. Only one left who knows for sure is your mama, and I'm not sure given the state she was in she'll ever really know what happened at the top of those stairs," Nathaniel said, squeezing my hands in his. "One thing I do know for certain, you had nothing to do with your daddy's dying, nothing at all, nor did your little sister," he added, staring toward the pantry as if he was looking for Adelaide. We were, he said, our father's bright, shining stars.

"Maizelle," Nathaniel called.

"Uh-huh," Maizelle answered from deep inside the pantry. She walked back into the kitchen with my sister's small hand still tightly clutched in hers.

"Why don't you help Miss Bezellia up to her room and get her all settled. She might want to rest a little bit. It's been a long morning, and it's not even noon yet."

Maizelle lifted me to my feet, and together we walked up the back staircase, careful to avoid the crowd of mournful-looking people who called my parents their friends. Those men and women looked as though they could just as easily have been going to a cocktail party as to a funeral. And now, when they weren't busy talking behind my mother's back about her drinking and her unfaithful husband, they wanted to comfort her, hug her, tell her everything would be all right. I hated them all.

Maizelle was afraid my mother might not ever recover from los-ing Mr. Grove. She was afraid she would blame herself. She was afraid the guilt might spread through her body like some kind of cancer, that it might take her life as swiftly as Mr. Grove's had been taken from him. She said that happens sometimes.

My mother's door was closed. I walked into her room without knocking. The curtains were drawn, and not even a small slice of sunlight had found its way past the heavy fabrics. With my arms outstretched in front of me, I felt my way to her bed and then reached for the lamp by my mother's side. She covered her head with her blanket but didn't snap at me for blinding her like she had done when I was little and rushed in to show her a necklace I had made out of dried macaroni and yarn. That time, she'd grabbed the necklace out of my hands and thrown it across the room. Now I sat down on the edge of her bed and gently pulled the blanket back so that I could see my mother's eyes. They were more than swollen and red. They were empty and broken.

"Everybody thinks I killed your father," she said in a voice so weak and fragile that I had to put my ear next to her mouth just so I could understand what she was saying. "I guess they're right, Bezellia. I guess I did." She started to cry, and between deep, tearful sobs, she could barely catch her breath. She mumbled something more about my father, but I couldn't understand what she was saying. All I knew was that, in the midst of my mother's confession, she had called me *Bezellia*. Whether she had done so out of guilt or affection didn't really matter. I had never heard my mother speak my given name. And even though her voice was almost inaudible, and even though I knew my attention should be someplace else, I desperately wanted to hear her say my name one more time.

Father, she admitted, had come home late last night, smelling of alcohol. He sat next to her on the bed so that she could almost taste the remnants of the other woman on his skin. He leaned down and kissed her on the forehead. She didn't know why—maybe he was feeling guilty or lonely or simply unsatisfied. And she wasn't sure she really cared. She wanted to tell him that she missed him. She wanted to ask him to stay with her, to lie next to her, to love her. But instead she said nothing and rolled onto her side, turning her back to him as she must have done so many other nights since they married. He got up and walked out of the bedroom. She heard the back door open and close and understood that he had gone to be with someone else. She picked up the silver-framed wedding photo that sat on her dressing table and threw it across the room and searched for a bottle of gin she had hidden under the mattress.

Shards of broken glass scattered on the bedroom floor and an empty bottle of gin now sitting on my mother's dresser were both testaments to the truth of her account. And now a desperate, repentant soul was curled up in a tiny ball, weeping into her pillow. I crawled in bed next to her and wrapped my arms around her trembling body. She cried until she fell asleep, and even then I could tell that she was grieving. I stayed there for a while, rubbing her back and thinking of every time she had forced me to smile.

When my toe was broken and I had to go to the cotillion because Rawley Montgomery wanted to dance with me, Mother told me to smile. When Jan Hobdy invited me to her thirteenth birthday party but Mother made me go shopping with her instead, she told me to smile. When Megan Scott's mother asked me to spend the weekend with them at the lake but Mother said I wasn't wasting my time with a girl who couldn't talk, she told me to quit crying and smile. Tomorrow, I whispered in her ear, she would get dressed, fix her hair, come downstairs, and greet her friends, and she would do it all with the perfect smile.

My mother slept the rest of the day. I bathed and changed clothes, and even though my eyes were heavy and tired, I couldn't sleep. So I found myself back downstairs looking for a little something to eat and a little comfort in the kitchen. After Maizelle fed me,

Nathaniel handed me a tray stacked with glasses of lemonade and told me to walk through the living room and see if anybody who had come to pay respects was feeling parched and thirsty. He said it's better to be moving around at a time like this than just standing there lost in your own dark thoughts. Maizelle and Adelaide kept their places in the kitchen, finding it easier to hide behind the stove and another chicken artichoke casserole.

Nana and Pop arrived shortly before dinner. Nana said Ruddy came by not long after I left. He said he was sorry for keeping me out so late, and he was really sorry to hear about my daddy. He wanted to drive his daddy's truck down here to see me, but Nana told him that my mother would not likely appreciate the concerns of a guitar-picking country boy who'd kept her daughter out till daybreak. I imagined I wouldn't hear from Ruddy again. Probably just as well.

Thankfully Uncle Thad stayed at the house until the last guest had left. He talked to my grandparents mostly, somehow knowing the longer he kept them on the front porch the easier it would be for my mother. He said he wanted to make sure his baby girls were okay and even offered to stay the night. Cornelia would be flying home from Boston tomorrow. She was worried sick about me, he said. She had already called the house twice this evening just to check on me.

Uncle Thad had insisted Cornelia go to college above the Mason-Dixon Line. He always said he wanted her to see how the *other* people lived. But I always figured what he really wanted was for Cornelia to come to know her mother, who had been living in New England since her daughter was two years old. Apparently the great New York painters were not very impressed with my cousin's mother. But she found the people in Boston loved her and her ability to paint one rugged seascape after another.

"You know, I was thinking on my way over here this morning, Beetle Bug, that it was a damn good thing my brother insisted on calling you Bezellia," Uncle Thad told me as he rubbed my shoulder with his strong right hand. "Your mother really didn't care for the name. I guess you've figured that out by now," he said with a tender grin on his face. "But you know, I think you're probably the first Grove to wear that name well since the first Bezellia fought those Indians down at Fort Nashborough.

"Now I know you're not going to be fighting any Indians around these parts, but I'm afraid you may have an even tougher battle up ahead of you—although you surely know that by now too. People can be mighty cutting without knives in their hands. They can say all sorts of things that aren't true. Damn near make you bleed. Hell, sometimes I think they just make up some of this shit so they have something to spread about town like manure on a vegetable crop. Look, Bee, your mother ain't no angel. But she's not all devil either. Sometimes life just forces the good right out of you so that nobody can see anything else but the bad. And your father, my brother, he wasn't perfect either. But be careful, sweetie, because when somebody dies, it's easy to start seeing them that way. Perfect, you know. And it's real easy to start blaming yourself and everybody else for everything that went wrong." Uncle Thad put his hand on the back of my head and drew me close to his body. I felt warm tears rolling down my cheeks.

"Your daddy wouldn't want you to hang your head in shame. No sir. He'd want you to be proud, proud of yourself, proud of your family, and especially proud of that big name he gave you," he told me, and then leaned down and kissed my forehead and whispered in my ear. "It will carry you through this, Bezellia. Don't you forget it."

The next morning, Mother came downstairs for her coffee. She was wearing a black silk suit with her diamond-encrusted *G* pinned to her lapel. Her hair was pulled neatly into a black barrette. She looked as beautiful as any new widow could hope to look. Maizelle rushed to pour her a cup of fresh, hot coffee, and Nathaniel helped her into one of the kitchen chairs. Her mother and father kept their distance on the far side of the table, not offering their daughter anything more than a weak "good morning." When the doorbell rang, I took my mother's hand and led her to the front door.

"Thank you for coming. We're holding up. Yes, it's very hard, but we'll make it. Oh, yes, the flowers are lovely. Thank you. Red roses were my father's favorite." And so on and so on. I must have repeated those same words at least a hundred times, each time sounding just as sincere as one of Mother's perfectly coiffed friends who was trying to pump me for information about my father's sudden and mysterious death. I wouldn't have known what to tell them even if I had wanted to share my family's latest and darkest secret.

And in the few hours since my father died, we had all become more at ease with what we needed to do. The etiquette of death had apparently given us something to hide behind as though we were performing some ancient burial ritual I had studied in school, not really understanding why or what we were doing but comforted by our faithful obedience to the task.

And again, after a day of serving lemonade and shaking hands, I found myself sitting at the kitchen table, staring into space as I had seen my own mother do many times after an evening of entertaining. Nathaniel was picking up glasses and napkins left scattered about the living room. Nana and Pop had gone to bed. They said our friends were downright draining. Adelaide was balled up in front of the television with Baby Stella tucked underneath her arm. Mother was back in her room, soundly sleeping after one of Father's friends from the hospital had personally delivered a handful of Valium. Maizelle was buzzing back and forth from the dining room to the kitchen, wrapping Pyrex dishes in Saran Wrap and singing the same old song about the number of artichoke and chicken casseroles she would need to freeze . . . or throw away. She stopped to pat my back and tell me that my father would have been proud of me today and then scooted into the laundry room with another armful of dirty linens.

I heard what she was saying, but I wasn't really listening. My thoughts were already drifting farther and farther away from Grove Hill, back beyond the house, somewhere on the other side of the creek, away from all the fake and phony people who claimed my parents were their dearest friends. And just when I thought I could escape for a moment, a faint and steady knock at the back door demanded my return. I dreaded the thought of having to make nice, polite conversation with one more person, but I dutifully pulled myself up and straightened my skirt. I even rubbed my hands across my head, making sure my hair was neatly in place.

But there on the other side of the glass stood Samuel, his warm, familiar smile begging me to open the door. My hands fumbled for the lock, and that old kitchen door suddenly seemed stubborn and heavy. Samuel smiled a little bigger as I struggled with the latch, his eyes encouraging me to try a little harder. And just when I was about to give up, the door flung open and I fell into his arms, sobbing so that I could barely hear him whispering in my ear, promising me that everything would be all right. People had told me that all day long, but when Samuel said it, I wanted to believe it was true.

"Good Lord, whatcha doing here, Samuel?" I heard Maizelle's voice asking from somewhere behind me. But instead of giving Samuel time to answer, I grabbed him by the hand and dragged him into the yard, slamming the door behind us both. We started walking in the dark, holding tightly on to each other's hands. We may have walked in circles for all I know. Neither one of us said a word about where we were going. We just kept walking, and after a while, we found ourselves standing at the edge of the creek, those grand cherrybark oaks inviting us to come and rest under their strong, graceful branches.

We sat down in the grass among a thousand chiggers and mosquitoes. But neither one of us cared about that either. Still, not a word spoken between us. Every movement of my body told Samuel exactly what he needed to know, and I didn't care if Nathaniel was mad at me for the rest of my life or if my mother rose up from her bed and slapped me across the face. I was where I needed to be.

"It's not fair," I finally said, my voice joining the choir of cicadas and crickets that seemed to have been singing a mournful, plaintive dirge. A long time passed before Samuel answered. It was as if he was letting my pain float far into space, among the stars and the moon.

"I'm real sorry, Bezellia. You're right. It's absolutely not fair for anybody to die like that, falling down the stairs in his own house," he said at last, wrapping his left arm tightly around my waist.

"He didn't fall, Samuel." I said it so matter-of-factly that it almost scared me.

"What do you mean? Somebody push him?"

"No. Lord, I don't know. Maybe. You know what Mrs. Holder told me today? She told me about some poor lawyer down in Williamson County that was just about my father's age that *hanged* himself last week. She said it must be terrible for a young girl like myself to lose my father at such a young age, although she imagined it was better that he fell down a flight of stairs than was found hanging from a pipe in the basement. Thing is, she wasn't sorry. She was just fishing for information, examining my face for any twitch or tear that would prove her suspicions true.

"Of course, everybody else crowding into my house wanted to be sure I knew that all of this, someday, would make me stronger. Stronger for what? Funny, don't you think, that whatever killed my own father is somehow going to make me stronger. Truth of the matter is, Samuel, I don't really care about my father right now. I just don't care. Bet that sounds pretty awful. But if he had only loved her. Or she had loved him. Hell, I don't know. I just know things would be different."

Samuel kissed my lips, maybe only hoping to seal my mouth shut for a minute or two so I'd quit saying such hurtful things about a man who could no longer stand up and defend himself. He kept talking. I kept hearing words. But as I rubbed my finger across my lips, my thoughts started wandering away from my father and toward the boy sitting next to me, the boy who had once called me a princess, the boy who had just kissed me for the first time.

"I don't think there's any sin in thinking things, Bezellia. Can't hardly help what passes through your mind," he said, taking my hand in his.

I dropped my head onto his shoulder and tried to focus my thoughts on my father. "Yeah. But maybe that's where things need to stay, locked up tight in your head."

"Maybe. But maybe it's better to set those thoughts free, instead of locking them up like some wild animal caught and thrown in a cage, pacing around and around till it loses its mind. Maybe that's kind of what happened to your mama and daddy. They weren't able to tell each other what they were thinking."

"I don't know. Maybe," I said, turning my body so I could look Samuel square in the eyes. "I never was meant to be here. I never wanted any of this. I just wanted to be in a normal family, any family that really loved each other. Hell, I'd even be in yours."

"Even mine?" Samuel said with a raised eyebrow.

"Even yours," I said, this time ignoring his insinuation, although I imagine I had insulted him without even trying. "In the past two days, I have done nothing but entertain all these people lurking about my house as if they were my best friends. Damn it, Samuel, I was good at it, being fake and genuine all at the same time. It almost felt like a gift, a strange God-given gift. And now I'm afraid, terrified really, that's what's in store for me—a lifetime of luncheons and parties and pretty suits and white cotton gloves. In the end, I proba-bly will go crazy, like my dead daddy, my drunken mama, and my little sister, who's going to carry that damn baby doll to the eighth grade.

"God, what is wrong with me? All I'm thinking about is me and what's going to happen to me."

"Bezellia, there's nothing wrong with thinking about yourself and what's going to happen to you at a time like this. It's only natural. But I can promise you that everything will, eventually, get better. Not tomorrow or the next day, but on down the road a ways. Like Daddy always tells me, you can't climb a mountain if it's smooth." His voice sounded so certain, so convincing, but I wasn't sure I'd ever find my way to the top of this rocky slope.

"Everybody who walked through that house today thinks my mother killed my father," I blurted into the darkness. "Maybe she did. Maybe we all did—Adelaide and me too. Little by little, maybe we all pushed him down those stairs."

Samuel lowered his head between his knees and rocked his body back and forth. "Lord, I don't know what it's like to be a Grove—nor do I want to, really. But I do know what it's like for people to make their minds up about you without knowing the truth. You can't let it shake you, Bezellia. You just can't."

"Shit, this is not about being black, Samuel. Not everything is about being black."

"Well, there you're wrong, Bezellia. Everything about me is about being black, just like everything about you is about being a Grove."

"Okay, then, what do you think I'm supposed to do? Go to a luncheon and play bridge? Hide behind a gin and tonic? Look for a boy who wears cashmere?"

"Cashmere?"

"Forget it."

Samuel took a deep breath, and I could tell he was trying to put his words together in an order that I could follow. "Bezellia, do you remember what you told me the first time we met?" I stared at him as if to say no. "You said I'd never forget you. And contrary to what you think, it's not because of that crazy name of yours. I'll never forget you because you are this incredible girl with this absolutely huge heart. Your family's kind of strange, that name of yours is definitely strange, but you're not."

Maizelle had promised me that someday I would be loved right, and now, sitting here next to Samuel, I was beginning to believe her. Yesterday I'd been hoping maybe Ruddy could give me some of that love, at least a tiny taste of it. But it wasn't like that with Samuel. He saw the very worst of me, the rotten part, the part I hated myself, and he still loved me. And I didn't think I was going to need a ring on my finger to prove how much I loved him either.

"Oh, God, I'm going to hell for sure," I said, my voice sounding soft and weary.

"Now how do you figure that?"

"Because I want you, to be with you. My father's been dead barely two whole days, and I'm not wearing black and crying into a monogrammed handkerchief. I'm sitting by the creek in the pitch dark wanting nothing more than to be with you."

Samuel leaned across my body, and I fell to the ground beneath the weight of his chest. He kissed me on each cheek, and then on the mouth, and then we kissed again with our mouths open wide. He lifted himself up on his hands and looked down at my face, and I knew if I was going to hell, then Samuel was going with me.

He pulled down his pants and pulled up my skirt and then wedged his body between my legs. He eased himself inside of me, carefully and slowly, stopping every so often to make sure I was okay. His body rocked back and forth as he kissed my face, gently at first. Then his movements became stronger and more deliberate. My body hurt with all of Samuel inside me, but I didn't want him to stop. He raised his head, and I could see that he was lost in a world of his own.

And when we were done, exhausted and sweaty from the effort of loving each other so fully, I started to cry. Samuel wiped my tears with his rough, callused hands, and I fell asleep feeling loved and protected just like a little baby must feel all snugly wrapped in her mother's arms.

chapter nine

*L*ife goes on, so they say. And for everybody else in town, I guess it did. But after my father died, everything around me seemed to change. Maizelle changed for sure. Although she'd never say it, I think she felt like the Lord had let her down the day of the *tragic event,* the formal name that soon became synonymous with my father's death. Now she was always scared, scared that she'd trip down the stairs and break her own neck, or that Adelaide would suffocate under her bedcovers, or that I'd choke on a piece of chicken. Maizelle said bad things always come in threes, and we were just one-third of the way there. Nathaniel told her she was acting childish, but that didn't stop her from fretting over everybody and everything. She said little prayers all day long, hopeful the Lord was listening better this time.

Nathaniel changed too. He wasn't scared or anything. He was just quiet. He never talked to Mother's impatiens anymore or whistled old hymns while sweeping the front porch. He never sat on the back steps at the end of the day, sipping a cold glass of lemonade and teasing Maizelle as she finished cooking our dinner. He talked to me some, mostly to see how I was doing. But he talked to the horses more. I think he was convinced that they better understood his loneliness. As the days passed, Nathaniel acted more and more like his old self, but there was a sadness covering his eyes that never seemed to go away.

Mother, well, she changed the most. She missed her *precious* Charles terribly. And just like Uncle Thad had warned might happen, she talked about my dead father as if he had been the most loyal and devoted husband in all of Nashville, a saint really, the patron saint of marital bliss. And now, with him gone, she cried a river of tears and wore black for weeks. And after going to the funeral, she just kept going, to church that is. Before long, she had traded her bottle of gin for a Bible and was attending church more often than she had bridge parties at the country club. She was now stoic and sober and overflowing with the Holy Spirit.

Nathaniel said we had God almighty to thank for this miraculous transformation, but I was not so sure. I had, quite truthfully, spent many tearful nights praying for a new mother, but the one that had been delivered was not exactly what I had hoped for. This one walked around the house quoting Scripture and praising Jesus and seemed to actually care about other people more than herself. I even heard her tell Maizelle that she finally understood what it must be like to be colored, to be a slave to the evil in the world. Maizelle just rolled her eyes. I think she might have even spit in Mother's coffee just for good measure.

Mother confessed that, after her dear Charles died, she had desperately tried to talk to her own daddy about the sadness she had endured for so long. And for once I wondered if her running away from home had more to do with her parents than with any heartsick boy or small country town. I even overheard Mother ask if they felt any regret for treating her the way they had, the three of them whispering in the den late one night, their voices growing louder and louder with every word spoken. Nana finally stormed out of the room just like I'd seen my own mother do at least a hundred times before.

The next morning, Pop told his only daughter that all her grieving had worn him out and he needed to get back to the lake and rest before his heart gave out for good. Before he left, though, he handed Mother an old leather-bound Bible, said it had been her grandmother's but it looked like she needed it more than he did. Mother admitted that at first she thought about throwing it at him. But instead she opened it squarely in the middle and started reading. She read for hours and then fell to her knees and found she really liked it there. With her head bent in prayer, she poured all of her hurt and grief and anger out on the one Father who, by the very nature of his job description, had to patiently listen.

For months after that, the Bible was the only book Mother ever read. And when she dared to pick up the afternoon paper, she promptly tossed the society page aside and read only Billy Graham's "My Answer" and "Hints from Heloise," one suggesting she cleanse her soul, the other her kitchen cabinets.

One morning I saw her in front of the house, sitting awkwardly behind the steering wheel of the Cadillac. I'm not really sure where she was headed, but she looked afraid, frozen in place like a block of ice. She finally shifted the car into reverse and pulled it back into the garage. The very same day she started redecorating the house. But this time, she said, the Lord was directing her. She was on a holy mission of sorts to make Grove Hill a haven from Satan's influence in the world, which apparently included everybody and everything from the Beatles to short skirts and go-go boots.

First she repainted the front parlor a heavenly blue, at least that's what Mother called it, but, to be honest, it looked more like the mold that grows on an old piece of cheese. Then she ordered a new rug for the library, reupholstered the sofa in the living room, bought new curtains for the kitchen, and had Nathaniel rearrange the furniture in my bedroom, even though I told her I liked it the way it was. And when she found an old Magic 8 Ball, a birthday gift from Cornelia, stuffed under my mattress, she had Nathaniel put on his heaviest work gloves and throw it away for fear that her even touching it would invite the devil into our lives.

Finally, one evening as the sun was turning a soft amber-red, Mother announced that the house was in perfect order. Then she promptly invited Reverend Foster and his wife over for Sunday lunch. She said she wanted a man of God to sit at her dining room table. Only then, she said, after we had bowed our heads and asked for the Lord's grace and protection, would the house feel truly blessed.

And while Mother was preoccupied with God, my little sister hid in her room. Mother thought nothing of it at first, a grieving daughter mourning the loss of her loving, devoted father. She just needed some time to herself, Mother said. She would snap out of it before long now. The Lord would heal her daughter's wounded heart. But when Mother found Baby Stella's head in the trash can, even she thought it might be time to call for help.

Maizelle said she knew a woman on the other side of the river who, for no more than fifty dollars, could rid Adelaide of all the evil that was haunting her, not to mention the darkness that Maizelle was absolutely certain was lurking about the stairs. Mother hesitated, as if she was genuinely considering the offer, but then thanked her and said Reverend Foster suggested she take Adelaide to Atlanta, where the medical care was surely more sophisticated. And more important, Mother added, the doctors did not belong to the Nashville Town and Country Club.

Reverend Foster came by to check on me every day while Mother was away. He said he was worried that my father's death and Adelaide's delicate condition might just be too much for one young girl to bear and thought I might need some comfort at this difficult time. His skin smelled of cheap cologne, and his yellowed teeth looked ghoulish, almost evil. He would touch my shoulder, letting his hand linger there longer than he should have. Today, he said, I looked particularly sad, and then he stroked my cheek. I tried to talk. I tried to scream. But I couldn't catch my breath. He pressed his body into mine, pushing us both against the living room wall, and I felt his hand slither down my thigh.

Maizelle was in the kitchen. She said there was corn needing to be shucked. I closed my eyes and started begging God for help. He must have been listening better this time, because suddenly I felt Maizelle's body force its way between me and Reverend Foster. And in that moment, I knew I was saved.

"She don't need any comfort from you," Maizelle's voice boomed.

Reverend Foster took a step back and, with a smirk painted across his face, looked at Maizelle as if she wasn't even there. "I'd be careful what you say, old woman."

"I only answer to one man, and that's the good Lord. So I suggest you go on and get out of here, Reverend Foster, 'cause taking you out of here myself might just be the biggest thrill I've had in a long time."

Reverend Foster picked up his Bible left on the table by the front door and turned around and smiled. "God bless you both," he said and then walked out the door.

Maizelle asked me if I was all right. She said that was a man sent from the devil himself, and then she spit right there on my mother's new imported wool rug. That was all we ever said about that day. Maizelle and I never spoke of Reverend Foster again. He still came around, always wanting something from my mother, but Maizelle always made sure she was nearby.

Mother and Adelaide ended up spending three whole weeks in Atlanta, and when they returned, Mother said the best the doctors could determine was that Adelaide had suffered some sort of nervous breakdown, although Mother preferred to call it an *emotional disruption*. Either way, sweet little Adelaide truly believed it was her fault that our father had tumbled down the stairs, and she was punishing herself since no one else was willing to do it.

The night my father died, Adelaide never took the cold medicine Maizelle had given her. She had only pretended to be asleep. When the house was quiet, she slipped out of bed and started playing with her babies, bathing them and dressing them for the night. She could have saved him, so she thought, had she not been running the water in her bathroom sink. The doctors reassured her that she had nothing to do with her father's accident, and then they doped her up on Haldol and suggested she write in a journal instead of playing with dolls. A girl who would be thirteen soon, they said, should be chatting with her girlfriends, not bathing a plastic toy.

They told Mother that there was no medical reason for her daughter's immature development and asked if Adelaide had suffered some sort of childhood trauma, other than her father's recent death. Mother said she couldn't think of anything at all but was certain that her daughter would grow out of her childish ways in time. She appreciated their care and gratefully put their prescriptions in her purse.

But after a while, Mother tossed the pills down the sink. She said she had prayed long and hard about that, too, and the Lord did not want Adelaide walking around drugged and dazed. Then she gave her daughter a notebook filled with paper and a box of new ballpoint pens. Again, Adelaide hid in her room for days, this time hunched over her desk, writing until her fingers cramped. Maizelle soaked her right hand in warm, soapy water at night and rubbed it with lotion that smelled like lilac and jasmine. Mother let Adelaide be, figuring it was better that she write till her hand hurt than that she be secretly changing Baby Stella's diaper.

Late one night, I spied Adelaide sitting in front of the fireplace. At first I thought she couldn't sleep and was just watching the light dance across the logs. But then I saw her rip a piece of paper from her notebook and throw it into the fire. She tossed her entire journal, page by page, into the flames and watched her words, her truest confessions, burn to ash.

Adelaide got a little better after that. She went back to school before Thanksgiving. Her teacher thought it might be best, given Adelaide's long absence and still improving health, that she take the full year to recuperate and repeat the eighth grade next fall. But Mother wouldn't hear of it. She said it would be an embarrassment her family could not endure at this difficult time, and besides, there was nothing wrong with her daughter, and a really good teacher would be able to see that.

Not long after Christmas, Mother finally persuaded Adelaide to pack most of her babies in cardboard boxes and store them in the top of her closet. She said they would only be napping and promised to retrieve them if Adelaide heard them crying. Maizelle even made little flannel blankets for each and every one of them, hoping she could convince my sister that her babies were cozy and warm.

Maizelle did not want to touch Baby Stella, who was still in two pieces and stuffed under Adelaide's bed ever since the night my sister tore that poor doll apart. Maizelle got down on her knees and prayed for her own protection, beads of sweat pooling across her forehead as she held her breath and reached under the bed, blindly grasping for Baby Stella's head and then her body. She taped the doll back together and placed her in a cardboard box, separate from all the other dolls, and carefully hid the box in the far corner of the attic.

And as for me, I smiled and told everyone I was fine, but most days I felt like I was suffocating. I missed Samuel desperately. Some nights I fell asleep wanting him so bad that my body ached for him, and some days I felt only numb. I wondered what my mother would consider my greatest sin—having sex before marriage or having sex with a man of a different color. The God she talked about certainly would not have cared for either. And sometimes, I wondered if I had done something wrong. As the days went by and I didn't hear from Samuel, I became more and more convinced that I had.

I called his house a couple of times, hoping that he would answer. But when I heard his mother's voice on the other end of the telephone, I hung up, never finding the courage to tell her who I was. He'd said he loved me, but he didn't call or write. I guessed he'd changed his mind.

Maizelle told me he was transferring to Morehouse College the first of September. The president of the school had personally offered him a full academic scholarship. It wasn't Grambling State, but he was excited to be going all the same. And even though Atlanta was only five hours away, I knew good and well that the distance that separated us could not be measured in miles.

I thought about Ruddy too. He did call once or twice after Father died. He said he loved me. He said he sure hated the thought of living without me. But he also said he knew I wouldn't be happy packed into a little house with a prizewinning bird for an alarm clock. But if I'd be patient, he would give me everything I ever wanted. He was going to be as famous as Johnny Cash someday. I wanted to love him; it just seemed it would be so much easier in the end. But I couldn't find my way there, and I still couldn't catch my breath.

Mother thought I was only missing my father. So she kept encouraging me to call my friends—to go to movies and parties and sleepovers—I guess thinking a busy social calendar would put an end to a teenage girl's grieving heart. But all the girls at school wanted to talk about was the Cotillion Club's winter formal. Every senior girl of superior social standing was invited, and my classmates chatted endlessly about their silk gowns and satin shoes and the dinner party at Mary Margaret Hunt's the night before the dance. I wanted to be like that for once, to not care about anyone or anything other than my next date to the big event. But I regretfully declined the invitation, knowing good and well that Mrs. Hunt had only included my name on the guest list out of some sense of guilt or repentance.

So instead of looking for party dresses, I started poring over college catalogs, looking for schools in faraway places like California and Vermont, schools like Pomona and Middlebury, schools that I knew absolutely nothing about except that their catalogs pictured happy coeds wearing lightweight cottons or heavy woolens. Unfortunately, unlike Uncle Thad, my mother, who really knew very little about going to college other than what she had picked up working as a sales-clerk at the Vanderbilt bookstore, did not believe there was a school worth going to that was either west or north of the Mason-Dixon Line.

In fact, she suggested that there was really no need to leave home at all with a perfectly fine university like Vanderbilt only miles from my front door. I begged Uncle Thad to talk to her. And she finally relented, although only after being held hostage behind closed doors for more than an hour, tortured with arguments about what her dead husband would have wanted for his baby girl.

Mother insisted that I apply to Sweet Briar, Hollins, and Agnes Scott. She was becoming increasingly convinced that, after four years of an all-girls' education, four more years might be even better. And although I suspected her logic had less to do with her interest in my education than it did her concern for my acceptance into a socially prominent institution, I couldn't help but wonder if she was right. After all, Mrs. Hunt herself was a Hollins graduate.

By spring, Mother and I took shifts waiting for the mailman. She confiscated every acceptance letter and took it to her room. She said she needed to pray over them, and she would get back to me as soon as the Lord had provided her some insight, some divine guidance of sorts. I only hoped that the Lord had taken the time to study the catalogs as carefully as I had. And then, one night at dinner, Mother made an unexpected announcement.

"Bezellia, after much thought and a lot of prayer, I think it would be best for you to go away to school. Not too far, mind you, and certainly not to California, where they seem to have lost all sense of moral decency. But you have been through a lot. I recognize that, and I do think a change of scenery would do you some good. Furthermore, I am convinced that the Blue Ridge Mountains will provide an inspiring backdrop for your academic studies, not to mention a natural reminder of the power of God, which is at work in our lives at all times. Reverend Foster agrees. So I have mailed Hollins College a deposit. They're expecting you in late August."

The great triumvirate—Mother, Reverend Foster, and God—had made the decision for me. I was Hollins bound. And even though I knew it was what my mother wanted, I was thrilled to be going. Mother and Adelaide both cried with excitement and took turns hugging my neck. They threw green and gold confetti all over the dining room and laughed some more. I had never seen Mother willingly make such a mess in her own house.

Maizelle poked her head into the room, and Mother motioned for her to come and join us. Maizelle disappeared for a moment on the other side of the door and then came back carrying a large bundle wrapped in yellow tissue paper and tied with a shiny white bow. She said she had been waiting to give this to me for some time now and then placed her gift before me with such solemnity and reverence that, for once in my life, I did feel like a real princess receiving some sort of royal offering.

I slowly untied the ribbon and carefully pulled the tissue away. And there, in front of me, was a brightly colored quilt, every stitch perfectly sewn with Maizelle's own two hands, now knotted with age and wear. She said she'd started this quilt the day I went to kindergarten, holding on tight to Nathaniel's hand. She said I didn't want to let go, and it took the both of them just to get me in the car and convince me that everything was going to be just fine.

Scraps of my old clothes—skirts, blouses, hair ribbons—were all sewn into the patchwork. Even one of my father's dress shirts was cut and pieced into the band. My father would always be with me, she said, pointing to the quilt's blue-striped edge. And down in the bottom right corner, she had embroidered a deep red heart with a thin green bean stretched across it. Maizelle and I looked at each other, both of us wiping tears from our eyes. In that warm, dark, round face, I found something I had always wanted.

chapter ten

*M*other helped pack my trunk and even insisted on driving to Roanoke with me. I was actually glad she came, though there were times when we rambled along for miles in silence, none of us, not even Nathaniel, knowing what to say. Of course, the moment the Cadillac passed through the heavy, iron gates of the Hollins campus, my mother bowed her head in prayer and profusely thanked the Lord for our safe arrival and her daughter's future academic success.

The grounds were a deep, dull green, tired from the hot summer days but well kept and welcoming all the same. A few grand brick buildings nestled in the foothills of the Blue Ridge Mountains acted like a kind reminder that you had, in fact, come here to learn. Girls dressed in Bermuda shorts and cotton skirts were already swarming about the campus, trying to find their dorm rooms, greeting old friends with squeals and hugs, and kissing teary-eyed parents good-bye. I felt oddly at home in a place I had only seen in photographs.

By late afternoon, I was settled in my room in Randolph Hall. Mother insisted that Nathaniel move my bed next to the window, and I insisted that it was fine against the wall. My roommate had not yet arrived to voice any opinion or objection, so Nathaniel did as he was told. Mother felt it was very important that the morning light splash across my face. I should greet each day, she said, staring at the power of God.

Then she made my bed, something I had never seen her do. She neatly tucked the sheets and blanket underneath the mattress, then fluffed the pillows so they looked twice their size. She gently placed Maizelle's quilt across the foot of my bed, meticulously smoothing it as if she was trying to absorb the details of my life sewn into the fabric by another mother's hands. Even Nathaniel seemed surprised to see Mrs. Grove manage a domestic task with such resolve and capability.

Of course, when she was done, she left a Bible by my bed and instructed me to read the Scripture daily. "There are too many temptations out there, Bezellia, and you must arm yourself in the fight against the devil."

I thanked her for everything she had done—for letting me go away to school, for driving to Roanoke, even for giving me a new Bible. My mother seemed so proud of herself that day, so proud of a job well done. We left my room arm in arm and then joined the other freshmen and their parents at a punch reception in the dormitory's formal parlor.

And while Mother and I nibbled on carrot sticks and pimento cheese sandwiches, Nathaniel took his place by the car. He said he had packed some peanut butter crackers in the glove box and that would be enough to tide him over till later. I was not the only girl with a dark-skinned man waiting outside under a magnolia tree. Yet I imagined when Nathaniel took Samuel to Morehouse in another week or two, he would be the one nibbling on carrot sticks and dainty little sandwiches.

Finally the dorm mother stood in the center of the room and politely asked the parents to begin saying their good-byes. The hour had come for their daughters to take their first steps as young Hollins women, and surely, she said, they did not want to stand in our way. A tall, forceful woman with white hair swept tightly on top of her head, she promised to keep a watchful eye on their girls, and I think everyone believed that she would.

Mother and I walked to the car side by side, her arm tightly wrapped around my waist. We hugged and cried; apparently neither one of us had expected the good-bye to be so difficult. Even Nathaniel had tears in his eyes. He said he didn't, but I watched him wipe his eyes with the soft white handkerchief he kept in his back pants pocket. Then I watched them both climb into the Cadillac, and suddenly I felt like that little girl going to kindergarten for the first time, wanting to grab Nathaniel's big, strong hand and beg him not to leave me alone underneath this magnolia tree. I couldn't take my eyes off the car as it wound its way up the long, narrow drive and back out the gate. And when the Cadillac finally disappeared on the other side of the green, grassy slope, I turned around and took a very deep breath.

My roommate was from Troutville, a small town north of Roanoke. I had imagined she would be like Ruddy's little sister, poor and simple, but she was neither of those things. Sarah Stanton Miller was smartly dressed in a light blue pantsuit and moved her body more like a ballerina than a nervous freshman. She was the great-great-great niece, or something like that, of Elizabeth Cady Stanton and said she had come to Hollins to write. With words, she said, she was going to fight for all women who had been denied their rightful place in society as well as any other poor soul she considered in need of an authorial champion. *The Feminine Mystique* was her Bible, and she taped pictures of her aunt Lizzie, Gloria Steinem, and some woman named Betty Friedan to the back of our door. I wondered if Samuel had heard of this Betty Friedan. I wondered if my mother and Reverend Foster had known that girls like Sarah Stanton Miller went to Hollins. Surely if they had, they would have prayed a bit more diligently, waited a bit more patiently, for an answer that would have led me to a more *traditional* campus.

Sarah was nothing like the girls I had known at Miss Harding's

Preparatory School. She was interested in politics and equal rights
and men like John and Robert Kennedy, Martin Luther King, Jr.,
and Norman Mailer. I'm not sure whether she wanted to make out
with them, practice writing their names, or dream of their wedding
day, but she loved them all the same. In fact, sometimes I wondered
if Sarah really liked boys at all.

"Bezellia, have you ever done it? I mean sex. Have you ever had
sex?" she asked me late one night while we were lying in our beds, our
faces hidden in the room's darkness. I told her that I had. Once.

"Did you like it?" Sarah seemed uncomfortable with her questions and asked them slowly, as if the pace eased her apprehension.

"Yes and no. It wasn't what I expected entirely. I mean it was a
little uncomfortable at first, but then again I don't really have anything to compare it to. The best part was just being that close to
someone. I guess you just can't get any closer than that. I'm hoping
the sheer pleasure of it comes with more practice. At least that's what
my cousin Cornelia says will happen. She's had a steady boyfriend for
a year now and has had sex lots of times. She even takes those birth
control pills."

I could hear Sarah breathing as if her body was slowly absorbing
everything I had told her.

"I guess I don't know if I want it that much," she said at last. "I
mean the practicing and all . . . for what really?"

"Maybe you've just got your mind on other things, bigger things,
more important things," I reassured her. "Maybe later it will seem
worth it. When you're ready."

"Maybe."

And that was all we ever said about boys, both preferring to keep
our fantasies and our realities to ourselves. But I faithfully signed her
petitions, mailed her letters to Washington, and posted her flyers
from one end of campus to the other. We were, Sarah said, merely
foot soldiers, sisters on the battlefield, in this fight for equality, and

Gloria Steinem was our long-haired, braless leader, forging our path to liberation. Sometimes I think I did what Sarah wanted as much for Samuel as I did for myself . . . and my sisters on the battlefield. And although some days I felt like I was trapped in the middle of a never-ending political protest, I have to admit that I learned more from this girl from Troutville, Virginia, than I did from any of my professors who were determined to teach me the differences between Rousseau and Voltaire and Hemingway and Faulkner.

One cool, breezy evening in October, Sarah asked me to go to a lecture across campus. I begged her to let me stay in our room and study for a French test, but she said French was inconsequential to a woman who couldn't even claim dominion over her own body. Gloria Steinem had come to Hollins, and she had brought a friend. And Sarah was, of course, determined to stake out a seat on the front row. *"Quel dommage,"* I whispered to myself and obediently followed my roommate to the chapel.

Gloria Steinem was already there, talking to young girls eager to say something smart and impressive. Sarah had taped so many pictures of her over her bed that she almost seemed like an old friend to me by now. Standing next to Ms. Steinem was a woman I didn't recognize, a beautiful black woman with a large Afro that perfectly framed her face. Her smile was kind and accepting—even if she was surrounded by a hundred white girls chanting for change and wearing little Bobbie Brooks blouses and coordinating pleated skirts.

Back home, I knew a lot of black women. But they were all like Maizelle, maids who worked long hours for white families or who were neatly hidden in the kitchen at the country club or who came to our church on Sundays to tend to the white babies while their mothers worshipped in the sanctuary.

I remember when I was a little girl shopping downtown with my mother and we approached a black woman and her two little girls on the sidewalk. This mother, nicely dressed in a wool skirt and silk blouse, obediently moved out of the way, pulling her two daughters along with her and allowing my mother and me to pass without missing a step. I'll never forget the expression on her face, the weary look of frustration and humiliation as she turned her head, certain not to stare at the white woman and her little girl. But this Dorothy Pitman stared right at me as I took my seat on the front row.

She had come to Hollins, she said, looking for a true humanist, for the young woman who understood that racism and sexism are inexplicably bound. She smiled and then clapped her hands to further punctuate her point, and the crowd let out a thunderous roar, as if they already knew this to be so.

"And black southern women, my friends, suffer the most," she said and struck her hand against the wooden podium. That was it. Nine simple words. And I knew Maizelle was that black southern woman she was talking about. She had lived in that dark, cold basement for years. She had watched the crows gobble up her pound cake. She had listened to my mother call her useless and lazy. And in that moment, I felt sad, a sadness that was so deep I couldn't tell where it stopped or started.

Sarah and I walked back to the dorm in silence. I knew I had a confession to make, a declaration of sorts. I suddenly needed to tell her about the one woman who had genuinely cared for me since the day I was born but had been forced to sleep in a cold, dark basement. I needed to tell her about the woman who had loved me like a daughter— fed me, bathed me, dressed me, listened to my stories—but would never be called *Mother*. I needed to tell her about Maizelle, but nothing came out of my mouth. We walked on in silence, my shame and guilt making every step difficult and sluggish.

A few weeks later, a letter came from my mother. I started reading it aloud, wanting to share with Sarah something about my life back in Nashville. But as I began to grasp the meaning of every word, I fell quiet. I couldn't talk. I couldn't cry. I think I was shocked into silence as Maizelle would say. Sarah demanded to know what was wrong, and I simply pushed the crumpled letter into the palm of her hand. She began reading it out loud, and then she, too, grew silent. The letter fell to the floor, but Samuel would soon be on his way to boot camp.

He shouldn't be going, I cried, looking to Sarah for some sort of explanation. He didn't have to go. He was going to college. He was going to law school after that. The war he needed to fight was right here, not on the other side of the world. He had said so himself a hundred times. There had to be a mistake. College boys didn't go to Vietnam, not even the black ones. Sarah held me in her arms, never once trying to convince me that everything was going to be just fine.

But Mother said there was no mistake. She said that Samuel never showed up at Morehouse. Instead he had driven over to Mississippi to listen to some civil rights activist who preached on and on about the young black man's duty to fight injustice at any cost. And even though she figured all this *fighting* talk must certainly have influenced Samuel's decision not to go back to school, she thinks that, in the end, it had more to do with events that occurred after he left the state of Mississippi.

Somewhere west of Tuscaloosa, an Alabama sheriff stopped Samuel for *speeding*. He and his two friends were pulled out of the car and forced to strip down to their underwear. Nathaniel wouldn't say what all happened after that, but his son came back to Tennessee a changed man. He said he was angry. He said he was desperate. He said he started rambling on and on about his moral obligation to defend his brothers whose voices were never heard. Nathaniel said he wasn't making much sense, but he never thought his son would go looking for a fight.

Apparently Samuel came home just long enough to pack his bags and tell his mama and daddy good-bye and then caught a bus to New York City. He said his voice was going to be heard and that wasn't going to happen as long as he wasted his time marching with a preacher singing songs and promising a better day. But Uncle Sam figured out that Samuel Stephenson was no longer a student and sent him a letter, personally inviting him to come and participate in the *conflict* in Vietnam. Nathaniel said if his son was looking for a good fight, then, sadly, he had found one.

I had watched the evening news. I had seen boys my own age, who should have been playing baseball and making out with their girlfriends in the backseats of their daddies' cars, lying dead in a rice paddy. I had seen babies and their mothers with warm brown skin and almond-shaped eyes huddled together—crying, wounded, hungry.

When my father died, I knew that people expected to find me huddled in a corner, somber and red-eyed. I could see the surprise on their faces when I wasn't. But now I couldn't stop crying. Only this time, I knew no one would understand the brokenness I was feeling. The handsome men and women who had put on their well-tailored black suits and had carried casseroles to my front door would not want to see these tears. So I climbed to the top of Tinker Mountain and screamed Samuel's name for the entire world to hear. I screamed until I had no voice, and I cried until I had no strength. Then I stumbled back down the mountain not knowing whether Samuel Stephenson would be alive at the end of the day or not.

At first, I found it hard to concentrate, thinking any minute I would get another letter or maybe even a telegram, this time tersely informing me that Samuel had been killed. And without even needing to ask, Maizelle sent me his address, a secret the two of us kept to ourselves. I wrote to Samuel, reminding him to be careful, to come home alive, but I never heard anything back. And as the days fell into months, I became more confident, or maybe foolish, in thinking that my friend, wherever he was, would find his way back to Tennessee.

And while I waited, I pretended that life was normal. And peacefully tucked there against Virginia's Blue Ridge Mountains, I found it was easy to think that it was. I went to class and listened as one professor lectured about Jefferson's influence on the Declaration of Independence and another about the Pythagorean influence on Platonic philosophy. And somewhere along the way, I always found an opportunity to voice my opposition to the war, whether it was relevant to class discussion or not. I could see my classmates roll their eyes at my persistent protest, but I didn't care. Maybe they knew I was thinking only of Samuel, and not the thousands of other boys fighting in Vietnam. But I really didn't care.

I wrote for the school newspaper and even joined a new yoga club on campus, although I didn't dare tell Mother. She would insist that *this* yoga was surely some kind of devil worship for no other reason than what she had read about the Maharishi in some magazine, and would probably send Reverend Foster to bring me home straightaway now that I had learned to bend and stretch my body into awkward and unladylike poses.

I was, however, asked to join the Cotillion Club, something that I knew would please my mother immensely but that surprised me even more than Sarah, particularly given my new, more enlightened state of being. Apparently a girl's last name was still considered by some at Hollins to be one of her most important assets. And apparently my last name was still considered to be of value, although Sarah said she would be forced to find another roommate if I joined a group of girls who did nothing more than plan dances and other frivolous social outings so that we could parade ourselves in front of a bunch of salivating young men with absolutely no interest in our intellect. I told Sarah that my mother actually considered dancing to be one of life's most important talents. She rolled her eyes as if to say that I had proven her point.

Mother wrote me almost every day. She missed me terribly, she said, but knew the Lord would comfort her lonely heart. And as much as she missed me, she said Adelaide missed me even more. I wrote Mother back and suggested that my little sister come for a visit, that maybe a change of scenery would do her some good. Mother replied, offering no specific explanation, only to say that Adelaide was not able to travel at this time. I used the pay phone in the hallway outside my room and made a collect call to Uncle Thad. I needed him to tell me truthfully how everyone was doing at Grove Hill. He hesitated for a moment. And I told him if he didn't speak up soon, I was hanging up the phone and jumping on the next bus home.

He paused again and stuttered a bit but finally admitted that everyone was doing much better now, although it had been quite a difficult few weeks. He said Mother had been taking Adelaide to church on a regular basis for several months now, convinced that a perfect attendance record would somehow cure Adelaide of any of her peculiarities. But Adelaide finally told Mother she had had enough of her religion and neither she nor Reverend Foster, or even God himself, understood the pounding pain inside her head. This time Mother believed her, so she threw her in the Cadillac and took her back down to Atlanta. The doctors said Adelaide was merely screaming for attention, but they would be more than happy to admit her to a psychiatric hospital for therapeutic rehabilitation. Mother didn't care for their diagnosis much, so she brought her daughter, along with another very large bottle of pills, back home.

As soon as they returned to Grove Hill, Mother moved Maizelle upstairs, thinking it was better to have two sets of ears listening for her baby girl. Then she asked Maizelle if she still knew how to reach that voodoo witch on the other side of the river, the one who had been born and raised in New Orleans. I guess Mother was thinking that this was going to require the skill and expertise of someone more in touch with the underworld than her precious Reverend Foster.

Besides, she probably preferred he know nothing about this, even if she had convinced herself that it wouldn't really be contrary to any biblical teachings she knew if all you were wanting to do was rid your child of an evil spirit. Even Jesus had been known to do an exorcism or two. But she grew so nervous about this woman coming to her house, especially after the sky turned cloudy and dark, that she telephoned Uncle Thad at the very last minute and begged him to run over just in case they needed some masculine and, of course, discreet protection.

By the time he got to Grove Hill, not long before midnight, the cleansing ritual, as Mother preferred to call it, had already begun. Uncle Thad said the woman did in fact look like some kind of voodoo witch he had seen down in New Orleans. She was dressed in a ratty old cotton dress with a bright orange cotton cloth wrapped around her head and was comfortably settled on the living room sofa, right next to Adelaide, chanting some kind of nonsense and burning homemade candles that smelled like rotten eggs.

She kept a muslin bag filled with roots and herbs tied to her waist and told Mother to boil some water on the stove. Then she placed her hands on Adelaide's head and chanted and sang for more than an hour, filling the room with words that none of them understood. She gave Adelaide a bitter tea to drink. My little sister took one sip and promptly fell asleep. Mother screamed out loud, thinking she had gone and hired a witch to kill her baby girl.

The woman told her to hush and promised that Adelaide had been finally freed from the evil that had kept such a strong hold on her. She told Mother to put her to bed and keep a cool cloth on her head during the night. When Adelaide finally opened her eyes, a day and a half later, she said her head wasn't hurting anymore.

Adelaide did seem better, but Mother just kept trying to fix her, trying to turn her into something she was never meant to be. Maybe Mother felt guilty, or maybe she felt embarrassed by her slightly awkward daughter. But either way, she never gave up trying to make Adelaide into a girl she was more comfortable knowing.

Mother continued to write. She said nothing about Samuel, only that Adelaide was always asking for me, even crying out for me in the middle of the night. I wasn't sure if that was the truth or if Mother needed me at home so desperately she was willing to say anything to get me there. She and Adelaide had certainly convinced themselves that life at Grove Hill would be better only if I was there. And by May, I found myself dreading the thought of going back home, where I would certainly be suffocated by their constant attention.

So instead of packing my trunk like the others girls excited about leaving for the summer, I found myself lying about needing to stay at Hollins. A visiting English professor, I said, had come all the way from Boston and selected me as his assistant. It was an honor, an opportunity I just couldn't forgo. He said my writing had promise. And if she would let me stay, I would even register for two additional classes so that I might be able to graduate a full semester early. Mother wrote me a brief letter and said she hoped this was indeed a once in a lifetime opportunity. She and Adelaide would both be looking for me at the end of July.

Only a few hundred of us stayed behind for summer study; even Sarah went home. She said she was going to organize a local chapter of the National Organization for Women in Troutville. Well, she was going to try. And, to be honest, I was glad she would be gone for at least a few weeks so I could finally think about something other than equal rights and congressional legislation. Instead I took an English class and wrote a short story about a wealthy family with an alcoholic mother and a doctor father who mysteriously died in his own home while everyone was sleeping. My professor thought it was brilliant, a rich and dark insight into the privileged American family. He gave me an A, said I should continue writing, and then asked if I'd like to join him for a cup of coffee.

Mitchell Franklin was more of a graduate student from Boston University than a full-fledged professor. He was finishing his doctorate degree in American folk literature and was spending the summer researching and teaching at Hollins. Before long, we were having coffee together every morning. And not long after that, we were meeting in his tiny apartment on the edge of campus every afternoon. He would open a bottle of wine and pour me a glass as if I was comfortable drinking the alcohol that made me feel both warm and slightly confused. We listened to Led Zeppelin and made out on the couch. And when our bodies started feeling relaxed and our heads slightly numb, Mitchell would take my hand and lead me to his bed.

"Bezellia," he'd whisper in my ear, lying next to me with nothing but a thin, cotton sheet covering our bodies. "You are so intoxicating, like a sweet, sweet nectar on my lips," and then he'd pull himself on top of me and work his way inside. So instead of studying, I found myself wandering across campus and knocking on Mitchell's door, every time discovering more and more about the sheer pleasure of sex. He was always there, always eager to invite me in and show me to his bedroom, always willing, if only for a few hours, to take my mind off Samuel.

"Hey, Mitchell, you in there?" I hollered late one afternoon, standing outside his apartment. I knocked again and again, banging my fist against the door until my hand started to ache. Everything about this day felt oddly the same as the one before except the stereo in his front room was playing Elton John, not Led Zeppelin. "Mitchell, Mitchell Franklin. Hey, it's me, Bezellia. Open up."

The door finally opened just wide enough to reveal a hint of Mitchell's face, his bare chest, a towel wrapped around his waist. "I've been standing out here knocking. Were you in the shower or something?" But his hair was still noticeably dry.

"No."

"Didn't you hear me?" I stepped toward him, but he didn't move to the side making room for me in the doorway.

"I thought you were studying for your exam tomorrow," Mitchell said with a blank expression smeared across his face. "You really should be, you know. It's going to be a tough one."

"I was. But I . . . What's going on? Why are you just standing there all of a sudden acting like some kind of English teacher?" My voice began to tremble, and I was afraid I already knew the answer.

"Sorry, Bee. I wasn't expecting you. I made other plans today. I thought you'd be busy with finals."

"Other plans? I leave you alone for one day, and you need to make other plans?" I screeched, my voice sounding ridiculously high-pitched as a leggy brunette walked up behind Mitchell and wrapped her arms around his waist. I tripped and stumbled as I stepped back off the front stoop. All I remember after that is the smooth sound of Elton John's voice calling after me.

"I hope you don't mind that I put down in words
How wonderful life is while you're in the world."

But I never looked back.

My grades revealed my summer affair better that any diary could have—a C− in French conversation and an A+ in creative writing, even though my exam book was not filled with the answers to Mitchell Franklin's inane questions about Plath and Poe. But it was full all the same. It read very simply, "Mitchell Franklin is an ass. Mitchell Franklin is an ass. Mitchell Franklin is an ass." Three hundred and fifty-three times, until every line, every page of my blue book was filled. Mitchell Franklin left Hollins at the end of the summer session and never returned my exam.

I desperately wanted to talk to Samuel, now more than ever. I wanted to tell him that I loved him and needed him to come home, that I had done a stupid thing while I was trying to forget how much it hurt without him here. But he was too far away to hear me, fighting in some mosquito-infested jungle while I was drinking too much wine and having too much sex. Maybe Samuel didn't need to hear this. Maybe I just needed to pay for my transgressions. So I went home. Mother was right after all. There was too much temptation and evil in the world.

chapter eleven

*N*athaniel opened the back door of the Cadillac, and I stepped into my mother's arms. She pulled me close, drawing my face into her neck. Her skin felt soft and warm but had a familiar and unsettling scent, a smell I hadn't been able to identify as a little girl but had learned in time was an unsavory blend of Chanel No. 5 and stale Tanqueray. I pushed myself back from my mother's embrace. Her eyes looked a little dull and distant, but she smiled and kissed me on the cheek. Surely, I thought to myself, I had made a mistake.

Adelaide and Maizelle, who had been patiently waiting on the front steps, rushed toward me. Maizelle's tummy jiggled up and down as she tried to keep pace with my little sister. They both flung their arms around me and cradled my body between theirs as they had the morning after my father died, neither one of them willing to let go. Maizelle said I had grown a full foot taller since Christmas, maybe more. I laughed and reminded her that I hadn't grown an inch since my senior year in high school and that maybe she was shrinking instead. She swatted my bottom and said she was going to stand me against the doorframe in the kitchen, where she had monitored my growth since I was a baby barely able to stand on my own two feet.

Now that I was here, everything about Grove Hill seemed new and fresh, as if I was seeing it for the first time—the marble columns, the pink impatiens that highlighted the flower beds along the side of the house, the sweeping front lawn. A part of me felt oddly homesick for something that was right in front of me. And yet another part of me dreaded being here.

Nathaniel was keeping pace right behind me. He started whistling an old hymn, one about surrendering everything to Jesus. He used to sing this to me on my way to school in the morning, and now I wondered if he was humming that old familiar tune just to calm me down. Mother quickly turned her head and with one scathing glance told him to hush. Maizelle's body stiffened, and I could see Nathaniel patting her arm as if to remind her that Mrs. Grove's reprimand would never keep his heart from singing. And true as that may have been, the voice in my head telling me to run was all but shouting now.

As soon as we stepped into the house, Nathaniel headed directly up the stairs, carrying my bags in both hands. He hollered that he'd bring the trunk up in a minute if he didn't break his back carrying the load he had with him. Then he laughed and disappeared above the landing. Mother covered her ears, as if to say that Nathaniel's voice was too loud and too rude.

Nathaniel had not said one word about Samuel on the ride home from the bus station. I had kept my mouth shut, not wanting him to see how much I missed his son, still not sure if he would understand that dull, persistent throbbing in my heart that had never gone away. But for the first time in my life, I thought Nathaniel looked different, and not just because what little hair was left on his head had turned completely white. No, it was more than that. His eyes seemed weary and his shoulders were hunched forward, and I understood that Samuel's absence had turned my friend into an old man.

Maizelle hurriedly shuffled back to the kitchen to finish up the evening meal. She said she had made all of my favorites, including a fresh pound cake that was cooling on top of the stove. She hoped I had packed a healthy appetite along with all those dirty clothes she imagined needed washing.

Mother immediately shooed me toward the stairs. She insisted that I unpack my bags before doing anything else. Dirty clothes must not sit in those suitcases, she said, or we'd never get the smell out of that new set of luggage. She told me to unpack my bags at least three more times, each time as if she had forgotten the one before. She tugged on Adelaide's hand and pulled her toward me.

"Surely you two sisters would enjoy spending the afternoon together, catching up and all. Adelaide, I bet you have so much to tell Bezellia about your first year in high school." But Adelaide only stared at the floor, desperately trying to ignore our mother. I realized at that very moment that while I had been away at school, my little sister had grown into a teenage girl who was determined to spend the afternoon exactly as she had planned.

"I wanted to finish something for Bezellia," she finally mumbled.

"Sweetie, you're going to wear those fingers out. Now go on," Mother insisted. "All you've been talking about for months is Bezellia coming home. Now here she is."

"Adelaide, what are you making?" I asked, and I pointed to the knitting needles clutched in her right hand. "I didn't know you could knit."

"She knows how to knit, all right. She's been knitting all day," Mother quipped, now sounding impatient and desperate for her daughters to leave her alone. "Adelaide, I want you to put those needles down and give your fingers a rest and help Bezellia with her unpacking. You hear me?" And she pushed my sister's body closer to the stairs.

Adelaide just rolled her eyes. And when she knew Mother wasn't looking, she glanced at me and smiled real big and motioned that she would see me later. Then she ran up the stairs, two at a time, and I

could tell by the sound of her footsteps on the floor above that my
sister had passed my room and gone into her own. Her door slammed
shut, and Mother shook her head in frustration and promptly turned
her attention to me.

"Okay, then, you start unpacking. At least one of you is going to
mind me. Maizelle will need to get started on that laundry before
going to bed if she's ever going to get it all done. I'll be out in the
garden. I want to put together an arrangement for the table before we
sit down to eat. My roses are particularly stunning this year, if I may
say so myself."

"Mother," I said as I reached for the handrail, a habit I had developed since my father's accident, more out of concern for Maizelle's
anxious disposition than for my personal safety. "Do you think
Maizelle and Nathaniel could eat at the table with us tonight? I mean,
since it is my first night home and all?"

Mother tucked her chin against her chest and moaned. Obviously
I should have known better than to ask such a presumptuous question, even if it was my first night home.

"Don't put me in that position, Bezellia. You know I can't allow
that."

"Why not? They're practically family."

"Why are you asking me this now? Tonight? I have enough on
my mind already. I don't need to be dealing with this. And what you
need to remember," Mother said, her voice rapidly becoming more
cutting and bitter, "is that we all love Maizelle and Nathaniel, but
they are not our family and they never will be. Now go on and get
those clothes unpacked."

I didn't dare tell Mother that Sarah Stanton Miller, Gloria
Steinem, and Dorothy Pitman, the feminist triumvirate who would
argue that even God was female, would be appalled to know that our
black help had never once been invited to share an evening meal with
the family they had served for most of a lifetime. And truthfully, I

wasn't really sure if it was a moral sensibility that was guiding my desire right now or just a need to be with the people I loved. I had hoped that in the months since Father's death and her own rebirth, Mother might have become a bit more accepting of the two people who had never left her side. But apparently history and hatred were proving much more powerful than years of faithful service and recent Christian conversion.

I climbed the stairs two at a time, just like Adelaide had done, just like I used to do when I was little and wanted to run from my mother after she had spent the day playing bridge at the club. Now I was afraid she was hiding in the garden, pulling weeds and cutting flowers and drinking gin disguised in a glass of Maizelle's homemade lemonade. I fell on my bed and stared up at the ceiling, at the fine lines that had carved their way into the plaster, spreading out in different directions like a spider's intricately woven web. It was as if the sadness filling the rooms of this old house was so thick and heavy it was splitting the walls apart right in front of me. I wondered if the Bezellias before me had watched this web grow as carefully as I had.

Everything else about my room was perfect. My bed was crisply made. The pillowcases were freshly starched. My collection of German teddy bears was neatly lined up on the window seat. The silver-framed photograph of Mother and Father holding me on my first birthday, even the jewelry box made out of Popsicle sticks and the pincushion I had needlepointed years ago were all perfectly placed about my room, another shrine, it seemed, to another lost daughter.

Subtle, muffled noises drifted up from the kitchen. I could hear them, faintly, but they were there—the same soothing sounds that had always reminded me I was never alone here. I left my suitcases untouched right where Nathaniel had put them at the foot of my bed and wandered back downstairs, following the familiar smells of corn bread and cake and fresh green beans simmering in bacon fat. Maizelle had the kitchen windows open wide and a fan running on high. She was standing at the stove stirring a pan of creamed corn. A light blue dish towel was thrown across her shoulder, and every so often she would lift it to her forehead and wipe her brow. Nathaniel was sitting at the table peeling potatoes, helping with the hash brown casserole just like he always did.

"Lookie here. If it's not the big college girl come to pay us a visit, Maizelle," Nathaniel said and laughed, never taking his eyes off the sharp knife in his hand. "We thought maybe you had gotten too big for the likes of us."

"Never," I said and sat down at the table in an old wooden chair with one leg shorter than the others so it left you rocking back and forth whether you wanted to or not. Nathaniel had promised to fix this chair years ago, but I told him not to. I never had to sit still in this chair. And right here, in this chair, in this kitchen, was my favorite place to be in the whole wide world. If Mother dared to ask where all I had been, I would tell her that I didn't need to travel the world to know that there was no better place on earth than here with Nathaniel and Maizelle.

Then out of nowhere, still staring intently at the potato and knife in his hands, Nathaniel started talking about his son. It was almost as if he had a tightly held confession to make, and I was certainly ready to listen. He admitted that every day that passed without a Marine in uniform showing up at his front door was a good one. He prayed without ceasing that Samuel would come home safe and in one piece. And best he could tell, his son should be out of that godforsaken place in little less than a year if Uncle Sam didn't go and change his mind. If he had to go back, Nathaniel sighed, it might very well kill his mama.

"I just thought you'd want to know that, Miss Bezellia," he said, and then Nathaniel lowered his head and went back to peeling his potatoes.

"Thank you," I replied rather weakly and leaned across the table and kissed him lightly on the cheek. Maizelle just kept shaking her head, as if she wanted us both to know that Samuel's leaving had broken her heart too. Every once in a while she stopped to rub her hands together. I think it made her nervous imagining Samuel tiptoeing through some jungle in the dead of night. But she said her arthritis was only getting worse and even rolling out the biscuits was getting to be a chore.

Although she was real sorry about the circumstances, she sure was glad that my mother had seen fit to move her upstairs. She just didn't think her body could handle the chill that never left that old basement room of hers. Adelaide, in her opinion, was doing much better. She was growing out of her affliction, just like Maizelle knew she would. She wasn't sure my mother had noticed yet. I walked over to the counter and took the rolling pin from Maizelle's hands. She wiped her eye with the corner of her apron.

"What's gotten into us?" Nathaniel laughed real gently. "Bezellia comes home from school and we're all sitting here crying like a bunch of newborn babies." Then he winked at me. "You know, Maizelle, we're not the only ones crying. I heard those babies of Adelaide's bawling up a storm in the attic the other afternoon. Don't you ever hear 'em?"

"Shut your mouth right now. That ain't funny. And don't you say one word about those dolls, Nathaniel Stephenson," Maizelle popped. "They're nothing but evil, pure evil," and then she spit in the sink and threw some salt over her shoulder.

"Maizelle, Lord, quit throwing that salt all over my kitchen floor. How many times do I have to tell you that now?" Mother quipped, startling all of us with her sudden entrance. She was wearing her garden gloves and a wide-brimmed hat to protect her face from the sun, but it completely hid her eyes. She asked where Adelaide was, and Maizelle explained with her hands that she had no idea. Mother's lips tightened, and then she told Maizelle to pour her another glass of lemonade and suggested that I go and check on my little sister instead of playing with the biscuit dough.

"Mother! I'm hardly playing here," I said, surprised and embarrassed that she would insinuate I was wasting my time helping Maizelle with the dinner. But she just waved her garden gloves in my face and said she'd be out back if anybody needed her.

"Don't mind her, Bezellia," Maizelle said in an unexpected and understanding tone. "Who would've thought she'd have it in her to last this long? Ever since your daddy died, she's had a lot to take care of all by herself, not to mention your little sister. Lord, your mama frets over that girl.

"First she had her writing in that journal, then she plunked her down in the garden, thinking if she kept her hands busy in the dirt her head would calm a bit. But it was no time at all and Adelaide starting making them mud pies again. 'Cept these didn't look quite like the ones she used to make, looked more like balls really. Not sure what that girl was thinking. But you can imagine your mama put an end to that real fast. Now she's got her knitting. And you know Adelaide, once she puts her mind to something, you can't barely get her to stop to eat. But it does seem your sister is doing so much better. Always knew she was gonna be just fine. Like I've always said, some babies just need more time than others to get comfortable with this world."

"That sister of yours sure has been knitting up a storm," Nathaniel added with a fresh lilt in his voice. "She's done taken to that knitting like a fish to water. Surprised she hasn't figured out a way to knit a fishing pole, come to think of it."

"You ain't funny, old man," Maizelle scolded and then laughed a bit herself. "It might not be perfect. But at least we ain't seen that Baby Stella lurking about the house for a long, long time now. Lord, that doll scares the living daylights out of me. I would have done burned her in the incinerator years ago and then thrown them ashes in the creek. That's right, washed every last trace of that doll right out of here."

Maizelle stood in front of the stove twitching from side to side. "See. Lookie here. See the shivers running up and down my spine. That's just from thinking about that crazy doll."

"To tell the truth," Nathaniel added, "your sister's knitting is really nice. Your mama's given dozens and dozens of baby blankets to the home for unwed mothers. There's probably not an illegitimate child in this town that's not wearing a pair of your sister's little knitted booties."

"But what about Mother? Does she ever see any of her old friends, even for lunch now and again?" I asked, the smell of my mother's embrace still lingering in my head. I looked at Nathaniel and then at Maizelle, but neither one of them looked at me.

"To tell the truth, Miss Bezellia, your mama hardly leaves Grove Hill 'cept to go to church or to Castner Knott to buy some more yarn," Maizelle finally admitted. "Lord, I never thought a person could get too much religion, but I'm afraid that's about what has happened to your mama. I think she's done gotten it into her head, or that Reverend Foster's done put it there, that your sister's peculiarities are some kind of punishment for a sin she done committed long ago. Not sure what he's preaching, but it sure don't seem like there's too much talk of forgiveness.

"Never have liked that man," Maizelle declared and cast a stern look in my direction. "He still comes around here all the time, says he's checking on your mama, but I think he's doing nothing but looking for her checkbook. He shore don't act like a certified man of God to me, more like a beggar than a preacher."

"What are you talking about, Maizelle? What sin is Mother paying for? Father's accident?"

"Lord, child, I don't know. I've said way too much already. Nathaniel, how's them potatoes coming?" Maizelle wanted me to know what was on her heart. She wanted me to know everything, but she turned and faced the stove, carefully stirring her creamed corn and waiting for Nathaniel to tell me what she couldn't say.

Nathaniel put the potato he was holding back in the bowl and carefully set the knife down on the table. He looked at Maizelle, and then he looked at me. He cleared his throat and sat forward in his chair. He spoke very carefully, as if he had been rehearsing this speech for some time now. And once he started talking, I was sure that he had.

"Your mama's been thinking it might be best for Adelaide to go to school somewhere else. Away from home. Reverend Foster believes it would be the best thing for the both of them. He thinks your mama needs an opportunity to fully devote her time and talent to the Lord's work. Never known a preacher not to think of raising a child as the Lord's work. Anyway, there's some Baptist school up in Kentucky that's supposed to be real good for all these Christian teens with problems that their own parents can't seem to handle. It's on a lake. You know how your mama feels about you girls being on the water."

"Oh, Lord, Nathaniel, you wasn't supposed to say nothing about that," Maizelle scolded, obviously relieved that *it* had been said, that *it* had all been said.

My skin instantly turned warm and then red-hot. "I don't believe that. Mother wouldn't do that. She knows how Adelaide feels being away from home. That doesn't make any sense at all."

"It's probably nothing more than talk, Miss Bezellia," Nathaniel said. "But I do think you need to know that Reverend Foster's been putting all sorts of ideas in your mama's head, and some of them seem to be costing her a whole lot of money."

Reverend Foster was older than my mother but not by much. And even though I had learned he was nothing but evil, he spoke with the authority of a parent or a respected teacher, and my mother had willingly deferred to his opinion from their very first meeting, just a day or so before my father's funeral. But now the thought of Reverend Foster anywhere near Adelaide made me furious. I did not trust his advice or his intentions, and I certainly didn't hear much of anything else Nathaniel had to say, because I was already out the back door, looking for my mother.

She was in her garden as she had promised, bent at the waist, all but her hat hidden from view by a soft ribbon of purple and pink hydrangea flowers. A cloud of tireless gnats quietly danced above her head. She raised her gloved hand and swatted them away. I marched toward her, shaking the ground beneath me with every step. Slowly, she stood up straight, a pair of metal clippers clutched in one hand and a bouquet of perfect hydrangeas squeezed too tightly in the other.

"Mother, are you sending Adelaide away to school?" I asked, not bothering to preface my question with polite or pointless prattle.

"Lord, that woman couldn't keep her mouth locked tight if those lips of hers were glued shut," Mother said, as much to herself as to me, shaking her head with obvious irritation.

"It wasn't Maizelle who told me," I interrupted, no longer tolerant of my mother's unkind words. "And that's not the point. You can't do that to Adelaide. She needs to be here, at home, at Grove Hill."

"Bezellia dear, you really are not one to talk about what Adelaide needs or doesn't need," Mother snapped and then turned to clip another hydrangea. "You have not been here, or do I need to remind you of that?" she asked, refusing to take her eyes off her flowers.

"I'm here right now. None of your friends are here, Mother. But I am. And I do know that you can't dump Adelaide at some school just so you can hide her from everybody in town. She's not weird. She's not sick. She's not damaged. She's just a little different. She's just not like you. And there's nothing wrong with that."

"First of all, I am not *dumping* anyone anywhere," Mother

shouted. Then she took several steps toward me, stopping quickly to smile and regain her composure. "I think you'd best watch your mouth," she resumed, speaking with a slow and yet strained precision, the way she sounded after the afternoon's first gin and tonic. "Besides, you know nothing about this school. Reverend Foster says that everyone there is a born-again Christian and that it may be Adelaide's only chance for salvation." And then Mother paused for a moment. "It's by a lake, you know, and being by the water should be very good for her, Sister."

Sister. Sister. I'd heard it a thousand times before today, always said with a certain amount of meanness attached, never with love or even a playful sense of affection. I had never corrected her, never demanded an apology, and surely never admitted that I hated the very sound of it. But now, in that garden, among all those beautiful flowers, it was as if she had taken a match and lit a full keg of dynamite. Years of anger and disappointment came blowing right out of my mouth in one deadly explosion.

"My name is Bezellia, damn it! Do you hear me, Bezellia. B-E-Z-E-L-L-I-A!" I was screaming so loudly my mother took two steps back, afraid, I imagine, that the force of my words might knock her right down. But I just kept firing.

"Being by the water has nothing to do with this, and you know it! That's exactly what you told us when we were little. And if you remember, Adelaide cried and begged you to let her stay home. But that didn't matter to you then, so I guess there's no reason to think it's going to matter to you now." My mother began to step backward, hoping, I guess, to take refuge among her flowers. But I pressed on.

"You just wanted to go about your very important business. Remember, Mother, playing cards with your friends and getting so drunk Nathaniel would have to carry you home? So don't start acting like you're doing the *loving* thing here by sending Adelaide away where no one will see her knitting or making mud pies or anything else that embarrasses you. And I don't know what this Reverend Foster is telling you, Mother, but you need to start listening to those of us who still love you—who haven't abandoned you or who don't just want your money. Whatever soul you've got left, apparently he'd sell to the devil himself."

And by the time I was done, I was standing directly in front of my mother, digging my shoes into the soft, warm dirt. She raised the metal scissors toward my face and gripped the flowers, now surely suffocating in her grasp, even harder. "That's enough, Bezellia. Just watch your mouth," Mother shrieked, drenching us both with her anger and hate. And for once my name sounded so ugly that I wished she hadn't said it at all. "Do you have any idea what I've been through? Do you have any idea how long it's taken me to get Adelaide to the point she's at now? Do you? Do you?" Mother rambled on, her voice sounding more and more shrill with every syllable she spit into that garden.

"What point is that, Mother? Tell me, what point is that? Holed up in the house knitting baby booties?"

"I think you better shut your mouth. You don't know what you're talking about. Being away at college has certainly given you a healthy dose of attitude. But listen to me, Sister, it has been damn difficult since the tragic event. You wouldn't understand. You haven't been here. But since I'm the one left to deal with this mess, I will be the one making the decisions about what is best for this family."

"Lord, Mother, you can't even say it. There was no *tragic event*. There was an accident. And if *it* wasn't an accident, well, hell, the Lord's going to forgive you for that too. Father didn't treat you right. We all know that. Everybody in Nashville knows that. And his death, however it happened, maybe it's the best thing that ever happened to you. What do you think, Mother?"

My mother could barely catch her breath, and her body seemed to waver in the afternoon sun.

"I can tell you this for sure," I said, now speaking in a more hushed tone, "it took Father dying to get that bottle out of your hands for the first time in years. And you're right, I don't know what's going on now. I don't know if you're drinking again or if your head is just so messed up on God you can't think straight. Which is it, Mother? Huh? Which is it?"

"Shut up! Shut up, Bezellia! Just get out of here. You hear me? Take those damn suitcases of yours and get out of my house!" Mother cried, tears now streaming down her cheeks. She wiped her eyes with her gloves, smearing fresh dirt across both sides of her face.

"I am not leaving, Mother. Neither is Adelaide. And if Father were here, he would never let you send her away."

"Your father isn't here, damn it!" Mother screamed. "He was never here. He was either at that damn hospital or with another woman. But he was never here! He was a spineless, spoiled man. The most cowardly thing he ever did was fall down those stairs and leave me with four children to raise—two little white babies and two little colored ones."

Mother's hat was lying on the ground now. Her left foot was pressed against the brim, smashing it deep into the dirt. Nathaniel, Maizelle, and Adelaide were standing on the steps by the back door, absorbing everything that had been said. They looked confused, disappointed, maybe even scared. And I imagined there were times when I had looked just like they did.

"Maybe he was all those things, Mother," I said. "Maybe he was born that way. Maybe you made him that way. But one thing I do know for sure"—and my voice began to weaken—"is that you're no better." Then I turned away and walked into the house, leaving my poor mother standing motionless in the garden, the flowers clutched so tightly in her hand that the stems had broken in half.

Later that evening, Nathaniel carried a tray to Mother's room while Adelaide and I sat at the dining room table by ourselves, just like we had so many times when we were children. I asked Maizelle and Nathaniel if they wanted to join us, but they said they preferred to eat their meal in the kitchen. In front of me sat a silver vase full of hydrangeas, all of them drooping toward the table.

chapter twelve

Adelaide and I sat on the front porch for a while after dinner, staring at the sky and eating pieces of Maizelle's pound cake. It was so moist it melted in my mouth, and I knew without asking that Maizelle had added an extra stick of butter, something she did for real special occasions.

My sister started talking and only stopped to put another bite of cake in her mouth. She never said a word about what had been said in the garden. Instead she chattered on and on about school and about her new friend Lucy, the only girl in her class who wasn't afraid to talk to her. Lucy had even invited her to spend the night a couple of weeks ago, but Mother wouldn't let her go for fear she might embarrass herself. Adelaide knew she was a little different from the other girls, but that was okay. Maizelle had told her that was what made her special. Besides, she liked to be alone—it didn't scare her like it did most people. And Lucy understood that.

"I know Mother's always trying to fix me," Adelaide said softly. "But I'm not broken."

I reached for my sister's hand and told her I already knew that. She sighed, releasing a full and steady breath, seemingly relieved that somebody finally believed her.

"Adelaide, come on," I said and stood up, motioning for my sister to follow me.

"Where are we going?"

"Not far."

"How far?"

"You know a friend of mine told me once that if you weren't willing to walk to something, then it just wasn't worth seeing. I promise this is worth it. Now come on. Trust me."

I ran a few feet ahead of my sister, drawing in the evening's remaining heat with every stride. Adelaide followed, obviously giddy to be out of the house without Mother watching over her. We stepped through the grass and clover, easily finding our way across the familiar field behind our house. Even from a distance, I could see the moonlight dancing off the water in the creek and the weeping willow gently swaying in the breeze.

"This? This is what you wanted to show me? The creek? You know I've only seen this a few hundred times already," Adelaide puffed, sounding confused and slightly irritated. I put my finger to my mouth and motioned for her to hush. Then I sat down on the ground and gazed up at the stars and said a little prayer to anyone who might be listening, to anyone who might know what I should do when morning came pushing itself up and over those old trees. And then I picked up a handful of mud and started shaping a ball. I smashed it with my right hand and set it on the ground and started making another.

Adelaide looked at me. Her eyes were wide open, like two beautiful little moons set right in the middle of her face. I motioned for her to sit down. And this time, without question or reservation, she dutifully lowered herself to the ground and picked up a handful of mud. And there we sat, shaping pies and sharing stories, neither one of us keeping track of the time.

"Remember when Samuel made you a crown, a crown of clover? Do you, Bezellia? You didn't like being a princess. Remember that?"

"Yes. I do remember that. And do you remember wishing that Samuel was your big brother?"

"Yes. But I still wish that," Adelaide said in a hushed tone, allowing her wish to float away into the still summer night. She made another mud pie and set it down on the ground next to mine. "When do you think Samuel's coming home?"

"I don't know for sure. Nathaniel is hoping by Christmas."

"Is he your boyfriend?"

"No," I said, but my answer was so slow and deliberate that even Adelaide seemed to understand I wished he was. She stood up with her back to the creek and her hands on her hips, looking just like Maizelle for a moment, and admired our collection of freshly made pies. She smiled and then started giggling.

"You know Mother told me if I ever made another mud pie she would rub my face in it. Kind of wish she had, always thought that sounded like fun," my little sister said, and then she scooped up some mud in both hands and rubbed it on her cheeks. "Feels pretty good," she oozed and started laughing again.

When Adelaide was a tiny girl and would stomp her feet and snort and squeal, Maizelle would beg me to be patient with her. "Just like a fuzzy little caterpillar," she'd say, "someday your sister will bloom into a beautiful butterfly." I was never so sure if she was telling the truth. But tonight, admiring my beautiful little sister with mud streaked all over her face, I knew she *was* right.

I have no idea how long we sat there or how many mud pies we made. Finally, we realized we had made enough, so we picked ourselves up and walked back to the house. Every so often we just stopped to look at each other, with mud on our faces and in our hair, and laugh out loud. By the time we got back to the house, Maizelle was standing outside the kitchen door, her hands resting on her hips. She didn't see a butterfly like I did.

"Where you two been? Lord, I knew something wasn't right in this house. You girls came to me in a dream. You were drowning in that creek, holding on to each other and hollering for help. I could hear you but couldn't get to you." She squinted her eyes and moved a step closer. "Is that mud? Oh, my Lord, your mama's gonna have a fit. What in the world has got into you, Bezellia? Lord, child." Maizelle was no longer worried about us drowning.

"Your mama's gonna hit the ceiling when she finds out you had Adelaide out in the middle of the night playing in that mud. Oh, dear, precious Jesus."

"Maizelle, calm down," I said as I smacked my hand over Adelaide's mouth to keep her from laughing right in Maizelle's face.

"Don't tell me to calm down, child. Your mama's gonna wear your hide out. And mine too. She's already on edge. Lord have mercy! Get the garden hose and get yourself washed off. And then your sister. Take them clothes off and put 'em here on the porch. Don't you bring one speck of mud in this house. Your mama will find it. Those eyes of hers have magnifiers on them. Lord, Bezellia, you know your mama don't like your sister playing in the mud." Maizelle groaned and rubbed her hands together and then walked back into the house mumbling something about Jesus and mud and a miracle.

Mother was asleep in the den by the time I got cleaned up. Her body, partly buried in the down-filled cushions of the club chair by the large picture window, looked unusually small and frail in the soft moonlight. An open Bible was resting across her chest, and an almost empty glass was wedged under her hand. "The Star-Spangled Banner" played quietly on the television set. Her head bobbed slightly up and down as the bombs began bursting in air. The black-and-white test pattern flickered on the screen, and the room went silent except for the hushed sound of my mother's breathing.

I carefully reached for the glass under her hand and lifted it to my nose. I wondered if Nathaniel had fixed her a drink with crushed ice and fresh mint from the garden, then left for the evening, tipping his hat as he walked through the back door. I wondered if Maizelle had covered her with a blanket before heading upstairs and if Adelaide had kissed her good night and, seeing the glass filled with ice and gin, simply whispered that tomorrow she would be a good girl and knit another sweater.

No one was more to blame than I was, hiding at school and ignoring her letters, not really wanting to know how she was doing. When Mother woke in the morning, she wouldn't remember much of this day. And maybe it was just as well.

MINISTER LEAVES METHODIST CHURCH IN DEAD OF NIGHT
REV. EDWIN C. FOSTER ALLEGEDLY STEALS FROM CHURCH

Church Members Report Suspicious Activities to Police

Reverend Edwin C. Foster, senior pastor of Broadway United Methodist Church, is currently under police investigation, according to local authorities. Foster, who has led one of the city's oldest churches for the past seven years, left his Grove Park home late last night and has yet to be located.

Local Methodist church officials confirmed that several thousand dollars from the church's checking account are missing, and police are concerned that Foster may have been stealing from church funds for several months now. A review of the church's financial records is ongoing at this time.

Foster had recently encouraged his congregation to donate large sums of money for needed improvements to the existing church structure as well as to fund architectural plans for a new fellowship hall. The close relative of one prominent donor, who prefers to remain anonymous, said he became suspicious when none of the improvements discussed were implemented.

He said he confronted the senior pastor in a private meeting earlier in the week and then approached the board of deacons with his concerns yesterday afternoon. The police were contacted when the church secretary could not locate Foster for Wednesday night services.

The Nashville Register
final edition
AUGUST 5, 1970

*U*ncle Thad made a few phone calls to Minnesota and then to the bank. Mother urgently needed another special vacation, but unfortunately this time there was no money to pay for it. She had withdrawn thousands of dollars from her savings account during the last six months, each transaction paid directly to Reverend Foster. I imagine with each payment she had hoped for some peace, some comfort that surely would come to such a faithful and generous servant. Now she was nearly broke and drunk, and Reverend Foster was on the lam, probably hiding out in some plush hotel on the South Florida coast.

Uncle Thad said we had a tough decision to make, probably one Mother was not going to like. He'd found a hospital right outside Chattanooga, situated on the banks of the Tennessee River. Nothing fancy, he warned, owned by the state. But the doctors there thought they might be able to help. He said it was something we could afford. He hoped that we could convince Mother to go on her own. But one way or another, he said, she would be going. He wasn't going to leave us girls alone with her when she was drowning in a bottle of gin.

"Bezellia, honey, I called your grandparents last night," Uncle Thad confessed as we sat at the kitchen table together. "At first I thought maybe your mother could stay with them for a while. They said no. Practically hung up on me, to tell you the truth. I just don't see that we have many other options. You can think about it for a day or two if you want. But the hospital needs to know by Friday."

Uncle Thad wrapped his hands around mine and scooted his chair a little closer. "Cornelia's home for a few weeks before heading back to Boston, Bee. Why don't you give her a call, probably be good for the two of you to talk. I know she's real eager to see you."

I smiled and felt a tear roll down my cheek. Just knowing my cousin was in town was a comfort.

Mother hid in her room, pretending to know nothing of our discussions, while Maizelle cooked one chicken noodle casserole after another, somehow hoping, I guess, that a full stomach would make everybody feel better. Nathaniel washed and waxed the car in case Mother needed to leave at a moment's notice. And Adelaide worked feverishly knitting a lightweight cotton sweater. She thought Mother might need it if she was going to be by the water.

"Bezellia," she asked one afternoon while we were sitting on the front porch together, "do you think Mother is going to get better this time? I mean stay that way?"

"I don't know. I sure hope so."

We sat there for a long time, neither one of us saying another word. I think we both were trying to accept the fact that our mother was not well, again, and maybe imagining what it would be like to know a mother who was. Then Adelaide shifted her rocking chair closer to mine and pulled something out from underneath her shirt. She was holding a small knitted sack made of soft pink yarn. Bright pink flowers were delicately embroidered along the bottom edge, each flower connected to the next by a green, leafy vine. A deep pink ribbon was laced through the top of the sack and tied in a neat little bow.

"I made this for you—well, at least part of it. I wanted to give it to you the day you came home, but it just never felt like quite the right time, especially after everything that happened in the garden and all. I don't want you to be mad, at Mother I mean. I don't think she means to do such awful things."

The real gift, she said, as she placed the knitted sack in my hands, was inside. With her eyes guiding my fingers toward the ribbon, I gently pulled one end and then the other, opening it just wide enough to glimpse an odd bundle of papers. Adelaide shook her head in excitement and silently clapped her hands together. They're letters, she gushed, letters from Samuel.

My mouth fell open, but nothing came out, not even a gasp or a moan. I held the letters next to my chest and looked at Adelaide for an explanation. She pulled her legs underneath her and sat a little taller. She was eager to tell me all she knew but wasn't sure where to start. She finally admitted that she had found them in Mother's room just a day or two before I came home. They were stuffed in a faded old pillowcase and tucked under her bathroom sink.

"I was looking for her dusting powder. You know the one that smells like gardenias? I just wanted to try a little. Cornelia gave me a subscription to *Seventeen* magazine for my birthday. And in the very first issue that came to the house, it said boys actually prefer the more subtle scent of a powder. Lucy said she bought some of that Jean Naté powder at the drugstore right before Easter and hasn't used a drop of perfume ever since."

I held the papers out in front of my sister, begging her to tell me more about the letters. Adelaide shook her head and again concentrated on the little bundle in my hands. She said she grabbed the pillowcase and ran to her room. She emptied every envelope and then filled each one with a blank piece of paper so Mother wouldn't notice anything was missing. Then she put the envelopes back in the pillowcase and the pillowcase back under the sink. She hid the real letters with Baby Stella, who was still tucked in a cardboard box in the far corner of the attic. She knew good and well that nobody would dare look for them there.

She promised she hadn't read them, well, maybe only part of one. But just between her and me, it sure seemed like Samuel still wanted to be my boyfriend, even if his skin was a whole lot darker than mine. She said she'd leave me alone now, figuring I'd want some time to read without a little sister leaning over my shoulder. She sure hoped this made me feel better.

My fingers were clumsy and stiff, and the small stack of papers suddenly felt very heavy in my hands. The first letter had been mailed months ago, not long after Mother had written to tell me Samuel had left for Vietnam. The paper was tattered and worn, and I wondered how far these words had traveled to find me. My entire body started shaking, and my stomach felt sick. But Samuel told me not to worry. He said he wasn't afraid. He said he'd now seen evil in the eyes of an Alabama sheriff and a North Vietnamese soldier. And from where he was standing, it looked pretty much the same.

He missed me and even drew a little heart next to my name. He confessed that he thought of us down by the creek every single night. It was what got him through the hell he'd found there on the other side of the world. Sometimes, in his dreams, he swore he could even smell my hair and the soapy scent of my skin. I started to cry and for a few moments allowed myself to fall back into Samuel's arms and feel the weight of his body on top of mine. I could feel his breath on my neck and his thigh pushing its way between my legs before I un-willingly drifted back to the porch. Another tear fell on the paper, and I quickly dried it with my blouse for fear I might wash away even one word that belonged to Samuel Stephenson.

He asked if I'd look after his dad. He knew he must be worried sick about his only son. He promised to write again as soon as he could and begged me to write him too. Any word from home sure meant a lot, but a word from me would mean everything. There were four more letters, but I couldn't bear to read them. Samuel had been gone almost a year, and he had never heard from me. He didn't know that I thought about him every day. He didn't know that I dreamed about him every night. He didn't know that I missed him so much it hurt. He didn't know that I had climbed to the top of Tinker Mountain and sobbed and screamed for Samuel Stephenson. He didn't know any of that. All he knew, or thought he knew, was that I didn't care, that I didn't love him anymore. Surely I loved someone else, someone different, someone better.

I found myself huddled in my bed, not really remembering how I got there. I hid under my pillow for the rest of the afternoon, crying for Samuel and hating my mother. I wished spitting in her coffee would make me feel better. But I knew there wasn't enough coffee or enough spit to make this right. Even with her Bible in her hand, she had found a way to be deceitful and cruel, prejudiced and judgmental. She might as well have slapped me across the face. This time I could see myself falling down the hard marble steps in front of our house, Samuel's letters swirling about my head. I reached for them. I tried to grab them. But they all blew away.

The sun was almost below the horizon by the time Adelaide knocked on my bedroom door. She looked like a cold, scared kitten, worried she had only made matters worse by sharing something that had always belonged to me. I could see the desperation in every limb of her body, the exhaustion from living with a mother who, in one way or another, had always been drunk. And even though Adelaide was beginning to look more and more like a woman, she still felt like a child to me, a little girl who needed to be loved right, as Maizelle would say. I held her hand and told her everything would be fine. I wasn't exactly sure how I knew that. I hadn't seen a sign of any kind or heard a voice from the great beyond. Just somehow, for the first time in my life, I knew it to be true. I stroked my sister's back, and after a while, she fell asleep.

I left Adelaide in my bed and snuck downstairs and called Uncle Thad. I didn't even wait for him to say hello. I told him to come to

Grove Hill. It was time to talk to Mother. I knew what I had to say, but I desperately needed my uncle with me. And while I waited for him on the front steps of my ancestral home, I looked across the lawn already covered in a light evening fog and saw the first Bezellia, hunched over her husband's dying body, the musket heavy in her hands and the smoke from the last shot burning her eyes. She looked about my age, no more than that. And there she was, holding her dying husband in her arms. In that moment, she was brave and fearless, maybe not by choice but certainly by circumstance. Father had said her blood was running through my veins, and now more than ever I hoped he was right.

Mother argued and fussed and cried when I told her she needed to go. She begged to stay at Grove Hill, sounding much like Adelaide when she was a little girl and was told she would be spending the summer with her grandparents. I told her that she was not well, but surely she already knew that. I told her she deserved this time away to care for herself after dealing with Father's death and Adelaide's peculiarities and everything else she deemed *tragic* that had been left for her to manage alone. Some time by the water would surely do her some good.

Uncle Thad, who had sat between us, silently offering us both some much needed strength and courage, took Mother's hands in his and told her that she really had no other choice. If she refused to go, then he could not allow Adelaide and me to stay at Grove Hill. He needed to know that we were safe in our own home. Mother burst into tears, and even though she pulled her hands away from Uncle Thad's, she just sat motionless in her chair, seemingly unsure of what to do next. I looked at her with a fixed expression, afraid that, if I even blinked, my resolve would also melt into tears. In the morning, Uncle Thad said, she should be packed and ready to go.

Then he helped her back to her room and stayed by her side till he was certain she was asleep. By the time Uncle Thad left, the rest of the house had grown unbearably quiet. Adelaide had drifted back to the den and was now knitting and watching television, neither activity fully capturing her attention. Maizelle was in bed reading her Bible. She left her door open slightly so she could listen for my little sister during the night. I told Maizelle that wasn't necessary anymore, but she said she would be listening for her babies till the day she died. I poked my head in her room and told her that I was headed out for a while. She furrowed her brow and looked up from her Bible and asked if I knew what I was doing. I told her I didn't know much of anything right now, I just needed a little fresh air, and then I headed downstairs and called Cornelia.

My cousin and I had both been so busy tending to our own lives that we hadn't talked in a very long time, at least not about anything of any importance. Now I was missing her, missing her terribly, and was so grateful she was home.

"Damn it, girl, I was wondering when were you going to get in touch with me." Cornelia was laughing on the other end of the telephone. "I was getting kind of tired of talking to dear Aunt Liz," she said, barely pausing to take a breath, admitting that she had called my house three or four times during the past week, apparently never trusting her aunt to tell the truth about my arrival.

I told her, given the circumstances, that was probably smart and that I'd be waiting for her on the front porch. A few minutes later, Cornelia sped up the driveway in the yellow Volkswagen Beetle that Uncle Thad had bought her when she came home from college after her freshman year. Mother always said that it was the worst looking car in town and that it reeked of those damn chickens. My cousin squealed when I jumped in the front seat. She leaned across the steering wheel and hugged my neck, accidentally hitting the horn with her left elbow. I told her she better hit the gas before my mother came looking for me, and then I dropped my head in my hands and started to cry.

"What's going on, Bee? What's Aunt Liz done now? Daddy said she's going to need another one of her special vacations. Except this time he said she's going to have to stay at the Motel Six and not the Ritz-Carlton, or something like that."

With my head still buried in my hands, I nodded and then muttered something about Adelaide's little knitted sack and Samuel's letters. Then words like Ruddy and Reverend Foster and Johnny Cash and Jesus Christ all started blending together, forming some kind of verbal cyclone that ripped a path right through my cousin's little car, none of it making any sense at all.

And when I finally ran out of strength, Cornelia told me to take a deep breath and start over again. "This time so I can understand you."

I tried to take a deep breath, but I started laughing instead.

"Girl, what has gotten into you? One minute you're crying and the next minute you're cracking up. You sure you're okay?"

"Your car really does smell like chickens," I said, ignoring Cornelia's concern.

"Ha. Very funny, Bee. That's because Daddy's always leaving the windows down and two of his favorite hens love to sleep in the backseat. Even laid a couple of eggs back there the other day. But what about you? Are you sure you're okay?"

"Yeah. I think I am. I had really hoped that the God my mother keeps praying to was paying better attention this time and had worked some kind of miracle and turned her into someone good, someone normal, hell, a magic fairy for all I care. But it was just an illusion, just a temporary illusion.

"You know, ever since I can remember, Cornelia, I've either hated her or felt sorry for her—nothing in between. And right this minute, I hate her *and* feel sorry for her. The only difference is that now I'm beginning to think I'm no better than she is—just another illusion of a nice girl when underneath it all I'm as much a mess as she is."

"Lord, don't tell me you've started drinking too," Cornelia teased, but she sounded a little more concerned than she had a moment ago.

"That's exactly what I've been doing. I've been doing nothing but drinking wine and listening to Led Zeppelin with an overachieving, oversexed English professor while Samuel's getting shot at and my little sister's knitting baby booties and my mother is sneaking gin into her lemonade."

"Wow. Back up. Start over. What oversexed English teacher are you talking about? What the hell have you been doing at that school, anyway?"

So sitting there in the driveway in my cousin's little yellow car, I shared the secrets of the past two years of my life. I started with Ruddy Semple and how I wanted to pull his pants off right there on Mount Juliet's white, sandy beach. I admitted that I wasn't really sure if it was genuine affection or outright lust that had left me tugging on his belt or just the need to feel a boy wrap his arms around me.

Then I told her about meeting Samuel Stephenson under the cherrybark oaks and offering up my heart and my virginity not more than a few hours after my own father died, not more than a few hours after saying good-bye to Ruddy. But I loved Samuel. I knew that. I also knew that my mother would die if she caught her daughter with a black man, and I couldn't help but wonder if loving him like that in my own backyard was as much to punish her as to satisfy me.

I told her everything about Sarah Stanton Miller and Gloria Steinem and their fight for equality, and Mitchell Franklin and his passion for afternoon sex. I told her about Samuel going to Vietnam and even showed her Adelaide's beautifully knitted sack and the letters she had found underneath my mother's bathroom sink. Cornelia took it all in, never interrupting to add an opinion or offer advice. She let me talk until there was really nothing more to say, and then she looked at me and smiled.

"Man, Bee. You just got home a couple of days ago."

We both started laughing again, and Cornelia knocked the gear-shift with her right knee. The car started rolling forward, and we both laughed even harder.

"You know, Bumble Bee," Cornelia finally said as she turned back to face the front of the car. "It's easy to get lost in that big name of yours. But I got news for you. There's a lot of people out there who don't care whether you're Bezellia Grove or Ophelia Rose. You know what I mean?"

But I just stared blankly, offering no sign of understanding.

"Okay, judging by that look on your face, I assume you don't. Let me spell it out for you in plain English. You do not have to do whatever you think it is a Grove is supposed to do. Take a lesson from Adelaide. Everybody thinks she's a little odd. Hell, I think she's the sanest one in that big old house of yours. Live your own life—not your mother's—no matter what anybody thinks. I don't want to be my mother probably any more than you want to be yours. I've seen my own mommy dearest all of about two times since I've been in Boston. She's too absorbed in her stupid paintings to pay me the least bit of attention.

"But, more importantly," she went on, and she put both hands on the steering wheel, "what you need to understand is that you really can 'forget all your troubles and forget all your cares, and go down-town. Things'll be great when you're downtown.'"

"What?" I stopped sniffling and started laughing again.

"That's right, Baby Bee. Petula Clark said it best. And that's where we're headed right now—downtown." My cousin shifted into first gear and stepped on the accelerator. The car lurched forward, the tires screeching as we headed down the drive. I glanced back at the house and saw Adelaide's face in her bedroom window, her nose pressed against the glass. She waved good-bye. I blew her a kiss, and she pretended to catch it in her hand.

Cornelia turned a sharp left out of our driveway and headed toward town. She rolled down her window, and I rolled down mine. Our hair was blowing in the wind, lashing across our faces. Cornelia turned the radio up even louder. We sang along with Elvis Presley and Carole King, making up words when we didn't know the lyrics, her little yellow Beetle vibrating to the beat of the music.

We sped past the country club and then past the Hunts' house. Cars were parked along both sides of the street. Mrs. Hunt was having another party. Apparently her husband had forgiven her or never really cared that much in the first place that she had spent countless evenings curled up in my father's arms. We passed churches and restaurants and Centennial Park.

Nashville had dubbed itself the Athens of the South long before I was born and built its very own Parthenon in the middle of this park just to prove it. It looked exactly like the one in Greece except this one was perfect, not standing in ruins. Mother had taken me there when I was five for a painting class. But I thought the giant marble statues were scary and stood whimpering behind my mother's back instead of brushing paint on my canvas like the other kids did. Mother marched me out to the car and spanked my bottom, said she hadn't brought me down here to act like a baby in front of her friends. I hated this park.

Cornelia turned the radio up a little louder and drove a little faster, and I started feeling a little better. Dimly lit office buildings and car dealerships blended into bars and tattoo parlors. Cruising downtown with the windows open and the radio blaring, I felt as bright and electric as all the lights and neon signs distinguishing one honky-tonk from another. I leaned my head out the window and let out a scream.

We passed Tootsies Orchid Lounge and The Stage. People were crowded on the sidewalks, trying to press into one bar or another, the music of different bands drifting into the street. We stopped by Rotiers on the way home to eat a cheeseburger and fried dill pickles.

A couple of boys from Vanderbilt lingered near our table and asked if we wanted some company. Cornelia scooted to the right, making just enough room for the boy with the dark brown hair to sit next to her. She cocked her head to the left and indicated that I should do the same. But I didn't budge. I wasn't looking for a college boy with a drawer full of cashmere to try to make me feel better.

"Sorry, boys," Cornelia said with such sugary affection that they both lingered a little longer hoping her friend would change her mind. But thankfully my cousin tossed her hair behind her back and grabbed her purse, indicating that we would be heading on our way, alone.

We got back in the car and just sat there for a few minutes, listening to the static on the radio, neither one of us bothering to find a better station. And somewhere beneath that constant, steady sound, I could still hear my mother crying, pleading with me not to send her away, and Samuel begging me to write him back. I rolled my window down and turned the radio up even louder. I told them both to hush, but they just kept making noise in my head.

I turned the knob to the left and then to the right, flipping the radio from one station to the next until an anonymous, velvet-toned DJ interrupted the static. A surprise was coming up next, he promised, a brand-new song from a boy who grew up just down the road a ways. "Here it is, folks, 'Big City Girl.'"

Cornelia swatted my hand, pushing it away from the radio. "This ought to be good," she said with a full, bold laugh.

The sound coming from the dashboard was slow and mournful. But with the first stroke of the guitar, the tempo and mood changed, and I knew that the voice that filled that little yellow Beetle had filled my head before.

"She wore pearls around her neck and went to fancy schools
She had pretty long legs that made the boys drool

*She wasn't looking for a country boy with holes in his jeans
But then she wasn't looking for love when she done found me."*

"Hey, this is pretty good . . . for country music," Cornelia shouted over the radio, slapping her thigh to the beat.

"Shut up," I popped and waved my left hand in her face, letting her know that I really meant it this time. But the voice inside the radio wouldn't hush. He just kept on singing.

*"She'd whisper French right in my ear, but it was all Greek to me
And I just wanted to meet her underneath the old oak tree.
And when we met one dark and starry night
That girl named Bezellia made me feel so right."*

Cornelia started hooting and hollering and now slapping me on the arm. "Oh, my God. Oh, my God" were the only words that came streaming out of her mouth. She screamed again and pounded the steering wheel with both hands. "Way to go, girl!" She swerved into the next lane, and I smacked her hard on the arm and told her to shut up before she got us both killed.

"I can't believe he did that," I shrieked. "I can't believe he used my name. Under a tree. Making him feel so right. Lord, when my mother hears this. Shit! She's going to kill me. Or at the very least send me to some Baptist reform school up in Kentucky. Damn it, if I could get my hands on him, I'd tie him up to that damn oak tree."

I could barely complete one thought before another crowded its way inside my head. I couldn't help but wonder if Ruddy was standing on a stage somewhere right now, maybe right here in downtown Nashville, with that big old smile painted across his face, strumming his guitar, singing about our secret night down on the beach. I felt completely exposed, naked as a little jaybird, as Maizelle used to say when she plucked me from the bathtub. Except now, the whole world was looking.

"What's your problem, Bee? This is so cool. You're gonna be famous—the girl who inspired Ruddy Semple's first big hit. You're his muse. Like June Carter."

"Lord, Cornelia, have you forgotten who my mother is? She's not going to want me to be anybody's muse, especially not some guitar-picking country boy's."

"Shit, Bee. Quit worrying. You and I both know that your mother doesn't care one iota about country music. And I seriously doubt where she's going tomorrow they're going to be sitting around listening to the radio. Besides, I thought you liked Ruddy."

"This isn't about liking him or not. He had no right to tell the whole world that we were fooling around underneath a tree. Shit, everybody's gonna think we did *it.*" By now my voice was sounding so loud and shrill that my own head was starting to hurt.

"See, I think you're looking at this all wrong. You've gone and gotten yourself a big singing star. That's a good thing. And so what if people think you did *it?* It's not like you're a virgin."

"What if Samuel hears this? What if he hears this stupid song while he's fighting in some jungle somewhere? Oh, God. Shit, Ruddy."

"Now see, there you go again, just thinking about this all wrong. Look on the bright side. One day Ruddy will be so rich and famous that the two of you can live in a big house and you can hire Samuel to be your Nathaniel. Then you can have him around you all the time."

"Shut up, Cornelia! Shit, for crying out loud, I cannot believe you of all people said that. Just shut up."

"Hell's bells, I'm just messing with you, Bee."

But I sat still and quiet, refusing to even look at my cousin.

"Oh shit," she said, breaking the silence, "you're still in love with him. Samuel, that is. You are. I mean really in love with him."

Cornelia stared at my face, searching for something to convince her that she had misunderstood.

"Nothing new. I've told you that," I quipped.

"Yeah, but I just thought you *liked-him-loved-him* not LOVED him. Look, Bee, you know I don't think there's anything wrong with the two of you having a thing for each other. There's nothing wrong with you two *liking-loving* each other or whatever you want to call it.

"But let's face facts, a real relationship ain't never going to work. Not here. Not now. Hell, twenty miles outside of town there are still little private clubs where all the members like to dress in white robes and wear funny cone-shaped hats on their heads, if you know what I mean."

"Do you even know how to shut up?" I cried. "And just for the record, you're the one who told me a long time ago that ours was a Shakespearean love, one to last for all time."

"Fine, I'll shut up. But just remember how Romeo and Juliet ended. It wasn't very pretty, as I recall."

We drove the rest of the way home in silence, neither one of us saying another word. I leaned my head out the window, still trying to muffle the sounds of Ruddy's voice rising above his guitar, my mother screaming at the kitchen table, and Samuel crying out in the dark— asking where I was, why I didn't write, why I didn't love him any-more, and why I had done *it* with another boy underneath an oak tree.

chapter fourteen

*M*other left without putting up much of a fuss. She still didn't understand why she needed to go. Doctors at a place like that, she whimpered with tears pooling in her eyes, would never understand a woman like her. But Uncle Thad told her that at the end of the day there wasn't much difference between one drunk and another, and then he swiftly led her to the car, not giving her another chance to argue or resist.

Nathaniel sat behind the steering wheel, and Uncle Thad took his place in the backseat, his arm snug around my mother's shoulder, her head resting on his chest. I waved good-bye until the car disappeared onto Davidson Road, and then I stood there a little longer, wondering what more I could have said to comfort my mother. Uncle Thad had thought it best that I stay at Grove Hill with Adelaide and Maizelle. They would surely need me at a time like this, he said. I had nodded as though I understood, but now I felt completely helpless. And I couldn't help but wonder if I had done the right thing. Maybe Mother really didn't belong in a place like that. Maybe she needed to be here, surrounded by the only people left who really cared about her. Maizelle appeared beside me and wrapped her thick, dark arm around my waist. She had tears in her eyes too.

Adelaide fled to the den and flipped on the television set, turning the volume up so loud that it almost hurt my ears. I stood right next to her so she had no choice but to hear me, and I told her that we could walk down to the creek a little bit later and make some more mud pies if she wanted. With the light rain we'd had during the night, the soil would be just perfect for cooking up a fresh batch. She scrunched her shoulders and nodded her head but then picked up her knitting so she was certain to have another excuse to avoid looking at me. I walked over to Mother's desk and pulled out a fresh pad of white paper and a ballpoint pen. I told Adelaide I'd be in the kitchen if she needed anything, but she just turned her back to me and stared at the TV.

The smell of freshly brewed coffee met me at the kitchen door. And even though I still didn't care for the bold, bitter taste, I held the metal percolator in my hand and poured some of it into one of Mother's heavy white mugs. I sat at the table with the mug in one hand and Mother's pen in the other and struggled to find the words I needed to explain that I would not be returning to Hollins in September. Family matters demanded my attention at home, I began, but someday soon I hoped to return to the school that I loved so dearly.

And when I was done, I sat there and stared at the next sheet of blank paper, knowing that there was more to say but not certain where to start. The coffee had grown cold, yet I still considered pouring myself another cup. Maizelle walked into the kitchen and opened the refrigerator. She filled a glass with orange juice and set it down in front of me, thought it would be more to my liking, she said. Then she picked up the mug and drained what was left down the kitchen sink. There was laundry to do, she added with a bit of a sigh, and I could find her in the basement. She slowly crept down the back staircase, balancing a basket full of dirty clothes in her hands and leaving me to stare at the same piece of paper.

I picked up the pen and began a letter to Ruddy. I'm not really sure why, except I wanted him to know that I had enjoyed spending time with him, especially our afternoons floating about in my grandfather's rowboat, checking fising lines for fresh catch and talking about music and roosters and everything in between. Those were perfect moments as the sun fell behind the water, and it felt as though we were the only ones on the lake to see it.

I told him I knew now that he really was going to be a big country music star just like Johnny Cash. I'd even heard him singing right there in Cornelia's car. I really appreciated him being such a gentleman that night on Mount Juliet's sandy beach, not doing, as he said himself, everything God intended a man and woman to do. I only wished he hadn't let the rest of the world, including my mother, think that we had.

Then I wrote to Mitchell Franklin and admitted that even though I enjoyed the sex I still thought he was an ass. I wished him the very best with his research and dissertation, but thanks to him, I was no longer considering a major in English. I told him I was still writing and had recently finished a short story about a young, ambitious professor who hid behind a long list of honors and degrees while he secretly seduced his female students. He eventually fathered nearly three hundred children, who all shared their father's brownish red hair and an unusual affection for Led Zeppelin.

I even wrote to Tommy Blanton. I wanted him to know that standing behind the coatrack in Mrs. Dempsey's sixth-grade classroom with his lips pressed against mine was the first time, in all of my life, that I had felt truly special. My quest for real love had begun at that moment, even if I had been too young to fully understand that then. And although I doubted he had ever thought about it too much, I wanted him to understand that those simple kisses had changed me forever. I would never be able to settle for anything less than a true and lasting love.

And finally, I wrote to Samuel. I told him that his letters had just arrived and that after all this time I understood if he no longer loved me. But I thought of him constantly and could still hear him saying my name for the very first time that day we talked in the barn. My name had never been spoken with such warmth and tenderness, nor had it ever sounded as beautiful as it did then.

I told him about my first year at college and walking to the top of Tinker Mountain and crying his name out loud. I wondered if somehow he had heard me. I liked to believe that he had. And when I was finished writing all that I had to say, I sprayed each page with some of my mother's perfume, hoping that even the faintest scent of May Rose would carry Samuel back to the creek, to that grassy bank underneath the cherrybark oaks.

As I sealed the last envelope, I could hear Maizelle slowly walking up the basement steps. I could tell she was tired and her aging body was aching by her grunting and moaning as she set her foot down on each step. I knew I should run to greet her and shift the load of clean clothes into my hands. I should urge her to stop and rest for a while. But I hurriedly gathered all of the letters on the table, keeping Samuel's clutched next to my chest, and ran to the mailbox at the end of the drive. And there, in that old metal box, I left my most secret thoughts to be carried away. Then I walked back to the house and turned my attention to Grove Hill.

While Mother was gone, Maizelle kept close to the stove, cooking chicken casseroles and pots of vegetable stew, even taking the time to can tomatoes and sweet cucumber pickles. I told her that the freezer was overflowing with plastic containers and Pyrex dishes and that Adelaide and I could never eat all the food waiting to be defrosted if we both lived to be a hundred. She ignored me and chatted nervously about a possible tornado or a nuclear war or some other unforeseen emergency that she needed to prepare for. She'd been reading the newspaper. It was only a matter of time, she said. But honestly, I think poor Maizelle was simply afraid that someday she'd be gone, too, and the poor little Grove girls would have nothing to eat.

Nathaniel waxed and buffed all the wood floors in the house and even repainted the outside of the barn. In the late afternoons, he spent his time sweeping the front porch, shaking the dust from the cushions, and watering the large concrete pots filled with more of Mother's impatiens. When he was satisfied with his work, he went inside and polished the silver tea service as if Mother was standing over him telling him to be more careful with the family's treasures. He said he wanted everything to look its best when Mrs. Grove finally came home. This time, he said, he had a feeling in his gut that things would be different.

He talked more and more about Samuel, mentioning him almost every day now. I loved that Nathaniel talked to me about his son, that he trusted me with this special information. Maybe he just felt, with Samuel so far away, not much harm could come from it. But his brows would lift and his eyes would brighten at just the mention of Samuel's name. He kept telling me that he would be home soon, and after a while, I think Nathaniel actually started to believe it. He said he had finally quit reading the newspaper, that it was a little bit easier getting through the days not knowing what was going on in the world.

My sister knitted for a while longer. It made her sad to think of our mother at that hospital alone, and keeping her fingers busy seemed to help. Besides, she said, there would always be a new baby needing something warm for its feet. Sometimes when she got tired of making tiny pink and blue booties, she would pull out a bright colored yarn and knit Maizelle a scarf. Poor Maizelle wore each one tied neatly about her neck, even if it was ninety degrees outside and sweat was dripping down her back. Then one day Adelaide came to me and handed me her needles. She said she was finally tired of knitting and was ready to give her hands a rest.

"I don't need to do this anymore, Bezellia," she said and walked out of the room and called her friend Lucy. Funny, I thought, how Mother's special vacation by the water seemed to have finally cured Adelaide too.

My sister went back to school in September, and this year she seemed to look forward to it. She spent more time primping in the mornings, sometimes asking me to braid her soft, curly hair, which now fell well beyond her shoulders, making her look more like a young movie star than a high school sophomore. Sometimes she would borrow a skirt or a pair of earrings from me, always wanting to make sure that she looked her best.

I drove her to school most days. Nathaniel himself had taught me to drive Mother's Cadillac just a month or so before leaving for college. He said driving a car was an important part of any young woman's education. But I'd never felt much of a need to do it until now, explaining to Nathaniel that sisters needed a little privacy to talk about boys and music and makeup. But more than anything else, we talked about Mother and Adelaide's new friend, Lucy. Sometimes Lucy would come home with us after school. The two of them would run upstairs whispering and giggling, then slam the door and lock themselves in my sister's room. Maizelle never stopped worrying, though, and always found an excuse to knock on Adelaide's door, whether it was to bring the girls a fresh piece of pound cake or to ask if Lucy wanted to stay for supper.

Uncle Thad came by Grove Hill most every afternoon. He spent hours at Mother's desk, tending to what was left of her money and talking to the bank on the telephone. With a few wise investments, he managed to repair my mother's checkbook so she would be comfortable, he said, in the years to come.

He called the hospital at the end of the day and checked on

Mother's progress. The doctors remained hopeful that she would return to Grove Hill prepared to lead a healthy, sober life. And even though they believed she no longer blamed herself for her husband's fatal fall, they suspected she was still holding on to a painful, deeply buried secret. Her drinking, they feared, would always be a problem until she was willing to confront her past.

They wanted to explore some more aggressive treatments, treatments that left Uncle Thad feeling cautious and unsettled. He wouldn't discuss them with me, only said that Mother had been a deeply depressed woman for a very long time and maybe it would take extraordinary measures to cure her once and for all. When I overheard him talking to the doctors about electricity and convulsions, I grew afraid that I had sent my mother away for good.

Uncle Thad also thought it was very important for Mother's well-being that I continue my education; my sitting around Grove Hill was not doing anyone any good. He said he had called a few old friends at Vanderbilt—people who had always been more than willing to relieve his brother of another sizable donation—and inquired about the possibility of my continuing my education there. Not long after that, I was awarded the Bezellia Grove Scholarship for study in American history. Uncle Thad couldn't help but laugh when he told me. Turned out, he said, that my father had finally found, thanks to cosmic fate or some sort of divine intervention, that young, bright academic who would surely see his family's history from his own generous perspective.

I made a few new friends, a nice girl from Atlanta and one from Charleston. Neither had ever heard of Dorothy Pitman or Betty Friedan, but both were willing to sign my petitions as long as they didn't have to dispose of any of their undergarments. In fact, Emily Louise Britain admitted that she desperately wanted to go to medical school. She had always dreamed of being a doctor like her father, but her mother was convinced that nursing would be a more suitable career for a young woman like herself. Patricia Davenport smiled and said that all sounded real exciting, but she preferred to marry a doctor and live in a big house on the Cooper River back home in Charleston.

Every once in a while, a wide-eyed fraternity boy would ask me if I had ever heard the song "Big City Girl," obviously hoping that I would be willing to meet him under some big old tree on campus and make him feel all right. I'd look kind of confused and vague and walk away, leaving him wondering what kind of pleasure he had missed. Most days, I kept to myself, and that was okay too. I guess, like Adelaide, I wasn't afraid of being on my own anymore, and before I knew it, life began to feel wonderfully predictable and normal, something I had always wanted.

Late one morning in early November, my grandmother telephoned the house. She said she had spent the past three days cleaning out my mother's room, and now she had all of her old knickknacks packed and ready to go. She asked me to send Nathaniel after them right away. She had looked at them for most of her life and didn't want them in her house one more day.

She said Elizabeth had called earlier in the week, demanding some kind of *god-damned* apology. She said her daughter was crazy if she thought she was going to apologize—for what? She hadn't done anything wrong. She was tired of her daughter's whining, and there was nothing more to talk about. She had her little girl's memories, the last bit of evidence that my mother was in fact a Morgan, stuffed in a box and waiting by the bedroom door. I told her I'd give Nathaniel the message. But by the time I hung up the telephone, I was feeling a desperate need, maybe more of a calling really, to find my way to the water.

Nathaniel pulled the car out of the garage for me. He wanted to know why I was heading out to the lake so late in the day. It was already after lunch, and the days were short this time of year. He thought it best that I wait till tomorrow. He thought it best that I let him go instead. He said he didn't feel comfortable with me driving on the interstate alone. He said if my mother were here, she would never allow it. I stood there with my coat over my arm and my hand resting on the kitchen door, reminding him that my mother was not here. He reluctantly pulled the keys from his front pants pocket and placed them in my hand.

"Be careful, Miss Bezellia. Call me as soon as you get there. I won't be leaving this house until I hear from you." Nathaniel followed me to the car and stood there while I started the engine and let it warm itself in the cold fall air, seemingly afraid to walk away and let me go on my own. I wasn't sure if he was scared of me driving on the interstate all by myself or of me heading straight into my grandmother's temper. Either way, I was ready to go.

"Nathaniel," I said, as I slipped the car into gear, suddenly feeling fearless behind the wheel of my mother's Cadillac, "I'll be okay. Don't forget, my name's Bezellia for a reason." I smiled and revved the engine louder.

Nathaniel shut the car door and took two steps back. "Now don't go pushing that gas pedal too hard. There's three hundred and forty-five horses under this hood, remember, and they'd love to take you for a wild ride," he cautioned, allowing a slight smile to cross his face.

I eased the car around the driveway and headed for the road, my heart beating faster with every passing mile. Not much more than an hour later, I pulled off the interstate onto Route 171. I rolled the car window down like I always did when I came to this stop, and even though it was fall and what leaves were left on the trees were golden and orange, I found the air here feeling oddly thick and stale. Everything else looked pretty much the same as it always had. The gas station on the far corner of the intersection still looked abandoned. And the old man dressed in his blue coveralls was still sitting in an old wooden chair and leaning against the building's dirty white wall. His triangle-shaped display of Quaker State motor oil still looked perfect; not a single can was missing.

The sun was lingering fairly high in the afternoon sky by the time I pulled into my grandparents' drive. Pop's old pickup was parked next to his John Deere, neither one looking like it had been moved in days. I pulled Mother's Cadillac alongside her father's truck. Surely my grandmother was standing watch in the kitchen window and would come running from the house any minute now with her hair falling loose behind her head. Surely supper was already waiting on the table.

But my grandparents' house looked dark, even lonely. The curtains were tucked shut, not a tiny sliver of light making its way through the windowpanes. Nobody was hurrying across the drive to greet me. I stepped closer to the house and heard muffled voices on the back porch. Nana and Pop, both of them bundled in heavy old sweaters, were there, sitting in their folding chairs. Their eyes were fixed on the water, which was still and glassy. The sun's soft reflection and a perfect mirrored image of the trees bordering the water rested on top of the lake's surface.

Neither one of my grandparents appeared surprised to see me. They didn't even bother taking their eyes off the water. Nana sat particularly still, almost as if she was frozen, her ratty chenille robe wrapped loosely over her sweater and her hair set in tight curls, held firmly against her head with a collection of bobby pins and old barrettes.

"Hello, Bezellia," she said, finally acknowledging my arrival.

"Hi there," I answered her cautiously, and then stood and waited for an explanation for their odd indifference. After a while, I knew I wasn't going to get one. "You two don't seem too surprised to see me," I added, begging for some sort of answer. "I figured you'd be expecting Nathaniel, not me."

"He called to tell us you was coming," my grandmother finally answered, still not taking her eyes off the water. "He was worried about you driving that big car of your mama's way out here. Would have appreciated it, dear, if you had given us a little notice."

"I didn't think I needed to ask permission to come and see you."

"Well, sweetie, company's company." My grandmother sat motionless in her folding chair, only pursing her lips and swatting at a slow-moving fly that had somehow managed to survive the first frost. Pop seemed too afraid to do any differently, so he just sat there too, staring at the lake and occasionally taking a puff on his Dutch Masters cigar. I pushed my way against their feet and stood directly in front of them both, resting my body against the black metal railing behind me.

"Is something bothering you, Nana? Are you mad at me for coming out here?"

"Why would I be mad at you, Bezellia? What have you done?"

"I haven't done anything. But it sure seems like you think I have."

My grandmother kept her eyes on the lake, and my grandfather just turned his head and looked away. I realized in that moment that Pop was no braver than my very own father.

"I guess sending my daughter off to some loony bin has me a bit bothered, if you must know the truth of it," she finally snipped as she sat firmly planted in her favorite folding chair.

"First of all, it's not a loony bin. It's a hospital. And she is doing much better. Thank you for asking."

"Oh, I know. Those crazy doctors called here. Wanted your grandfather and me to drive over there and talk to Elizabeth, said she was on the verge of some kind of breakthrough. Listen here, Bezellia, we went through hell with that girl when she was not much younger than you are now. Why do you think your grandfather has a bad heart? She wore him out. I can't get into her troubles no more. It'd damn near kill him, maybe me too."

I knelt down directly in front of my grandmother so she had no choice but to finally look at me. And even though my heart was racing, my voice sounded calm and insistent. "Why'd she leave, Nana?" I asked.

"Just let it be, Bezellia."

But I stayed very still and waited for a better answer. The sun had drifted quickly down toward the horizon, turning a bright, brilliant orange as it fell. Apparently the world was trying to tell me to proceed with caution.

"I just can't do that, Nana. I can't leave it be."

My grandmother shook her head and gripped the arms of her folding chair a little tighter, looking resigned at last to telling me something she felt certain I wouldn't want to hear. She kept her eyes focused on the water. I guess she figured that, if she searched hard and long enough, she would eventually find some kind of comfort out there. Then in a flat, distant tone, she began to share my mother's story, feeding it to me as if I was a little baby, one small bite at a time.

Apparently my mother was no more than sixteen when she fell "all crazy in love" with a boy who lived on the other side of Old Lebanon Dirt Road. His family didn't have much of anything, not hardly a pot to piss in, according to my grandmother.

"But that didn't seem to matter much to your mama back then. She just thought that boy hung the moon, even if his pockets were always empty.

"One night your mama and this boy done come into the kitchen and sat down and announced they were gonna have a baby." Nana stopped at this point and let out another long, steady sigh. "I told her no way in hell was my only daughter gonna have an illegitimate baby and ruin this family's good reputation.

"Turned out the boy wanted to marry her, try to make things

right. But his family said what they had done had been a sin. Said their boy had been led astray and that he could never see your mama again. They as much as called her a tramp." Even all these years later, my grandmother's voice was loud and offended.

"That boy was man enough to get her pregnant, but he wasn't man enough to stand up to his parents and do the right thing. He never called her again, and before long he left town to join the Army. Came back and everybody around here slapped him on the back and told him he was a great American. A couple weeks later, he up and married some poor white trash, and now it looks like their son is gonna be some famous country music singer. Isn't that something, Bezellia? His daddy gets my daughter pregnant, and then his son fools around with you and turns it into a hit song. Looks like you and your mama are just two peas in a pod after all."

My skin was hot to the touch, and my head was already crammed full of so many hateful thoughts I wanted to slap my grandmother's mouth just to make her hush. But I had come a long way, so had my mother, and we both needed to hear everything she had to say. So I just sat there and bit my tongue, bit it hard till it bled.

"I threw your mama in the car the day that boy enlisted and drove her over to the next county. There was a doctor there who had a reputation for taking care of girls who done been thinking with the wrong part of their body. And he did just that. He took care of your mama's little problem right there on his kitchen table. She put up a fight at first, but it was for her own good. I told her that was the end of that, and we weren't to ever talk about it again.

"Elizabeth never was the same. I'll admit that much. She was angry and mad at everything and everybody. Never once thanked me for making things right. She took off not six months later, leaving us nothing but a piece of paper taped to her bedroom door and a shoe box filled with a bunch of love letters from that good-for-nothing boy." Nana stopped talking for a minute. She quickly wiped a tear from her eye and crossed her arms against her chest.

"Lord, all I was ever trying to do was protect that girl's reputation. And look what you've gone and done. Locked her up in some mental institution. No telling what people are gonna think about us now."

The crickets started humming, their pitch picking up strength. The sound of my grandmother's voice had thankfully been swallowed in theirs. But I could hear my mother, loud and clear, screaming to keep her baby as they forced her onto that kitchen table and spread her legs apart. I needed the crickets to sing even louder. I needed to quiet that sound forever.

Nana finally tapped my thigh with the palm of her hand, signaling that she had shared all she intended to. Then she motioned for me to follow her into the house. On the floor, right outside my mother's bedroom door, was a large cardboard box. Her room was stripped bare. Every photo and keepsake was gone. Even the plaque with Jesus' picture on it, the one Mother had made in Vacation Bible School, was apparently now stuffed inside this box.

"Nana," I said, more like I was asking a question, desperately wanting to know why she had packed away her daughter's childhood.

"Time to let the past go, honey," she answered. And she picked up the box and carried it out to the Cadillac.

By the time I made my way back to the interstate, the old man in front of the gas station was gone. One single, ghostly light was left burning in the office, highlighting his display of motor oil. Suddenly I needed to see my mother. I needed her to know that she hadn't done anything wrong. She had loved a boy, that was all, a boy who probably didn't even know how to dance. There was nothing wrong with that, nothing at all. And now she just needed to come home.

Early the next morning, Uncle Thad called the hospital. The doctors were not very eager to release my mother, not even for a short visit home. They said her treatment was not going as well as expected. They needed more time. And Mrs. Grove, in their expert opinion, seemed very anxious about returning to Grove Hill. They said maybe we should instead consider a quick trip to the hospital one afternoon during regularly scheduled visiting hours. Our desire to have Mother home might be genuine, but it was not, in their expert opinion, in their patient's best interest.

Nothing about that sounded right to me or to Uncle Thad. Mother loved Grove Hill. And I knew, if given the opportunity, she would want to come home. Uncle Thad agreed and said that first thing in the morning he was driving over to Chattanooga and checking on Mother himself. He told me not to worry, but even his own voice sounded concerned.

The next morning Nathaniel hurriedly swept and cleaned every inch of the house. And Maizelle started fussing about the kitchen making chicken Kiev and tomato aspic, Mother's favorites. She would bake a lemon meringue pie before the end of the day, she promised.

Just three or four hours after Uncle Thad left Grove Hill, he called to say that he would be bringing Mother home immediately. He was packing her suitcase now, and they would be on the road by early afternoon. He said nothing more than that and then hung up the phone, his voice, firm and uncomfortably vague, resonating in my ear.

When Mother did arrive at Grove Hill, it was as if I was seeing her for the very first time. Her hair was pulled back neatly in a low ponytail, and her face was scrubbed clean. She was dressed in a pair of khaki pants, a white collared blouse, and a light blue cardigan sweater. She looked beautiful, at least so I thought, until I looked into her eyes. They were different. They were hollow and vacant, and she stared at me as if she had never seen me before.

I stepped toward her, wanting to welcome her home, to pull her into my arms and tell her that I understood now. But she inched closer to Uncle Thad, reaching for his hand, reminding me more of a child who has accidentally bumped into a stranger than my very own mother. Uncle Thad slowly guided her up the large marble steps. Mother stood on the porch for a moment, seeming a bit cautious or maybe confused. But Uncle Thad squeezed her hand a little tighter and led her back inside her home.

Uncle Thad stayed until dinner, and then he stayed some more, carefully watching over my mother's every move as if she was a little girl learning to walk. And in a way, she was. She did get better, slowly. She never drank again. She never spoke hatefully to Maizelle or Nathaniel. In fact, she didn't even seem to notice that the color of their skin was different from her own. She never called me Sister or forced Adelaide to knit. And yet sometimes I wished she had done those things, because the woman who came back to Grove Hill was timid and afraid. She was just not my mother.

LOCAL VIETNAM HERO COMES HOME
BLACK MARINE NOMINATED FOR BRONZE STAR

To Be Honored at Mt. Zion A.M.E. Church

Local black U.S. Marine Corps Private First Class Samuel Stephenson will arrive home in Nashville Thursday after being wounded while serving a tour of duty in Vietnam. Stephenson has been nominated for the Bronze Star for Valor, one of the military's highest recognitions of bravery on the battlefield, according to a U.S. Marine Corps spokesman at Camp Lejeune in North Carolina.

Stephenson, a graduate of Pearl High School, served in Vietnam outside Saigon. He had only been in Vietnam for three months when he demonstrated acts of heroism during a surprise attack by Vietcong forces just south of the Marine Corps base of Khe Sanh. According to official military reports, Stephenson, surrounded by enemy combatants, moved through a hail of gunfire to rally his unit's dazed infantrymen to redirect their fire on the advancing enemy.

Although wounded by an exploding grenade, Stephenson got to his feet and led a small counterattack force. Refusing medical treatment, he pressed the attack, killed several of the enemy, and reinforced his unit's defensive position. Stephenson's dauntless courage and heroism, according to the U.S. Marine Corps spokesman, inspired his fellow Marines to defeat a determined and numerically superior enemy force. Stephenson is being discharged early due to the injuries suffered in combat, for which he will be awarded the Purple Heart.

Stephenson is the son of Nathaniel and Celia Stephenson of

East Nashville. A service of thanksgiving will be held at Mt. Zion
A.M.E. Church at eleven o'clock on Saturday morning. A reception will follow in the church's fellowship hall.

The Nashville Register
early edition
DECEMBER 18, 1970

chapter fifteen

$\mathcal{S}$amuel was coming home. That's what the newspaper said, that's what Nathaniel said, but somehow I still couldn't believe it. And although Christmas was just a few days away, I honestly didn't spend one minute thinking about presents or lighted trees or shepherds standing watch by a manger in an old dilapidated stable outside of a two-bit town in the middle of a desert. Not this year. All I could think about was Samuel Stephenson, the beautiful boy who spoke my name with more tenderness than even Shakespeare or the Virgin Mary could have imagined.

We were all counting the days till he came home, even Mother, though I'm not sure she really remembered who Samuel was. She said she did, but I think she just wanted to share in the excitement. There were a lot of things Mother didn't remember anymore. Apparently when they send a bolt of lightning through your body one too many times, it can knock part of your memory right out of your head. But she was getting better, at least that's what Maizelle said. She said she could see it in her eyes. And even though there were brief moments when I had begun to recognize the mother I used to know, I wasn't quite so sure.

Adelaide had made a chain out of construction paper, the kind it seems we all learned to make in kindergarten as soon as the teacher trusted us with a pair of scissors and a jar of paste. She hung it all around the kitchen so Mother, Maizelle, and I could see with our very own eyes exactly how many days it would be until Samuel was home safe and sound. That chain seemed long enough to wrap around the world when she first made it. Now there were just a few pieces of paper left, dangling above the kitchen sink.

Nathaniel and his wife were planning a special prayer service and a big party afterward in the fellowship hall underneath the church's sanctuary. Samuel was a hero, and he deserved a hero's welcome, they said. They mailed handwritten invitations to everybody they knew, including us. But Nathaniel said that, before even one piece of cake was cut, we were all getting down on our knees and thanking the good Lord for bringing his son back in one piece. There were too many parents out there, he said, whose boys had come home in boxes. He didn't know why that had to be. He'd just add it to a very long list of things he figured he'd never fully understand until he stood at God's feet. So only after the good Lord was thanked and praised would we head downstairs for some of the best barbecue in all of Nashville.

Nathaniel could not stop smiling. Just talking about his son coming home left him trembling with excitement. He walked into the kitchen and looked up at Adelaide's paper chain and nearly shouted, "Three more days! Praise the Lord, three more days!" Then he headed into the dining room looking for Mother's tea service. Polishing the silver might just calm him down a bit, he thought. Maizelle said she thought it might take a shot of whiskey and then turned around and walked out of the room, laughing to herself.

The front doorbell rang shortly before noon. Adelaide, Mother, and I had all gathered in the den. Adelaide was sitting on the floor writing Christmas cards to a few of her friends. She had made them herself, using the rest of her construction paper and pieces of silver and gold foil left over from some long-forgotten school project.

Mother was relaxed on the sofa, knitting Samuel a sweater. Not long after she came home from the hospital, she'd picked up a pair of Adelaide's knitting needles, and she hadn't put them down since. I had never seen my mother knit, but she said she used to do all sorts of handiwork when she was a little girl.

She chose a deep red yarn for the body of the sweater and then placed a bright green Christmas tree, perfectly trimmed with shiny blue ornaments and topped with a yellow star, right in the middle. And even though I couldn't picture this sweater on a young military hero, I looked at my mother and reassured her that Samuel would love it.

Uncle Thad came in from the back and knelt down by the fire just before the bell rang. He had three logs tucked under his left arm and snowflakes stuck gently to the top of his head. He carefully stoked the fire, making room for fresh wood but careful not to throw sparks onto the rug. It had started snowing not long after breakfast, just enough to lightly cover the ground, just enough to make everyone want to sip hot chocolate and listen to Adelaide's collection of rock 'n' roll holiday albums on Father's old record player.

"Lord have mercy, if you don't look like a Christmas card yourself," Maizelle said as she walked to the front door. But when she saw a young, dark-skinned girl standing on the porch, she dropped to her knees and cried out loud. Nathaniel came running from the back of the house. He let out a scream from somewhere so deep within his belly that I was afraid his insides might come spilling right out of his mouth. The sound washed through my body, leaving me numb and scared, and for a brief moment I found myself hiding behind my mother. Sometimes, even now as an old woman when I dream about Samuel, when we're wrapped in each other's arms underneath the cherrybark oaks, I wake to the sound of that tortured cry. The young girl rushed into the house, not waiting for anyone to formally invite her in.

"Daddy, no, it's not what you think!" she cried. "It's not what you think. Samuel's fine. Samuel's here. He's home. He got here this morning, not long after you left. He wanted to surprise everybody. Mama told me to come and get you. Everybody's at the house now waiting for you. Daddy, stop crying," she pleaded softly, realizing that her sudden appearance had left her father thinking that his only son was dead and gone.

And like a set of dominoes tipping forward, we all seemed to fall to the ground, so overwhelmed with relief and joy that even the weight of our own bodies was too much to bear. Mother, in a fit of unexplainable tears, wrapped her arms first around Nathaniel and then Maizelle. And once we'd caught our breath, Adelaide and I started screaming with excitement. Adelaide said she just couldn't believe it because there were still two paper loops hanging over the kitchen sink. I'm really not sure how long we stood there. Time seemed to have no meaning that day. Finally my uncle mouthed something to me that I couldn't quite understand. He motioned for me to come closer and then spoke quietly in my ear.

"Bezellia, sweetie," he said, "go get Nathaniel's coat and hat. We need to drive those two on home. Neither Nathaniel nor his daughter is fit to be behind the wheel of a car right now. They're just too overwhelmed with emotion to think straight, let alone drive across town. I'm not sure how that girl got here without winding up in a ditch. The roads are already getting a little slick. I'll drive Nathaniel's truck, and then you follow in mine, just put some good snow tires on it the other day."

But I stood there, like a schoolgirl playing freeze tag and waiting for her turn to run. Shocked maybe by the excitement, at least that's what I think Maizelle would have said. My uncle kept talking to me. I guess repeating the same instructions until I finally nodded and stumbled down the hall, feeling my way with my hands. My eyes were clouded with tears, but I found the closet by the back door and reached for the brass knob in front of me. When I touched Nathaniel's hat, the soft, worn felt between my hands, my body started shaking uncontrollably. Nathaniel was wearing this hat the day he introduced me to Samuel. He was smiling so big, so proud of his boy. Now Samuel was finally home. That's what his sister had said. She walked right up to my front door and said it. But I was almost afraid to believe it was true. I wondered if Nathaniel felt the same way.

Uncle Thad drove directly in front of me, checking his rearview mirror every second or two, careful to keep me close in his sight. I could see Nathaniel and his daughter on the seat next to Uncle Thad. I could tell the two of them were laughing and crying just by the way their heads kept bobbing up and down. I had never been on the other side of the river. Mother used to say there was nothing over there worth seeing. "That's where the colored live, Sister. You cross that river and you just might get shot." That's what she used to say.

The houses were smaller and closer together, but the streets seemed tidy and well kept. Even under the gray December sky, the neighborhoods, all decorated for the holidays, looked welcoming and friendly. Small children bundled in heavy coats were walking on the sidewalks with their mothers, hand in hand. No one was carrying a gun. No one was lying drunk on the side of the road. I wondered if Mother had ever been over here or if she had just made all of that up.

Nathaniel's house was made of stone and topped with a black-shingled roof. A large porch wrapped around the front, just like ours. It was bigger than the other houses on the block, and his yard was planted with grand, aged boxwoods and scores of hydrangeas looking dormant and twiggy in the winter cold. A lush pine wreath was tied to the front door, and brightly colored lights tacked along the roof-line were blinking on and off again, seeming to welcome everyone who walked by. And right in the middle of the yard stood a bare old oak tree with a huge yellow ribbon tied around its trunk. It looked as though it had grown weary waiting for Samuel's return.

Cars were already parked along both sides of the street as far as I could see. Men in work clothes and dark suits and women in woolen coats and colorful hats had filled the yard, patiently waiting their turn to get inside the house and wrap their arms around their hometown hero. In a strange way, it reminded me a little of my father's dying and all the people who had come to pay their respects, except this time everyone truly cared.

Nathaniel jumped out of the car and rushed to the low gate that surrounded his property. He fumbled with the lock, and when the gate finally swung forward, he almost fell onto the grass. A large man grabbed him by the elbow and led him into the house. His daughter stumbled behind them. Every few steps somebody would grab her and give her a big hug and then set her free again. And just as soon as she'd regain her balance, someone else would scoop her up in his arms and hug her so tight it looked as if her tiny little back might snap in two just like one of Maizelle's green beans.

By now, everyone standing out in the front yard had turned around and was looking at Uncle Thad and me. No one readily spoke or invited us in, and I realized I felt as out of place in this world as Samuel must have felt in mine. Uncle Thad offered a few quick hellos and then gestured for me to get in the car. But again, I just stood there, seemingly frozen in place. I desperately needed to see Samuel. I needed to tell him that I'd got his letters. I needed to tell him that I'd read each one at least a hundred times. I needed to tell him that I still loved him. But I wasn't welcome here. I could see that.

Uncle Thad said this was a very emotional day for this family, and we needed to give them some time alone. Maybe so. Maybe I'd have a chance to talk to Samuel later. We didn't see Nathaniel again that week. His daughter called the house and said that her mother and father surely appreciated the large bouquet of flowers Mother had had the florist deliver as well as the country-baked ham. They had been eating on it for two days now. They sure looked forward to see-ing us at the church on Saturday, and she promised that her daddy would be in touch as soon as he could.

Maizelle visited the family two or three times, always carrying a chicken noodle casserole with her. She said Samuel's mama didn't need to be worrying about cooking any meals right now. She just needed to be loving on her baby boy. Maizelle always came back from the Stephensons' looking happy and kind of mad all at the same time—happy to see Samuel again and mad that he had been sent to that jungle in the first place. She said some days she felt like throwing a brick right through the president's big white house. Samuel had nearly given his life, she said, for a country that probably wasn't going to treat him any better now that he was home. "Not right. Just not right."

I asked her a thousand questions about Samuel every time she came back from a visit. And she patiently answered them all, although she'd look at me with one eye slightly closed and her head tilted sharply to the right. "Samuel coming home hasn't changed anything, sweetie. You remember that." But she was wrong. It had changed everything.

Late Friday afternoon, Nathaniel called the house. Mother spoke to him from the telephone in the kitchen. I could tell she was trying not to cry, but her voice quickly grew weak and teary. I didn't think too much of it really. Mother found more and more to cry about these days—a pretty sunset, a perfect rose, even one of Maizelle's fresh, hot pound cakes could reduce my mother to tears. She wiped her eyes with the back of her hand and lowered her body into one of the kitchen chairs, the one with the uneven legs, and gently started rocking back and forth.

Nathaniel and his wife wanted the Groves to sit with his family at the church service tomorrow. Mother told him she didn't deserve such an honor but promised we would all be there on time. And she'd be real happy to bring another ham if he thought they might need it. Nathaniel told her that their stomachs were good and full for now, but he would see her at the church tomorrow morning.

"Can you believe that?" Mother said as she handed me the

receiver. "Nathaniel wants us to sit with his family." She just sat there and smiled, big tears once again welling in the corners of her eyes. She was so pleased to be considered part of Nathaniel's family. I couldn't help but wonder if she could remember the way her daughter used to admire Nathaniel's son when he came to work at Grove Hill.

The next morning, precisely ten minutes before eleven, the Grove family walked into the sanctuary of Mt. Zion A.M.E. Church and took our seats on an old, hard wooden pew right behind Nathaniel and his wife. A crisp white bow was tied on its end, indicating that this space was reserved for the Stephensons' family. The church was packed with people waiting to welcome Samuel home, except everyone else was black. I knew they were looking at us. I could feel their stares falling across my back. But surely, I told myself, countless men and women had sat on this very same pew—praising God, begging for some needed strength and courage. So now I rubbed my hand against the wood, trying to absorb the gifts of the generations who had rested here before me, who might have even found my presence in their church strange and awkward too.

Adelaide snuggled up next to me, and I felt her slip her hand inside mine. I patted her arm and smiled, reassuring her we were right where we needed to be. And when I looked up, Samuel was standing at the front of the church. He was dressed in a dark Marine Corps uniform. He was holding a pure white hat with a short, shiny black bill firmly in his hands. He looked so handsome, so strong and brave and yet so peaceful and calm. His jaw was clenched tight at first, as if he was trying to maintain a Marine's perfect stance, but then I saw a glimpse, a hint really, of that beautiful smile starting to appear across his face. I whispered his name, but he couldn't hear me. Mother looked at me and gently put her finger to her lips.

Samuel sat down in a large but simple wooden chair. The preacher stepped in front of him and took his position behind the pulpit. He outstretched his arms and then announced that we had all come here today to welcome Samuel Stephenson home. Every man and woman in the church cried out almost simultaneously, chanting "Amen" and lifting their hands to the Lord as if they were offering up a gift of some kind. The minister repeated himself again and again, and then he paused for a moment and lowered his head.

"It wasn't the homecoming we had planned," he said softly. "It wasn't the homecoming his mama and daddy had been waiting for. It wasn't the homecoming they had dreamed about." His voice was growing louder and stronger and his arms were open and inviting.

"No. It is a thousand times better. Only God could imagine a homecoming like this!" And the church exploded with excitement—people praising God, thanking God—no one seemed afraid to express what was on his heart. "This special child of God is home at last, and his journey has just begun. He will not be defined by the evil he has seen. His heart will not be hardened. No. Not this child of God. He will be a better man because of it. He will be a better American because of it. He will be a better Christian because of it."

Then the minister grabbed the pulpit with both hands, as if his own emotions might carry him away if he didn't hold on tight. "These are not tears of sadness we are crying today. No. These are tears of joy, tears of happiness, tears of thanksgiving.

"And while we are grateful that Samuel is here with us, we must take a moment to pray for all the young men, men just like Samuel, who will not be coming home to their mothers and fathers, to their sisters and brothers. Have mercy, Lord. Have mercy."

Again, voices called out, echoing the words of the pastor. And now both men and women were crying out loud. Little girls, teenage girls, girls who looked about my age, girls I imagined might have loved Samuel like I had were crying out loud. Nathaniel and his wife held on to each other, their backs heaving. Samuel would look down at his parents and smile, always careful to reassure them that he was really and truly here.

The minister lifted his arms one last time toward the ceiling, and the choir started to sing. Their bodies swayed back and forth with the rhythm of the music, and before long everyone in the church was following their lead, standing and clapping their hands. Even my mother sang along. Her face was so full of emotion. And for a moment, everyone's voice blended together as if each of us was offering the others something we really didn't know we had. And by the time the last note had been sung, we all were exhausted from the effort. The choir sang one final amen, and the minister opened his arms as if to embrace us all. He announced that it was time at last to move this wonderful celebration downstairs.

Samuel and his parents left the sanctuary together, the three of them holding hands with the rest of the Stephenson family and the minister following close behind. And whether everyone else was eager to fill his aching stomach or to personally welcome Samuel home, I'm not really sure. But every single body in that church stood and headed in one fluid motion toward the stairs, making it almost impossible for the Groves, feeling a bit hesitant and out of place, to exit our pew and join the throng. A few men shook Uncle Thad's hand, and Mother smiled and spoke to every woman who stopped to welcome her to Mt. Zion A.M.E. Church. And when the sanctuary was finally empty, we took our places at the end of the line.

It was probably an hour before I could even see Samuel standing a few feet ahead of me. He spent so much time with everyone that for a while I thought it might be midnight before I got close enough to touch his hand. His smile was so big and his laugh was so wonderfully tender that, as I got closer, I only hoped he would have something left for me.

Mother spoke to Nathaniel's wife first and then to Nathaniel. She hugged him tightly around the neck and whispered something in his ear. He smiled and gently patted her shoulder. Then she moved forward one step and was standing right in front of Samuel. Samuel's smile faded just a bit, but his eyes were still warm and open. When Mother reached out to shake his hand, you could see his surprise. They exchanged a few words. They both smiled, and then Mother moved on.

I have no memory of what I said to Samuel's mother or to Nathaniel. All I really remember is standing in front of this boy who seemed so familiar and so distant all at the same time. He was dressed more like a G.I. Joe doll than the boy I used to know, who wore old, faded blue jeans and a ball cap on his head, the same boy who thought my name sounded funny, the same boy who fell on top of me and loved me the night my father died. I wanted to talk to him like I used to when we sat by Uncle Thad's swimming pool, dangling our feet in the water, sharing everything and nothing.

"Bezellia," Samuel said, and I closed my eyes for a moment and just let the sound of his voice fill my head. "Hey, how've you been?" he continued, warmly but cautiously.

"Pretty good," I said, and then I paused for a minute. "I sure did miss you," I said faintly, so not even Nathaniel could hear.

Samuel just shook his head. "Wrote you a bunch of letters."

"I know. I read them all . . . at least a hundred times." Samuel looked confused, and his smile began to fade away.

"I never heard from you."

"That's not true. I did write, not long after you left. Maizelle even gave me your address. But when I didn't hear from you, I thought . . ." My voice fell silent. Samuel didn't understand what I was saying, and I didn't know how to explain it to him. But I knew in that moment, sitting someplace on the other side of the world, Samuel Stephenson had already convinced himself that I didn't love him.

He just shook his head again. "Heard a great song about you too. Glad you've been feeling all right."

"It's just a song. He just made all that up."

"Doesn't really matter," he said and then seemed to be almost searching for the next person in line, someone else who would hug him and tell him how wonderful it was that he was home.

Nathaniel looked at us both as if he didn't approve of our lingering conversation. And before I could think of anything more to say, he leaned between us and announced that he needed to borrow his son for a minute. He wanted him to give the blessing, and there were a lot of hungry people waiting to hear him speak. As the two of them walked away, I felt like that little girl standing on the porch at Grove Hill, knowing then as I did now that Nathaniel didn't want us to exchange much more than a few nice words. Samuel looked at me as if to thank me for coming and then walked off with his father, maybe even feeling relieved that he had been whisked away. And while everyone bowed their heads and praised Jesus one more time, I snuck out the door and crawled into the backseat of my mother's Cadillac.

This was certainly not the homecoming I had imagined. In my dreams, Samuel was going to hug me and kiss me and not care who was looking. He was going to forgive me for not writing. He was going to tell me that he had missed me, that he still loved me. But that was just a dream, I guess. I'm not sure how long I was there in the backseat of that car or how hard I cried, but I woke to the sound of my mother tapping on the window glass.

"Bezellia, we've been looking for you. Didn't know where you'd gone off to. Did you get something to eat?" she asked as she opened the door and slid onto the front seat. "Looks like you've been crying. Why are you sad? We're supposed to be celebrating. Nathaniel's son has finally come home. I didn't remember him having a son that age. Sure seems like such a nice young man."

"I just got *overwrought*, I guess, isn't that what Maizelle would call it? But do you think we could go home? I really want to go home."

"Sure. I'll go find your sister and Uncle Thad. I last saw them waiting in line for a piece of that chocolate cake. You want me to bring you a piece? It sure looked good," she said, and then she stepped out of the car and disappeared back inside the church, fortunately not seeming to understand why I was hiding in the back of her car.

When we got back to Grove Hill, the sky had turned a dark, wet gray. I ran to my room and immediately fell on my knees. I couldn't really see what I was doing, but through the tears I reached under the bed and grabbed an old shoe box. I threw the lid aside and reached for the bundle of papers, the letters Samuel had written, the only proof that he had in fact loved me. I left the empty box on the floor and headed back downstairs.

Mother was on her way to bed; she said the day had exhausted her. She sure hoped I felt better in the morning. Maybe I was coming down with something. "I wouldn't know what to do if you got sick. Is Maizelle here?" she asked, already looking nervous at the thought of caring for a sick child. I reassured her that I was fine and that she should go on and get some rest. I could hear Adelaide on the phone in her room, telling Lucy all about the service and the whole pig roasting on a spit behind the church.

I flew down the back stairs, almost tripping on my own two feet, and then out the kitchen door, kicking my high heels off as I stepped off the concrete porch. I ran barefoot toward the creek. I couldn't even feel the freezing earth beneath me. By the time I got there, a light snow was starting to fall again from the sky. I watched for a moment as the water moved over the rocks, and then I dropped the letters into the current. I could hear Samuel calling me a princess as the papers floated on top of the water and drifted out of my sight.

chapter sixteen

*S*amuel was just on the other side of the river, but he felt a million miles away. We never saw each other. We never spoke. And Nathaniel no longer talked about his son, the Vietnam hero. I guess he was afraid that talking about Samuel could lead to something more dangerous than what he'd found in that jungle.

Maizelle said that Samuel was already back in school, even hoping to return to Morehouse in the fall. He thought it best to stick close to home for a while, though. He was a good boy, she said. He knew his parents needed some time with him before he up and left again. I just nodded like I knew I should, as if all of that made perfect sense to me. And then I went on pretending that everything else in my life was fine. And in some ways, I guess it was.

By early spring, Mother had begun to venture out into her garden. She still knitted and read her Bible most every day, but usually around four in the afternoon she would put on her wide-brimmed hat and spend some time among her flowers. Sometimes I think she just stood in the middle of her garden, not really sure what to do but enjoying the beauty of everything growing around her.

She even planted a few tomatoes, and she babied those vines until they started producing fruit ripe enough to pick. When she picked the first one, she seemed almost afraid to eat something that looked so perfect. But then Maizelle took it from her hand, sliced it, salted it, and put it back in front of Mother. When she ate it, she said it was the best thing she had ever put in her mouth.

Uncle Thad came over most evenings just as the sun started to drop toward the treetops. He helped Mother with the last of the weeding and the watering. Sometimes the two of them would linger in that garden until well after dark. A couple of times I even caught them running around catching lightning bugs between their hands. Maizelle thought they had both lost their minds. Maybe they had, but Mother seemed to find an awful lot of comfort in Uncle Thad's presence. And Uncle Thad seemed to enjoy having someone to care for now that Cornelia spent most of her time in Boston, working as diligently on another graduate degree as on her relationship with a Harvard doctor whose family tree was rooted so deep that Cornelia herself said it almost reached the center of the earth.

Maizelle didn't really leave Grove Hill much anymore. She said her nieces and nephews had all moved out of town by now, and there wasn't much left for her on the other side of the river. She guessed she felt more at home here than anywhere else, but I couldn't help but wonder if she missed the life she had all but given up to tend to a family that apparently had a hard time caring for itself.

She spent a lot of time on the front porch, stringing beans, mending clothes, or whatever else she considered important. And even though her hands were always busy, her body was now slow and deliberate. Sometimes she sat there for a couple of hours simply pulling the husks off a single bag of corn. And sometimes I'd find her sound asleep with an old cardboard fan from some funeral home resting in her lap. It made Mother very nervous when she found Maizelle sleeping like that. I think she was already growing afraid of living in this world without Maizelle by her side.

A couple of times I dreamed that Maizelle had passed. I saw myself sitting by her bed telling her stories about heaven that she had first told me when I was a little girl. I'd wake up crying and dripping in a cold sweat. Maizelle said when you dream about something three times, then it comes true. So some nights I tried to stay awake, desperately attempting to avoid a dream of any kind.

Maizelle had always promised me that Adelaide would grow out of her awkward ways, and now it seemed she had. She was getting ready to join Miss Clements and a small group of girls traveling to Rome to admire Italian art. Of course, when she asked Mother for permission to go, Mother simply looked at me for an answer. I told them both it was a wonderful, life-altering opportunity for Adelaide and she surely shouldn't miss it.

And even though I wanted the best for my little sister, secretly, honestly, I was mad that she was going and I was not. I was mad that somehow, without my even knowing it, my mother had become my child. The only time I escaped Grove Hill much anymore was in my stories. I'd probably written a hundred of them by now, all of them stuffed in a shoe box and hidden under my bed. And that's where I figured my dreams were going to stay, neatly tucked out of sight.

At least on paper, I had traveled the world and found true love on top of the Eiffel Tower and standing in the shadows of the Egyptian pyramids. I guess, in the end, Nathaniel's mother had been right. In a story, you can be anybody you want to be, even if it's just a girl who wants to be loved right. I made Adelaide promise to send me a postcard every day. I told her to memorize every detail. My next story would be set in a small village just outside of Rome. Of course, I never thought that my sister, the one who used to stand on the front steps with a grape-jelly biscuit in her hand, would be the one to take me there.

And just when life seemed to be feeling a little bit normal, my grandmother called the house. She had not telephoned since Mother was in the hospital, since before I had driven out there to pick up the memorabilia from my mother's childhood room. She had told me then she was done worrying about her girl, and apparently she'd meant it. Now, she was only calling for a favor.

"You want to talk to your daughter, Nana? I'm sure she'd love to hear from you."

"Don't really have the time to chat right now, Bezellia. I called for a reason, not to sit here and talk up a blue streak. I need to get Nathaniel's phone number from you. I've done torn the house apart looking for it, but figured Elizabeth would have it for sure."

"Why do you want Nathaniel's number?"

"I didn't know I needed to explain my business to you, dear. But apparently that's what it's gonna take to get that number from you. I'm trying to get ahold of that boy of his before he heads this way."

"Samuel?" Just hearing myself say his name left me feeling excited and sick, like a thousand butterflies were swarming in my stomach. My heart started to race, and the palms of my hands grew hot and sweaty.

"He's only got one boy, don't he? You got his number, Bezellia, or not? I really ain't got all day to sit here on this damn telephone."

"Why do you want to talk to Samuel?"

"Lord, child, if you must know he's fixing that damn dock. Thing is about to float right out into the lake, and your grandfather ain't strong enough to do it himself. But I need Samuel to stop on his way up here and get a couple of gallons of gasoline for the tractor. Your grandfather wants him to mow the yard. You got that number, Bezellia, or not?"

Mother had written it in pencil on the wall by the telephone not long after coming back from the hospital. Nathaniel had told her to call him night or day if she needed anything. Just knowing the number was there by the phone helped her sleep at night, she said. But I didn't need to look at those old pencil markings. I knew it by heart.

I gave my grandmother the number and then rushed into the kitchen and told Mother and Maizelle I was meeting some old friends over at the shopping center. I told them I didn't know when I'd be home. We might even stay for dinner and a movie. All I knew was that Samuel was leaving for Atlanta in a few weeks, and if I didn't get to that lake, I might not ever see him again. I grabbed my mother's keys from the nail where they were left hanging by the back door and ran to the garage without waiting for Mother or Maizelle to think of anything to say to stop me.

As I drove toward the lake, I realized somewhere deep inside that I had no idea what I was doing, but I couldn't turn back, not now. Something kept propelling me forward. When I pulled up to Route 171, I looked for the old man in his blue coveralls keeping watch over his collection of Quaker State motor oil. But he wasn't there. The building was empty, and the cans of motor oil were gone. I sat at the stop sign for a moment trying to make sense of his absence, wondering if I'd made a wrong turn. My window was down, and the air seemed particularly still and quiet. It was as if even the cows had disappeared. I finally turned left and headed toward the lake, still not really knowing what I was going to do when I got there.

Maybe I was feeling a little hungry or maybe I was stalling, still trying to come up with a plan, but just before turning onto the gravel road that led to my grandparents' house, I pulled in front of the little corner store where Pop came early in the mornings to buy his minnows for the day's fishing. It was an old wood-frame building that looked as though it might collapse if you sneezed real hard. Faded lettering above the front door read WATKINS BAIT AND TACKLE.

There were some high school boys standing in front of the concrete tank that held the fresh bait. They were drinking RC colas and talking about fishing and football. Every once in a while the biggest one, with sandy brown hair, would pick up the net hanging outside the tank and run it through the water. He'd lift the minnows into the air, and just when you imagined those poor little fish, flopping about in front of their captor were about to die, he would drop the net back into the water, giving them another chance to escape.

The boys stopped talking and stared real hard as I walked past them and opened the screen door before stepping inside to get a cold drink. The man behind the counter said I looked familiar and asked where I was headed. I reminded him that I was the Morgans' granddaughter and was just here for a short visit. He said he'd heard my mama wasn't doing well. Said he knew her when she was just a little girl and hated to hear that she had done gone and lost her mind. Spending time in the state hospital was no picnic, he knew that for sure, seeing how his own mama had been there a few years back.

"For some reason always thought your little sister was the one that was kind of special that way. Wasn't she the one that carried that baby doll around with her all the time, remember that? What she's up to these days anyway?"

I reassured him that my mother was doing much better and that Adelaide was actually vacationing in Italy with some friends from school. "Hmm," he said, as if I was telling some kind of tall tale to disguise my family's misfortune, "vacationing in Italy" being nothing more than a big-city, fancy way of lying about another *tragic event.*

I grabbed a bottle of Dr Pepper from the icebox in the back of the store and a bag of potato chips and took them to the counter to pay. I thanked the man for his concern and then stepped back outside, the bright sunlight blinding me for a moment. But even with my hand shielding my eyes, I could see the boys were still there. I could hear them whispering as if they were telling a joke meant only for them. And as I stepped toward the Cadillac, I heard one of them humming the tune of "Big City Girl." I turned my head and shot them all a scathing stare. But the three of them just laughed and took another sip of their RC colas. The big one licked his lips.

"Stick your tongue back in your mouth. You wouldn't even know what to do under that tree if you were ever lucky enough to get there," I shouted at him. And then I jumped behind the steering wheel of my mother's car and pushed the gas pedal to the floor, leaving the boys choking in a cloud of dust and me feeling more determined than ever to see Samuel Stephenson.

But I couldn't drive to my grandparents' house and admit that I had come to see the black boy working on the dock. And neither Nana nor Pop would believe for a minute that I had come to see them. So I slowed the car down, making certain not to stir any dust in the road and reveal my position. I coasted a few hundred yards past the final turn to the house and then pulled the Cadillac off the road and into a field dotted with nothing but a couple of cows and some Queen Anne's lace.

Perched on the hood of the car, I could see Nathaniel's old blue truck sitting in my grandparents' driveway. I sat there for what seemed like hours, making necklaces out of dandelions and drinking my Dr Pepper. And when I had to pee, I jumped off the hood and squatted low in the field, leaving my mark like a dog declaring his territory. I picked a bouquet of Queen Anne's lace, crawled back on top of the car, and counted the clouds floating across the sky.

Finally, just as the sky cleared and left me nothing to look at, the sound of my grandfather's John Deere tractor hummed in the distance, consuming the quiet of the late afternoon. I knew Samuel's work was almost done for the day, and he'd be heading home soon. I slipped off the top of the Cadillac and walked back to the small private road that led to my grandparents' drive. I had thought all afternoon about what I would say to Samuel when he saw me out here in the middle of nowhere, waiting for him. But now I couldn't remember anything that made any sense. I waited some more, and just as I was growing afraid that Samuel would never finish mowing that yard, the tractor grew silent.

I figured by now my grandmother was handing Samuel his pay for the day's work. She may have even offered him a cold Coca-Cola and a piece of buttered corn bread. He'd surely smile and say thank you and then promptly get in his truck and head on home. And as if

I was choreographing the scene myself, I saw his blue truck ease its way toward me.

I walked into the middle of the road, and as Samuel got closer I could see that his eyes were growing wide with surprise. He just stared at me, seemingly trying to make sense of my being there. And again I found myself wondering, as I had so many times during the afternoon, if I had made a mistake coming all the way out here. But then he smiled, gently at first, and the smile grew slowly until it stretched clear across his face. He slowed the truck and stopped a few feet in front of me. I walked around to the side, yanked the door open, and climbed onto the seat next to him. And without saying more than a few words, I directed him back down the road to the sandy beach that Ruddy had introduced me to some years ago now.

"A beach," Samuel said in surprise. "Never would have thought of putting a beach out here on the lake."

"Crazy, huh?"

"Yeah. Maybe not as crazy as seeing you here today." And then Samuel looked at me, obviously searching for some kind of explanation. I opened the door and motioned for him to join me on the sand.

"Yeah. That's pretty crazy too," I admitted. "Maizelle told me you were leaving for Atlanta soon. I don't know. I just never had much of a chance to talk to you. I just wanted to know . . ." I hesitated, hoping that Samuel would somehow reassure me, that he would let me know he was glad to see me. But he didn't. And just when I thought he might not say anything, he turned and looked out toward the water.

"I've missed you too," he said. Just hearing those few words left me feeling relaxed and reassured that I had done the right thing.

"You know, nothing has ever turned out the way I thought it would," I began. "And I don't know why I should expect it to now. But I'm tired of trying to convince myself that I don't love you,

Samuel. I just don't think that's ever going to be possible. And I don't care what anybody thinks." Samuel took my hand in his and held it so carefully, almost as if he was afraid it would break.

"But you do care, Bezellia. Why else would you have snuck all the way out here if you didn't care? You do care. I care. Everybody's going to care." And then he kissed me on the cheek and smiled. "Doesn't mean I don't love you."

Before I could make sense of anything Samuel had just said, I heard the sound of twigs snapping behind us. At first I didn't think much of it; maybe it was just a deer passing by. But the sound grew louder and more persistent, and I turned around to find the three boys from the corner market standing about fifty feet behind us.

"Well, ain't this cute. A little vanilla and chocolate right here in front of us," said the large boy with the sandy brown hair, the one the other two called Ritchie. "You think the two of them know this is a family beach?" he asked, and then he started grinning.

His buddies shook their heads as if to tell us we should have known better than to come here. Samuel didn't say a word, but he stood up and pulled me behind him, seemingly unafraid of the three boys moving toward us.

"Listen, boy, I don't think you ought to be touching that girl like that. Might get you into some awful trouble, and I sure would hate to see anything happen to you way out here," Ritchie said. But Samuel didn't flinch, and I could see the muscles in his entire body tighten.

"You *boys* do know that there's a war going on right now, don't ya? I just got back from there. Served in the United States Marine Corps. And even though it's clear you three don't have what it takes to be a Marine, I think you need to address me with a little more respect. Sure would hate to have to teach you a lesson . . . way out here."

"No nigger talks to me like that," Ritchie said and moved directly in front of us, his two buddies following close behind him.

Samuel pushed me out of the way, and I fell onto the sand. Ritchie raised his right arm and swung at Samuel. But Samuel stepped to the side, missing his blow, and just as quickly pulled his own arm back and hit the boy directly in the stomach, landing him flat on his butt. With their friend on the ground, the other two jumped on Samuel, punching and swinging. So many arms were flying in the air I couldn't tell who was hitting and who was getting hit.

Ritchie climbed to his feet and scrambled to reach a branch left lying on the beach. I saw him raise the branch above his head and aim for Samuel's back. And somewhere in that moment, I found a rock. I don't even remember how it got there. Maybe somehow Maizelle had shown me where it was, but I saw it hurtle threw the air and strike that boy's head. I saw him fall, and for minute I wondered if I had killed him. For a minute, I wished I had.

One of the other boys jumped off Samuel and came toward me.

"Looks like you need to be taught a lesson too," he said, and he reached for my shirt and tore it open, exposing my chest. He pushed me down on the sand and climbed on top of me. I was screaming and scratching, but all I could see was Ritchie, who had made his way to his feet and was now standing over Samuel with the branch raised above his head, this time striking Samuel across the back. Samuel fell still, blood from his forehead coloring the white sand red. I screamed even louder, begging for help, as the other two boys came toward me. I could smell their stinky, sweaty skin on top of me. And as I felt my pants being tugged down my legs, I heard a shotgun being pumped and loaded, and then the sound of my grandmother's voice.

"I sure would hate to shoot you boys, seeing how I've known all three of you since you were in diapers. But if you don't get off my granddaughter, I'm not going to have much of a choice, as far as I can tell." Thank God, there she was, my grandmother, standing on the edge of the sandy beach in her ratty old chenille bathrobe, her hair pinned in curls against her head, and a twelve-gauge shotgun resting on her shoulder.

The three boys climbed to their feet and, without taking their eyes off my grandmother, stumbled back among the trees beyond the beach mumbling something about the crazy old woman and her nigger-loving granddaughter. My grandmother kept her shotgun pointed at her target until she could no longer see the boys, and then she turned her attention to Samuel, who was lying motionless in the sand.

I crawled next to him and lifted his head into my lap. His forehead was split open, and the blood was now spreading onto my pants. My grandmother knelt down beside him and put her fingers against his throat.

"He's good and alive, but you better get him back to Nashville. A doctor's gonna need to put some stitches in his head," she told me and pulled an old dish towel from her robe pocket and tied it tightly around Samuel's forehead. Then she turned her attention to me. "Bezellia Grove, what the hell are you doing up here?" But I just sat there, not really knowing what to say. "I swear to heaven and back that you and your mama think you can do whatever the hell you feel like, no matter what it does to anybody else around you. But I tell you what. You cannot bring your colored boyfriend up here. Shit, are you crazy?

"Now the two of you better get on your way real fast, before there is more trouble. I'll stay here with him, and you take his pickup to my house and then get that damn Cadillac and get on back here. After you're on your way, I'll give Nathaniel a call so he knows what happened. Poor man, don't you think he's been through enough?"

"I didn't mean for any of this to happen," I muttered.

"Sweetie," she said, but she said it with all the sarcasm she could muster, "I think it's best if you don't ever come back to the lake. People around here don't forget things too quickly. And they're not likely to forget this anytime soon."

I nodded my head to let her know that I understood, that I would never come back. And even though I was crying so hard I could barely see, I managed to get the Cadillac back to the beach like my grandmother had told me to do. She helped me lift Samuel into the backseat, and even before I got to the interstate, my body was shaking so hard I could barely keep the car straight on the road. Samuel moaned and opened his eyes; his face was so swollen he didn't look much like himself. I told him not to worry. I was taking him home.

As I slowed to turn onto the interstate, I saw the man in the blue coveralls standing inside the gas station, stacking a new collection of Quaker State motor oil. His display was looking perfect, just like it always did. He stopped for a moment and looked at me and shook his head as if he already knew what I had been doing in his hometown, on his family beach. I slowly made my turn and headed back to Nashville.

I guess Nana was right after all. Samuel was right. Nathaniel was right. Maizelle was right. Hell, even Mother had been right a long time ago when she could remember that cashmere and convertibles were all a girl like me needed in life. Maybe I was meant to know nothing else.

BEZELLIA GROVE DIES AT 93

Bezellia Louise Grove, local writer and philanthropist, died Thursday morning. She was 93.

Best known for her short story collections like *Deep in the Grove* and *She Called Me Sister*, Grove deftly depicted the dark and sometimes tragic elements of affluent Southern life.

In 2038, the Nashville native, whose family's own rich history had been traced to the city's first settlement, wrote *Our Final Kiss* after her personal discovery of her foremother's diaries in the attic of her family home. Grove said the more than two-hundred-fifty-year-old diaries proved, once and for all, what she had long believed to be true—that her ancestor was a brave and fearless woman. It was her only novel and her final work.

A great philanthropist, Grove gave generously, of both time and money, to public schools and libraries throughout the metropolitan area, particularly to those east of the river. Now under construction, a new community library will open this fall on Trinity Lane bearing her name, according to the Nashville Public Library's executive director.

Grove established and funded the Samuel Stephenson Memorial Scholarship, named for one of the city's most successful African-Americans, who served as mayor in the late 1990s. She also donated the seed money for the first local chapter of the National Organization for Women and remained an avid supporter of women's rights both locally and nationwide.

Although Grove never married and led a relatively quiet life, it is believed that she was the inspiration for the 1970 country music sensation "Big City Girl" by Ruddy Semple. Grove repeatedly denied claims that she was Semple's muse, although he was known to spend afternoons on the Grove Hill estate when he was in town recording.

Grove died in the home that has belonged to her family for more than two hundred years, and private services will be held there Saturday afternoon.

She is survived by her sister, Adelaide Elizabeth Grove Ewing, of New York City, and two nieces, Bezellia Louise Davis, of Washington, D.C., and Elizabeth Maizelle Kilkelly, of Los Angeles, as well as four great-nieces and two great-nephews.

The Nashville Register
final edition
MAY 15, 2044

acknowledgments

*I*t took coming home again to find Bezellia Grove. But it took a family to find her voice. I want to thank the following people for loving us both.

Shaye Areheart, my beloved editor, whose kindness was always appreciated but whose faith in me was life changing.

Christine Kopprasch, who has never missed a step and now continues on this journey with me.

Barbara Braun, my agent, who trusts my love of storytelling and my commitment to share it with others.

Rick and Karen Miller, who invited me to a dinner party, but offered lifelong friendship and a girl named Bezellia.

Bonnie MacDonald, whose passion and courage was inspiration for Bezellia and continues to be for myself.

Lee Smith, whose generosity as writer, teacher, and friend has been a model to emulate.

Darnell Arnoult, who shares her love of storytelling as generously as she does her heart.

Roy Morris Jr., whose encouragement has been always appreciated and whose talent is always inspiring.

Becky Brothers, a Southern girl, who has a thirst for big stories and a patience for their telling.

Acknowledgments

Annaliese and Albert Vergara, who come whenever called.

Lisa Morse, Athena Wood, Carey McAniff, Kathleen Chapman, Ann Watkins, Babs Behar, Audrey Wilcox, Dana Battaglia, Mary Hackett, Kisha Campbell, Julie Schoerke, Ellen Ward, Karen Schettman, Jackie Tanase, Kaye Richardson, Christy Strick, Debbie Berletic, Nancy Ellen Libscomb, Paige Crutcher, women who have journeyed with me, some longer than others, some farther than others, but all willing to walk another mile.

Jamie Kyne, Susie Caro, Kate McReynolds, Beth Peshkin, Claudine Isaacs, Jan Price, Ingrid Meszoely, Emily Kurtz, Shannon Kilkelly, Rick and Karen Miller (again!), healers who may have been doing their jobs but whose kindhearted care, patience, and wisdom have reminded me that there is always hope, always joy, and we will find a cure.

And my big, wonderful, growing family, specifically, Mary Hall Gregg, Alice Gregg Haase and Vicky Gregg, Susan Moore, Tricia Gilmore and Fred Gregg, Tom Purdy, Dick Haase, and Chuck Gilmore, sisters and brothers, whose love and generosity is never-failing . . . and a whole passel of cousins, nieces, and nephews that I just downright adore!

My precious husband, Dan, and my three spectacular daughters, Claudia, Josephine, and Alice, every day you remind me of my greatest blessings.

And my sweet, kindhearted, tender mother, Mary, if only Bezellia had been loved like I am!

In order to provide reading groups with the most informed and thought-provoking questions possible, it is necessary to reveal important aspects of the plot of this novel—as well as the ending. If you have not finished reading *The Improper Life of Bezellia Grove,* we suggest that you wait before reviewing this guide.

reader's guide

1. Bezellia's mother detests her daughter's name to the point that she refuses to let it cross her lips, instead calling her oldest daughter only "Sister." What is implied in this nickname? How was Bezellia's life affected by this grand-sounding name?

2. Mrs. Grove warns her young daughter that she should look for only three things in a man: that he wears cashmere, drives a convertible, and can dance. Does she truly believe this credo, and what is Bezellia's reaction to this advice? Furthermore, how did Mrs. Grove's marriage into a socially prominent family affect her ability to parent?

3. Bezellia's relationship with her father is distant at best, and her relationship with her mother is very difficult. How do these two most important figures in Bezellia's life affect her attitude toward physical intimacy? How are her relationships with Samuel and Ruddy both similar and different?

4. Bezellia thinks that she and Samuel face some of the same issues and want the same things (p. 76). Do you agree? What are the similarities and differences in what they each must confront?

5. An interracial romance in the South during the late 1960s could be a very difficult, if not dangerous, relationship. How do Nathaniel and Mrs. Grove feel about seeing their children together? Later in the book, why didn't Bezellia encourage Samuel to leave the South so they could fully explore their relationship? And to what extent do you think these issues still exist for interracial couples both above and below the Mason-Dixon Line?

6. Maizelle shares a story with Bezellia about her own mother washing laundry for white people (p. 79), in which her mother endured hardships and was beaten after an altercation in which she was unjustly accused of not doing her work. What is Maizelle trying to teach this young woman?

7. After she is invited to Ruddy Semple's house for dinner, Bezellia daydreams about being Ruddy's wife. What does this vision reveal about the Groves' eldest daughter?

8. What is Bezellia's first impression of her grandparents, and how does that change during the course of the book? How does this change in perspective affect her thoughts toward her mother?

9. Several newspaper articles are interspersed throughout the book. How do these pieces affect the story line?

10. When Dr. Grove dies, a wake is held at the family home. How is the etiquette of death in the South different from other regions in the country? Does this formal process help the Groves through a difficult time?

11. Bezellia's little sister always walks to the beat of her own drum, to say the least. Adelaide herself talks about not being afraid to be alone, unlike most people. Do you think Adelaide is truly not well, as her mother believes, or is she just content to live her life differently from those around her? In that way, is she or is she not like her older sister?

12. Do you believe that Maizelle and Nathaniel are representative of those who worked for white families in the South? In what ways did Maizelle and Nathaniel change Bezellia's life? Do you think she would have become the same person without their influence? Do you think family is always about blood relationships, or can we create our own family?

13. The title of the book states that Bezellia's life is "improper." What is meant by that? How does Bezellia, if at all, affect the thoughts and attitudes of those in her 1960s Southern city? In the end, did she live up to her name?

about the author

SUSAN GREGG GILMORE is the author of the novel *Looking for Salvation at the Dairy Queen*. She has written for the *Chattanooga Times Free Press,* the *Los Angeles Times,* and the *Christian Science Monitor*. Born in Nashville, she lives in Tennessee with her husband and three daughters.